THE JUNGLE SOUTH OF THE MOUNTAIN

THE JUNGLE SOUTH OF THE MOUNTAIN

A Novel

Andrew Westoll

HARPER**AVENUE**

The Jungle South of the Mountain
Copyright © 2016 by Andrew Westoll.
All rights reserved.

Published by Harper Avenue, an imprint of HarperCollins Publishers Ltd

First edition

The author would like to thank the Canada Council for the Arts,
the Ontario Arts Council and the Toronto Arts Council for their support.

HarperCollins books may be purchased for educational, business or
sales promotional use through our Special Markets Department.

HarperCollins Publishers Ltd
2 Bloor Street East, 20th Floor
Toronto, Ontario, Canada
M4W 1A8

www.harpercollins.ca

Library and Archives Canada Cataloguing in Publication
information is available upon request.

ISBN 978-1-44344-185-8

Printed and bound in the United States

RRD 9 8 7 6 5 4 3 2 1

For Samantha and Remy

"A brave heart and a courteous tongue," said he.
"They shall carry thee far through the jungle, manling."
RUDYARD KIPLING, THE JUNGLE BOOK

CONTENTS

THE BAMBOO SEASON

I

~

THE LETTER ARRIVED WITH THE PROVISIONS, AND when Stanley spotted it among the bags of cassava flour and the cans of beans and the bottles of *palum* he understood the rains were on their way. It was that time of year again, the last weeks of the dry season, when Maria penned her annual letter and Stanley braced himself for the deluge. Before he'd unfurled his hammock for the night and cracked the rum, he had slipped the unopened letter and a fresh *jugo* of beer into his day pack. And now five hours had passed, the jungle had woken outside Camp Collymore, and Stanley was late for an appointment in the bush.

He pulled on his field gear, his binoculars, his machete, laced his boots, hefted his pack and unlatched the front door. Flipping on his headlamp he picked his way through the darkness to the bottom of Ant Hill, where the mist was thick and the river slid silently past his little beach. What harm could come from remembering? he thought to himself, as he always did on this day each year. But he knew the answer to this question: a great deal of harm could come from it, a very great deal. In the jungle, negative thoughts had a habit of conjuring things, of slipping their bounds and finding shape in the world. That's how Maria would have explained it. For Stanley, the harm of the memory would be more visceral: every year on this day his stomach turned to mush.

Turning east from the river onto the Voltzberg Trail he began the hike in. At Anyumara Falls, which were still just a trickle, he startled the capybara and her young at the water's edge. By the beam of his lamp Stanley watched the rodents nose the air, their plump bodies paralyzed with awareness. They were so still they might have been part of a natural history diorama—*Hydrochoerus hydrochaeris*, World's Largest Rodent, Tropical Rainforest Biome, South America. Of all the things Stanley had discovered about prey animals—and the capybara was the definition of prey, the prized quarry of the anaconda—it was this capacity for stillness, this ability to appear carved from stone at the moment of greatest peril, that impressed him most. After following monkeys for so many years Stanley had cultivated a similar ability to remain calm and still for long periods, but he often wondered if this skill would actually translate into real poise under pressure, as it did for the capybara, or if stillness would simply abandon him when he needed it most.

Stanley flipped off his lamp, stepped off-trail and slipped quietly past the capybara. This small ritual of courtesy had marked the beginning of his days for eight years now. When he and Maria had first walked the Voltz it had been Maria who had spotted the capybara at the falls. She had let out a gasp, gripped Stanley's arm, and in the darkness Stanley's initial reaction had been desirous, the pressure of his wife's fingers on his skin causing his insides to surge. But a moment later he had reached into his pocket, pulled out his notebook and set to work. They had arrived in Roosvallen only the day before and both were beyond exhilarated—the winding boat ride south from the coast that felt like they were slipping off the edge of the earth; their first evening in this forest, sitting around the campfire while their boss, the great Professor Collymore, pressed his case that this jungle was like no other; this capybara and her young, caught in the spotlight, a taxidermied family of four. This is our life, Stanley, Maria would say at moments like these, squeezing him tight. This is *our life*.

4

Now, eight years on, Stanley recalled that encounter with the capybara with deep sadness. Because as Maria, awestruck, had narrowed the beam of her headlamp that morning, and as Stanley had scribbled the time and approximate location of those motionless rodents into his notebook, the pair had embodied one of the great ironies of the scientific enterprise: that out in the field, science docs not make distinctions between the radicals and the rationalists, between those driven forward by the body and the spirit and those driven forward by the mind. For Maria, those capybara became members of a shared ecosystem that morning. For Stanley, those rodents became the project's first data point.

Up Kawati Top and down the other side Stanley took Domineestraat south. Here the jungle was at its thickest, and in the weeks since he'd last walked this trail the forest had made every effort to reclaim it. Spiny creepers criss-crossed the path at head-height, several epiphytes had slipped from their moorings and drifted to the earth, and about halfway down the trail a fallen tree barred the way. Stanley decided against his machete and quietly rounded these obstacles, the only human-made sounds his breath, his footfalls and the occasional clank of his camp chair against his pack, while the forest around him built towards the dawn crescendo. The peeping tree frogs of every denomination, the purr of nocturnal insects nearing the end of their shifts, the far-off moan of a dove or a bush dog, Stanley had never been able to tell which. At the bottom of Domineestraat stood a lone heliconia plant. As he passed Stanley flicked open his knife and sliced off an impressive set of bracts, the half-heart-shaped appendages seeming to glow in the dark they were such a brilliant red. Heliconia had been Maria's favourite.

On that first day in the jungle Stanley and Maria had bushwhacked for seven hours straight but had failed to find a single primate—no capuchins, no bearded sakis, not even a lowly squirrel monkey. Collymore had sent them out alone that morning to christen their new study site, to begin exploring and laying claim to the place that might one day become as productive as Corcovado or Manú. And now his protégés would return to camp with nothing to show for it.

Nothing? said Maria, when Stanley voiced these concerns. Sweetheart, open your eyes.

They had, of course, seen the menagerie that day. It had started with that capybara, then the caracara up on Kawati, then the trumpeter birds. And for the rest of the day, Stanley barely had time to stash his notebook before another wild feature of the jungle revealed itself. By midmorning they had spotted a tapir, an armadillo, two yellow-footed tortoises and the tail end of a giant anteater. During a water break Maria had noticed a kinkajou, or honey bear, peering down at them from the mid-canopy. Both were amateur ophidiologists—a result of having spent years chasing primates through rainforest environments—but they were only able to identify two of the twelve snakes they saw that day, the vicious bushmaster and the nasty fer-de-lance. There was something unique about this jungle, as Collymore claimed—something magical about the way it was put together. At noon the pair ate their lunch next to a large stand of heliconia, and as Stanley had reviewed his notes from the morning Maria had disappeared into this stand and reemerged five minutes later, a broad smile on her face and a long set of heliconia bracts in her hand. It had already fallen off, she said, before Stanley could accuse her, with gentle ridicule, of "defiling Mother Earth." They were just sitting there on the ground, she said, like little broken hearts.

That afternoon Maria had carried those bracts all the way back to Ant Hill. She had strung them up above their tent, and when Professor Collymore had returned from the river he had scoffed at the gesture. It's stunning, my dear, he had said, towelling himself off with an old T-shirt, his Scottish brogue echoing back from the canopy. From the family *Heliconiaceae*. It will be rotten by morning.

South from Domineestraat now, Stanley carried his fresh heliconia with both hands, felt the satisfying heft of life still present in the plant, and soon the trail opened up into a grove of massive *kankan* trees. Their trunks were many feet across and their buttress roots nearly overlapped. Through the high canopy Stanley could see the mauve sky. I'm late, he thought. This should have been done before dawn. He walked faster, unencumbered now by the collapsing forest, his pack clanging through the grove, his route memorized, but as he neared his destination a lump formed in his throat. He slowed when he caught the glint of glass amid the roots of a particular tree. Flipping off his lamp and leaning the heliconia against a buttress, he dropped his gear and stood silently before the towering *kankan*.

At the foot of this tree stood a collection of empty beer bottles. In the dimness Stanley saw that a few of them had tipped over, so he reached down and righted them. Eight empty bottles. Seven years since he'd lost his boy. Beneath this makeshift shrine, a few feet down in the soil, lay the remains of Stanley and Maria's only child.

Stanley dug in his pack for the *jugo*, snapped off the cap and began pouring the fresh beer over the old bottles. He knew what he was supposed to do next—kneel at the foot of the tree, surrender to the moment and allow the memories to rush in, rub the beer into his skin and speak a prayer to the spirits who held sway over this forest—but in seven years he'd never been able to oblige. Instead he remained standing, sprinkling the beer without pattern or intention, as if he had been asked this favour by a stranger. It wasn't my fault, he said, tears slipping down his face, the *jugo* nearing on empty, the gloom gradually lifting from the grove. I'm sorry, little man, but your mother is wrong. It had nothing to do with me.

When the *jugo* was finished Stanley placed it beside the others at the foot of the tree. Then he dug the stem of the heliconia into the earth and carefully leaned it back against the buttress. Hefting his pack he sniffed hard, spat, said his goodbyes for the year and turned to leave, but as he exited the grove his stomach turned, and at the bottom of Domineestraat he had to drop his gear again and race into the understory. Stanley crouched beside a slim tree, leaned back against the trunk and emptied his bowels, the contents slapping into the little hole he'd managed to kick into the earth at the last second. The urge had come so quickly that he had neglected to tap the tree trunk with the hilt of his machete first, a ritual that would ensure he wasn't about to drop his pants beneath a nest of bullet ants. While he waited, he craned his neck to keep an eye above him, just in case his choice had been a poor one.

With this additional ceremony complete Stanley returned to the trail and began searching for his monkeys. Back on the Voltzberg he went east for a few hundred yards and then hung a right on Downing Street. He returned to the spot where he'd left the troop the previous evening, a nondescript section of high canopy about halfway down the trail, but of course they weren't there. They could be anywhere. He considered heading straight to the bamboo but it was still early, a little after six o'clock, and usually the monkeys had only just begun to stir by now. Over to the Danforth and then up to the Voltz again, he took Broadway south, and once he had gone all the way down to Pikin River he began to get the sense that this might be one of those infuriating days with no monkeys and, therefore, no data. Coming up Saramaccastraat he felt his mood darken further, and by the time he passed Yonge Street his skin had begun to prickle with anger.

And then he heard a soft crash from somewhere to the north of his position and a lightness came over him. He found them just south of the Voltzberg, a family of nineteen brown capuchin monkeys that Maria had nicknamed the Longfellows, after her favourite Romantic poet.

The monkeys paid no attention to Stanley, just continued their slow progression through the trees, their quiet conversations of soft *ke-junks*, the requisite storm of branches, leaves, nutshells and invertebrates showering the ground beneath them. Stanley dropped his gear and pulled out his data binder, made a note of their location on the daily map. Then he performed the first group scan of the day, doing the best he could through the fog and the semi-darkness to evaluate the troop's spread. He only spotted thirteen monkey-like shapes in the trees, and under these conditions he couldn't identify anyone except Johan, the alpha. By the rough direction of their movement, though, Stanley surmised where they were headed, and his mood dropped once again.

Then, from somewhere to the west, Stanley heard voices. He stopped writing, listened carefully, and when he heard them again he quietly closed his binder. With his visit to the *kankan* grove still fresh in his mind, and with at least a half-hour before he'd be able to collect much worthwhile data from the Longfellows, Stanley made his way north to the Voltzberg, a plan taking root that would perhaps go a small way toward cheering him up.

2

~

WHEN HE WASN'T WITH THE MONKEYS OR transcribing his data or reading the latest issue of *Animal Behaviour* or clearing trails or drinking *palum* or smoking hash on the island or lying in his hammock and trying to think of nothing, Stanley's favourite pastime in the rainforest was playing pranks on the tourists. Like all pranks his were successful even when they failed miserably, but this one would stand out for its striking imperfection. It was now seven o'clock but the understory was still obscured by fog. The Longfellows had left their sleeping site and were traplining to the bamboo, as they'd done every morning for the past six weeks, and Stanley could hear them twittering to each other as they made their way north through the canopy. But he could also hear a tour group approaching, the clink of titanium, the swish of synthetic fibres. He had about ten minutes before the monkeys would cross overhead, so he stepped off the Voltzberg Trail and hid between the high buttress roots of a *kankan* tree.

Stanley had met these tourists two nights ago at a party on the island, and as usual he had loathed them. The Roos Boyz had been in fine form, the *kawina* drums pounding, the Courvoisier flowing, and if you could find Shike and he was feeling generous he would hook you up with a fistful of hash so strong the tropical lightning would flicker straight inside you. The Boyz had regaled the tourists with the usual horror stories, of tour groups gone missing, of old-time explorers who'd lost their minds in the jungle. As employees of the domestic conservation agency, and as young men who'd been plucked from their home villages downstream and dumped off at Roosvallen with little training, it was the Roos Boyz' job to host and entertain the tourists; how exactly they accomplished this was up to them. As always, one of the women from the group—in this case a fit, long-legged German—disappeared for a while, and one of the *kawina* sat abandoned for a time. No matter where they came from, one of the tourists always tried to bed a wild Maroon.

Petrus, who was the patriarch of the Maroons on the island, was the first to emerge from the gloom that morning, his machete in one hand, a chainsaw balanced on his opposite shoulder. Stanley smiled and settled deeper into his hiding spot; he and Petrus hadn't worked together for a long time. Petrus mounted the rotten log that lay across Treefall Creek and his tour group came into view behind him, their wobbly arms outstretched for balance, their giggles rising into the trees. They looked like a group of children being led through the murk. Stanley tapped a buttress with the hilt of his machete. A low boom rose up the trunk. He waited two minutes and tapped again, a little harder this time, and the boom went straight through him. Petrus slowed. He'd heard the signal.

Showtime.

Stanley slammed the hilt into the buttress as hard as he could. An ethereal sound, a thousand timpani drums being struck at once, rose through the canopy. He did it again, the boom reverberating from his wooden cave and echoing through the forest, abolishing all other sound and causing his throat to tighten. He realized for the hundredth time that he should really carry earplugs. Then, after the third boom Stanley heard one of the tourists scream. He stopped, sat back and listened.

This was his favourite part: the moment when it dawned on the Germans or the Dutch or the Americans or the French that they

were, in fact, being extraordinarily stupid—that they were break-
ing one of those hard-bargained evolutionary contracts Stanley's
generation had somehow been grandfathered into by wandering
through a remote neotropical wilderness at dawn, a place filled
with jaguar and puma and three of the most poisonous snakes on
earth, without so much as a walking stick to protect themselves.
Not to mention the stories they'd been told the previous evening, which had already put them on edge. It was priceless, this
moment, and Stanley knew the sound that always accompanied it:
the scream, then the silence. He could hear that silence now. He
could also hear his monkeys, so he resumed the cacophony.

He played those buttress roots like *kawina*, this one now that
one, the hilt of his machete and his bare fist against the rough
wood. A strange sound rose in his throat, a high-pitched wailing, a forest banshee, some demon from the jungle south of the
mountain. He did not resist it. Stanley rolled in the dewy muck
between the roots, pounding and wailing and kicking, coating
himself in a stinky loam of rotten leaves and dead insects, opening
his knuckles to the kapok wood. If Maria or Professor Collymore
or perhaps a government official back in the capital were to watch
a video of Stanley thrashing around between those buttress roots
that morning, howling in the dawn light and slamming his fists,
a manic smile spread across his face, they might be tempted to
conclude that this was the moment everything started to fall apart
for Stanley, the very instant when he began to lose his footing. But
they would be wrong about that.

Every tourist was screaming now. Stanley took a break to
sneak a peek. They were huddled together on the trail, shoulder
to shoulder, inching backwards and shaking and pointing at a spot
halfway up the trunk of his tree. The stories had come alive. The
mist had risen and Stanley could see the outlier. There was always
an outlier. It was that long-legged girl from last night, frozen in
fear down the trail, unable to join her countrymen and women,

her knees cantilevered inwards, her hand raised to her mouth, tears pouring down her cheeks. Just as Stanley began to feel badly for this woman, Petrus pulled the cord on his chainsaw and the industrial howl silenced everything.

Petrus brandished the saw and pointed it in Stanley's direction. One of the tourists, a bratwurst of a man, thrust out his hand and hollered as he realized what Petrus was about to do. Unmoved, Petrus let loose a howl of his own, revved the saw and crashed off-trail towards his colleague. For a moment the sight of Petrus running towards him with that mad look, his machine churning *maka* palms to pieces, caused Stanley's stomach to turn anew. It always did; Petrus was a wonderful actor. Petrus ducked down between the buttresses of a neighbouring *kankan*, his saw blubbering on standby, his conservation agency uniform still freshly pressed, his trademark professional calm intact. Hard to believe Petrus is pushing sixty-five, thought Stanley, as the old man gave one last blood-curdling cry and flipped off the saw. The tourists shrank closer together, shaking and whimpering now, their lone protector having offered himself up to some forest ghoul.

Down the trail, the tall German tilted backwards, looked like she might topple, then caught herself as if suddenly waking. Eyes wide, she turned and began running back towards Treefall Creek. She was gazelle-like in her escape; Stanley made a mental note to find out which of the Boyz had slept with her the night before. Ex-Olympian, a bag of hash says so. Unfortunately, in her panic, the woman caught her left foot on a root just in front of the rotten log that bridges the creek and commenced one of the most extravagant falls from grace Stanley had ever seen. Her foot stuck, her long body planked into the earth. Her face bounced off the end of the log with a crunch and her long legs scorpioned over her back. The whiplash alone was surely enough to knock her cold.

Stanley cringed, looked over at Petrus, who had popped his head up to watch the finale. The old man grimaced, then shrugged his shoulders, lifted his ball cap to wipe the sweat from his brow, and slipped back out of sight. Up above, old lady Agnes wheeled through the canopy, bamboo on her mind. She was followed by Johan, Beatrix and Mignon. The others wouldn't be far behind.

The woman's tragic escape jolted the Germans into action. They rushed back up-trail, many of them still holding hands, and swept the woman's limp body from the bog, carrying her away like a phalanx of panicked ants. The fat man, however, didn't move. He stayed put, transfixed by what he'd spotted in the trees.

Affen, he said quietly to himself, reaching out his hand to Agnes, Johan and Beatrix. His fear softened into a faint smile.

Here, monkey monkey.

3

THAT WAS A LONELY DAY. IT WAS ALWAYS LONELY after a tour group went through, but to make matters worse the capuchins had spent the entire day in the bamboo patch, as they usually did during the dry season when fruit was harder to come by. The bamboo, which covered twelve acres in the middle of Stanley's study site, sprouted year-round and was a vital food source during the driest months, providing reliable calories at a time when the rest of the jungle was at its stingiest. But nothing could make a person feel more forlorn than spending eight hours staring at an immovable wall of *Bambusoideae*. Back in the day Stanley and Maria would kill time during the dry season by imagining absurd scenarios for the monkeys. Deep inside the patch was a poker table. Johan was the dealer, Wacky was the risk-taker, and Beatrix was the mysterious vixen who was secretly in the house's pocket. Wacky would come close to carrying the day but inevitably, on the last hand, Beatrix would throw all in. The subordinate Wacky wouldn't be able to resist her charms, and Johan would provide the heartbreak.

Anthropomorphism might be the cardinal sin for an animal behaviour researcher, but fuck that, thought Stanley—nothing comes more naturally to humans in the wild.

Stanley spent the majority of those eight hours sitting on his camp chair, elbows on his knees, head in his hands, listening for the monkeys but thinking about nothing. The only time he actually considered pulling Maria's letter out and opening it was during his hourly walks around the circumference of the patch, but every time he sat down again and resumed his vigil the impulse left him. In order to dwell on something, to really ruminate, he had to be moving. Or perhaps the forest had to be moving; he was never sure if it was his own momentum or the perception of the jungle moving past him that caused his mind to get stuck in such a variety of ruts.

They had met as first-year doctoral students, two of the unlucky few to be assigned as teaching assistants to The Story of Animal Behaviour, a notorious third-year undergraduate course. Monday mornings at nine o'clock, a windowless lecture hall in the basement of the Anthropology wing, a cohort of 145 privileged and uniformly arrogant twenty-year-olds for whom the class was, both figuratively and literally, a bird course. A few minutes before the first class, Stanley had found a woman of approximately his age crouched beside the door to the lecture hall, the olive skin of her neck and shoulders swollen with insect bites, her black hair twisted into a ragged braid so long that it brushed the floor, the assigned textbook open beneath her as if she were offering it libations.

Maria?

The woman started, looked up, peered at Stanley confusedly as if he had wrenched her from a deep sleep. Then, slowly, her face relaxed into a warm smile.

Stanley, she said, reaching out her hand. Colleague. Compatriot. Fellow martyr. Drew the short straw, too, huh?

Maria returned her gaze to the book at her feet, read a few more lines while slowly folding the corner of the page she was on. Stanley noticed her elegant fingers as they searched for purchase.

So you're actually reading it?

This isn't a textbook, said Maria. It's a book about how to live. I haven't had the chance.

Oh, you must, Stanley. Gorchenski is a fucking genius.

Where'd you get those bites?

Maria closed the book, looked up, smiled again.

Bioko.

Colobus?

Pennant's red. You?

Stanley rubbed his neck.

Lemuroidea.

No.

What?

You're a walking cliché, Stanley. Lemurs?

Island biogeography was Darwin's shortcut. Why shouldn't it be ours?

Maria let out a loud snore, closed her eyes, allowed herself to fall back into the lockers with a crash. Stanley laughed.

Not endangered enough for you?

They're highly endangered. But that's not why you were there.

How would you know?

Maria stood, cocked her head at Stanley. She was taller than he was, long and lithe, her batik dress unfurling to her sandals and casting a golden light through the subterranean hallway.

Maria reached out and tapped Stanley's forehead with her index finger.

Monkeys can't eat theory, she said.

They met like this for the next thirteen weeks, every Monday morning before class, and each time they would arrive earlier than the last, under the pretense of discussing the readings ahead of the lecture. Maria had been right about the textbook; once he'd cracked it, Stanley couldn't put it down. Gorchenski, an early-twentieth-century scholar of avian mating rituals, had taken a distinctly unorthodox approach to the discussion of animal behaviour. Instead of organizing his text through the lens of evolutionary theory—with the usual chapters on proximate causes, the role of genes, neural mechanisms and reproductive tactics—the book applied a narrative perspective to the study of animal behaviour. In his introduction, Gorchenski laid out his now-infamous proposal: that every animal has a life story, a biography, and the only way to tell the truth about that animal and to imbue its life with authentic meaning is to embed our understanding of its behaviour within a biographical frame. He took this concept to the extreme in his textbook, with each chapter based not on a theoretical concept but on a universal aspect of human life—birth, hunger, adolescence, jealousy, love, procreation, parenthood, the search for a home, old age, death. He then used this framework, along with the latest behavioural scholarship, to tell the life stories of seven individual animals: a monarch butterfly, a sea horse, a Siberian tiger, a West African hammer-headed bat, an emperor penguin, a chimpanzee and a fruit fly.

The result was a slim volume that treated animals not as the subjects of human science but of their own subjective experiences in the world. It was both a guide to animal behaviour and an ethological thought-experiment, employing the tools of the literary writer—scene setting, rising tension, thwarted desire, lyricism, and even (in the example of the chimpanzee) characterization—to guide the reader to the conclusion that animals lead objectively meaningful lives whether or not we are there to observe and record their behaviour.

In his introduction Gorchenski admitted to being inspired by the philosopher Thomas Nagel and his attacks on reductionism. But when the book was first published in 1940 many believed Gorchenski had reduced his field—and his career, for that matter—to a long series of banalities. This was the era of the modern synthesis, when the burgeoning field of molecular genetics promised to revolutionize the way scholars interacted with Darwinian theory. Critics at the time accused Gorchenski of promoting sentimentality, of veering into metaphysics, of co-opting the emotionally manipulative strategies of nature documentary and of engaging in anthropomorphism. But a smaller group of scholars, most of them fringe ecologists and literary theorists and philosophers, believed Gorchenski had invented a robust new framework for communicating the marvels of nature, one that reframed animal behaviour not as a human construct but as a powerful, enigmatic force with which animals themselves construct meaning in the world.

Don't you see? said Maria, one Monday morning near the end of term. Gorchenski founded the field of eco-criticism before anyone knew what to call it. A decade before Imanishi, two decades before Goodall. He could see that science is nothing without storytelling. This class should be cross-listed with the English department.

Fuck the Huxleys, said Stanley.

Don't laugh, Stanley. Matthew Arnold was right. Without the eloquence of the humanities, how can we really learn anything? If there is no meaning behind the endless streams of data, what the hell are we doing this for?

Maria's great strength as a researcher was her ability to see connections between things, the importance of the seemingly insignificant to the whole. Her doctoral thesis was a groundbreaking investigation of seed dispersal in Pennant's red colobus monkeys on the island of Bioko in the Gulf of Guinea. Her results had suggested, incredibly, that the monkeys might actually know what they are doing when they "deliver" digested seeds a certain distance away from nearby fruit trees, and that this knowledge is passed down through the generations. Monkeys as farmers, primates as stewards of the forest; a real coup for the field of conservation biology. (The project was a media darling, with Maria's favourite headline appearing in *Smithsonian*: "Colobus Monkeys Put the 'Culture' in Agriculture.")

Stanley's dissertation was nowhere near as sexy as Maria's, a brute-force comparison of activity budgets with social status in wild lemurs. But his grasp of the most arcane corners of evolutionary theory was watertight and his data-set was stunningly comprehensive, consisting of more than five hundred individual follows on over one hundred animals—the work of a researcher with unheard of endurance in the bush.

By Christmas, The Story of Animal Behaviour was over, Stanley and Maria were spending every waking moment together, and the two had made plans to become each other's field assistants. They spent three months on Bioko that winter and then ten weeks in Madagascar, toiling in some of the most challenging field conditions on earth, and the combination of Maria's nuanced thinking with Stanley's attention to detail caused both projects to flourish in exciting new directions. On the last day of fieldwork before flying home for the summer, Maria led Stanley blindfolded to her favourite spot in his forest, southwest of the Tsinjoarivo commune in the Onive River basin, where the Onive dropped into a gorgeous waterfall. When Stanley removed his blindfold and found Maria on bended knee the two burst out laughing, and that summer they were married. Three years later they had defended their dissertations, and six months after that they were disembarking at Pangol International, the air so thick with humidity and aviation fuel and charred vegetation it felt to Stanley as if the collective breath of the entire South American continent had risen to its northern coast. Maria had given up the colobus, and Stanley had forsaken the lemur. They'd been given the opportunity of a lifetime, to spearhead a project under the world's most prolific primatologist. The brown capuchin monkey, the chimpanzee of the New World, would now become the subject of their science.

4

LATE IN THE AFTERNOON STANLEY FOUND THE Longfellows popping out from the bamboo on Pancho Villa. They zipped over the Voltzberg and returned to where he had left them the previous evening, to where he'd left them the previous five evenings, somewhere in the high forest of the south. Assholes, said Stanley, as he began the long hike home, knowing the monkeys would have given him the slip again by morning. They're fucking with me. They've been fucking with me for eight years.

The most direct route back to camp was usually the Voltz. That night Stanley was about three miles out, so the last mile would surely be in darkness. When the project started he and Maria had been warned to never be out after dark, to always give themselves enough time to get home before the forest shifted, as it did every day at dusk, from a semi-benign tourist mecca to a world of malignancy. The most reliable way to accomplish this was to leave the bush before they heard the chirping of the *siksi-yuru*, cicadas who struck up every night around six o'clock. But ever since his boy had died and Maria had left, Stanley's attention to detail had slipped, and he would routinely end his day to the score of the cicadas and by the beam of his headlamp, negotiating a jungle set loose from its moorings. Perhaps he'd been out there too long but Stanley had come to love those walks. In a certain frame of mind it's very soothing to walk alone in the dark.

In an hour Stanley had reached the top of Ant Hill. He opened the front door to Camp Collymore, flipped on the lights and began to undress. Headlamp, binoculars, camp chair, machete, backpack, walkie-talkie, switchblade, wristwatch, notebook, boots, socks, belt, field shirt, field pants. His sweat-soaked clothes landed with a slap on the floor. Naked, he grabbed his towel and walked back down the hill to the little beach. He plunged into the river to bathe. The cold water woke him. As he walked back uphill Stanley observed that his annoyance with the monkeys had passed and he was able to love them again.

Camp Collymore was not faring well. Eight years in a tropical rainforest is equivalent to more than a century in a temperate clime; the studs were rotten, the house wore a skirt of mould and the zinc roofing had almost rusted through. Inside, the snakes, geckoes, bats, mice and butterflies waged war with the spiders in every corner, their corpses scattered throughout. As for the attic, no one had climbed the ladder for about five years. Stanley would occasionally hear footsteps up there—not the scratch and scamper of rodents but actual footsteps, with purpose and heft, a gentle reminder that a rainforest will greet colonialism of all forms with belligerence. One day the jungle will take back this small tract of hilltop land overlooking the river, thought Stanley. I just hope I'm dead and gone when it does.

The camp foundations were cement, a point of great pride among the Maroons who had poured it, as this was the first building with reliable foundations to have been raised in the park since the late 1980s, when the military government cut off the electricity, halted all flights and firebombed the villages up and down the Cariban River. Petrus worked here back then, and one of his favourite stories to frighten the tourists with from those days is that by cutting off air transport, officials had unknowingly stranded a group of Dutch college students and their guide, a famous ecology professor from a famous European university. They'd been sitting up on the airstrip, flush with excitement from their first bushwalk and awaiting their flight back to the city's nightclubs and whores, when the nation's only two bombers arrived and laid waste. Benny, who had worked at Roosvallen almost as long as Petrus, never believed this story, and the tale had become a singular bone of contention between the older Maroons who lived on the island, especially when the *palum* was flowing. Petrus doesn't drink, and he tells every group of tourists who come to Roosvallen that the remains of those teenagers and their prof were buried at the foot of a *kankan* tree somewhere in the nearby jungle. Benny drinks profusely, and he tells the tourists that Petrus is *fukkup*.

After his beans and rice Stanley sat at the data table and transcribed his notes from the day. There wasn't much, a long series of OOVs (out-of-views) from seven o'clock on. He made sure to note the presence of the Germans, in case a graduate student might one day consider writing a thesis on the impact of ecotourism on primate biogeography, even though Stanley knew the odds of this occurring were extremely low. Ever since news had spread about Collymore's disappearance and the catastrophe that soon followed, Roosvallen had earned the reputation for being somewhat cursed, and no graduate students or researchers of any kind had inquired about visiting for a very long time. In fact, Stanley hadn't received a single piece of correspondence from the university for many years now, a somewhat unorthodox state of affairs but one that Stanley relished. They know my real value, he told himself whenever he pondered the administration's silence. A lecture hall is the last place I should be. Roosvallen continued to be funded, which was all Stanley really cared about.

The only other curiosity from the day was that Stanley's headcounts had been one short. He'd only been able to conduct three counts before the caps had disappeared into the patch that morning, but still, he couldn't remember another time when he'd missed counting a monkey three times in a row.

Once his notes were finished he filed them along with the map of his troop's movements into the appropriate three-ring binder, and returned this binder to the appropriate shelf in the camp library. The binder sat next to a battalion of identical binders, a six-foot bookshelf full of them, ninety-six months of pure monkey data. Above the binders, a large mason jar filled with the preserved remains of a three-toed sloth that Maria had found one day. She had planned to bleach the skeleton and rebuild it, museum-style, with pins and steel joints and little labels. Next to the jarred sloth, a metal box containing five hundred samples of tapir shit, the raw materials for yet another project that never got off the ground.

On the walls, laminated conference posters authored by Stanley himself—"A Unique Ecological Niche for *Cebus apella*"; "Precursory Tool Use in *Cebus apella*"; "Fruit Harvest and Forest Traplining in *Cebus apella*"; "The Effects of Habitat Type on Aerial Predation Risk in *Cebus apella*." The posters were yellowed and curled at the edges, and the graphic elements would surely have appeared antique to a current undergraduate. But the scientific observations they contained were entirely fresh and beyond reproach. This was the first baseline field study of the brown capuchin monkey, *Cebus apella*, in an Amazonian habitat like this—a black-water forest uncharacteristically rich in nutrients, a near-impenetrable understory thicketed with vines, a fruit density unparalleled by any other forest in the tropical world. How had the brown capuchin monkey—by far the most intelligent and socially complex primate species in the forest—adjusted to life in this particular jungle? How had it evolved to take advantage of the unique opportunities presented by such an ecologically generous place? These questions were Stanley's lodestones, his prime directive, and one does not simply discard one's prime directive when one's life falls apart. When the rest of the world abandons you, your questions are all you have left. Along with grant money from UNESCO, the Leakey Foundation and the National Science Foundation, of course, which the university continued to dispense.

After Maria's departure Stanley had buried himself in the work, spending sixteen hours a day in the field and publishing at an incredible rate. Over the first three years he saw nine papers in print, with two appearing simultaneously in *Science* and *Nature*, something no researcher had ever done before. The rains came and went, the trail system grew, the data binders multiplied and Stanley found solace in the only place he knew to look for it: the ultra-rational pursuit of his science. He attended every conference he could—the American Society of Primatologists, the International Primatological Society, Calgary, Cancún, Vienna, Rio de Janeiro, Beijing—and introduced audiences around the world to the Longfellows, who had inspired Stanley's most provocative papers. To Johan, the only alpha-male monkey known to have reached the most powerful position in the troop without siring a single off-spring. To Wacky, the first capuchin monkey on earth to have been observed using tools in the wild. To Banana, the juvenile female who invented the sleeping nest, something chimpanzees make routinely in the wild but that monkeys never have. To Lucy and Agnes, at forty-six the oldest capuchins on record. And, of course, to the youngest member of the troop, Charlie, for whom Stanley had a serious soft spot.

At each meeting Stanley would reveal the latest breakthrough from Roosvallen, and it didn't take long for a compelling story to emerge and for the project to acquire near-mythic status. In those first few years of conference-going, whenever he stepped to the lectern the audience would applaud and whistle and cheer with uncharacteristic enthusiasm. But Stanley knew there was more to these boisterous receptions than just professional cour-tesy; his international colleagues may have been impressed with his scholarly output and the growing reputation of Roosvallen, but beneath their applause lay a collective pity, as if every paper he gave represented some small triumph over unimaginable devastation. They probably weren't wrong about that, Stanley figured, but sometimes he felt like a cancer survivor at these conferences, or like a POW returned home. Rumours had always flown within the primatology community about what had really happened to Professor Collymore—it had become a favourite pastime at social gatherings to devise new theories about his true fate—but there was never any doubt about what had happened to Stanley and Maria. It never failed that one colleague or another would find Stanley in the bar after one of his talks and tell him how they could never have stayed, how they would have left that jungle as quickly as possible and perhaps even sworn off fieldwork forever. It was during one such encounter in Beijing, when the world's foremost authority on the Philippine tarsier became so distraught he could barely speak, when Stanley decided to stop publishing altogether, to stop attending conferences and speaking about his monkeys, to hole up at Roosvallen and continue collecting the data and never leave again.

Maria must have been horrified by this decision. Not only would it be more difficult to attract money without publishing, but the local conservation movement would grind to a halt if Roosvallen went quiet. The stories of this place need to be told! she would have said. The monkeys need our voice! But Stanley figured he could maintain his funding through reputation alone, at least for a good few years. He simply no longer had it in him to sit at a computer and distill what he was finding in the forest into words for no one aside from his pitying colleagues to read. Someone else can tell the story of this place, he thought to himself. Someone else can find the meaning in all of this.

And besides, he thought, Maria will come back one day. And when she does she will find the monkey project in perfect working order. She will find seven years of data logged, of group scans and phenology studies and individual follows, and they will pick up right where they'd left off. She will be impressed by the precision of Stanley's observations since her departure, and she will use them to begin publishing the stories of Roosvallen again. She will find her hairbrush and her tulsi tea bags and her dog-eared issues of *Conservation Biology* and her autographed copies of Gorchenski's *Story* and Berry's *Life Is a Miracle* and her collection of colobus photographs exactly where she'd left them, and she will forgive him his dishevelment. Then she will bring his head to her chest and they will weep one last time together before hiking out and finding the monkeys anew.

The story is stronger than I am, thought Stanley, as he reached into his pack and retrieved Maria's latest letter. One last ceremony to complete. He fetched the same three-ring binder from the camp library, flipped it open and slipped the envelope in between the pages at random. Then he closed the binder and returned it to its shelf.

With his data filed Stanley visited the outhouse, brushed his teeth, grabbed the bottle of *palum*, rolled a joint and hooked the hammock across the living room. Camp Collymore had two small bedrooms, a living room and a kitchen. In the kitchen was a sink, a propane range, a long countertop with a pantry beneath and a plywood table with bench seating. In the living room were the data table, the library, the storage cubbies, the hammocks, the front door and the doors to the bedrooms. This was Stanley's entire world in the evening hours, and he hadn't opened either of the bedroom doors in seven years. The walls of the house were made of screening nailed to a wooden frame. The screens protected against insects and allowed the heat of the day and the cool of the night to pass through. When the sun was up, the inhabitants could see out on all sides. When night came they knew nothing of the world beyond the glow of their solar lights. My solar lights, thought Stanley. They're beginning to dim and so am I. The zizz and whirr of the forest at night, the sweep of cool air to banish the hot, his bed an Amerindian pendulum of homespun cotton. The far-off buzz of an outboard motor. Howler monkeys miles away. The lights, my lights, going dark. A boat beaching at the bottom of Ant Hill. Footsteps slow, methodical.

Petrus outside his front door.

Glok, glok.

Bas-Pey.

Stan-ley. Everything fine?

Ai . . .

Petrus started to giggle. Stanley joined in.

She alive? asked Stanley.

Face *fukkup.*

She could run.

Ai.

I feel bad.

Stanley rolled partway out of the hammock. His head swam so he lay back down.

You want to come in?

Benny *taki* football tomorrow.

Okay.

Mi bring fish.

Thank you.

Silence.

Okay, *mi gwe.*

Okay . . . Bas-Pey . . . thank you.

On the doorstep, a plastic Tupperware filled with Stanley's favourite: deep-fried anyumara meat.

5

THE NEXT MORNING STANLEY LEFT CAMP AS USUAL at five o'clock. Hiking the Voltzberg Trail just before dawn was like wandering a battlefield moments after the bodies had been hauled away. In the early years it felt like trespassing to go out that early, as if the forest deserved its privacy, but soon this feeling faded and it was Stanley who was desperate to keep the jungle at arm's length. He hiked past Anyumara Falls, up the steep incline to Kawati Top, and then down into the main study site. As he descended, a flock of six trumpeter birds popped out in front of him and scurried down the trail, honking the whole way, relieved to have found the trail but terrified to suddenly be so exposed. Stanley watched them with half-interest, his mind elsewhere. The birds soon veered into the understory, their fear winning out.

The study site took the form of a rectangle, two miles wide and three miles long, with the Voltz running down the middle and then continuing for another six miles to the foot of the Voltzberg Mountain, an impressive basalt sugarloaf that rose up from the rainforest canopy and offered panoramic views to those hardy enough to reach her summit. At the bottom of Kawati Top, smaller trails branched off left and right. Compared to the Voltz, which had been cleared for those tourists and was the equivalent of a two-lane highway, Stanley's side trails were barely footpaths through the bush, many of them invisible to the untrained eye and most of them pathways that Stanley had struck and cleared himself. He spoke their names aloud as he passed, a routine he'd developed in the early years so he wouldn't get lost but that now served no other purpose than to make him feel at home. Domineestraat. Hollywood Boulevard. The Danforth. Fifth Avenue. Downing Street. Vilakazi Street. Broadway. Stanley had cut and named more than fifty trails since he'd arrived and by now the system was so complex that every couple of weeks he had to take a day away from the monkeys to hike the nether regions, the places the monkeys hadn't visited in a long time, to ensure the trails were clear. These were some of his favourite excursions, the inevitable tree-falls, collapsed lianas, riotous overgrowth and herds of jungle pigs reminding him just how quickly the forest could advance when you turned your back on it.

That morning the monkeys were right where he'd left them. On Casanova, Stanley dropped his pack, chugged some water and set up his camp chair for the first scans of the day. It was too early to identify individuals; they were up too high and the light was still poor. But Stanley could begin counting, which he was eager to do. His first count was fourteen, understandable considering some of the young might still be on their mother's backs and the subordinate males were probably still on the periphery. Fifteen minutes later, he counted eighteen, one less than a full complement. As the troop moved north and began crossing the Voltz, Stanley packed up and rushed ahead of them. He took a shortcut through the bog, which was now dry but would become impassable with the rains. He emerged on Saki Trail and made straight for the amphitheatre, a semi-circular dome of foliage next to the bamboo patch. He dropped his camp chair, sat down and waited.

Jerry and Costanza were the first to arrive. Juvenile males of roughly the same age, the two could always be found in close proximity to each other and were often the ones leading the way into the bamboo. As they dropped into the amphitheatre Stanley could see their flashes, the triangular patches of blond hair that most capuchins had above each eye but that in Jerry and Costanza's case were uniquely bright. Next came Agnes and Lucy, the elder stateswomen of the troop whom Stanley knew by their slender, elderly bodies and protruding ears. Following the old ladies were the youngsters Mignon, Banana and Peanut, who dropped all the way to the amphitheatre floor and began wrestling each other at Stanley's feet. When he accidentally dropped his notebook the young monkeys jumped and voiced a series of high-pitched squeaks, the immature precursors to terrestrial predator alarms. Once they'd determined it was only Stanley the kids returned to their roughhousing, and the rest of the troop appeared overhead.

In primatological field studies, monkeys were usually assigned names from a small set of categories. The most common names referenced a monkey's appearance, the obvious example among the Longfellows being the adorable Mignon. Next came the monkeys named after foods, such as Banana and Peanut, and those named after researchers' family members, like Aunt Lucy and Granny Agnes. Then there were the icons of pop culture (Jerry and Costanza), sports (Holyfield and Martina), film (Denzel, Dustin and Marilyn) and religious figures both ancient and contemporary (Suri Rama, Athena and Moses). Finally, to allow for local flavour, monkeys might be named after domestic political leaders past and present. Johan, the alpha male of the Longfellows and a bruiser of a monkey, was named after Sir Johan Ferdinand, who served as the country's first president and who was almost deposed in the late '80s during the attempted coup d'état. Beatrix, the highest-ranking female, was named after the queen of the Netherlands.

But there were exceptions. Stanley had named Wacky during the first week of the project after he'd observed a large, sub-adult male slamming a *Phenakospermum guianense* nut against the fork of a tree. The nut eventually burst open, Wacky had fed voraciously on the sweet coating of the seeds inside, and the groundwork was laid for Stanley and Maria's first paper and a multi-year grant from the Leakey Foundation to study proto–tool use among capuchins. Wacky would eventually graduate from whacking nuts to fishing for termites, a form of tool use previously thought to be the sole domain of the apes.

Stanley had named Charlie just a few days after he'd been born, the day after Maria had left Camp Collymore. Charlie could be identified by the patch of bright white hair at the end of his tail.

Where the hell is Moses?

The troop had swept en masse into the bamboo, but Stanley had only counted eighteen and he'd identified them all. Moses? Where are you, little man? Stanley left the amphitheatre and ran down Saki in both directions. Maybe Moses had followed a different route into the patch? This was something Wacky might do but not Moses, a three-year-old who rarely strayed from his mother, Martina. Moses was a fuzzy-butt, so-called because he was so young his hair still stood on end. Fuzzy-butts were no trailblazers.

Moses! Stanley poked his head down the Appian Way.

Stanley did not expect the monkeys to come running at the sound of their names. The Longfellows were wild primates, the furthest things from domestic pets and only partially habituated to humans. Their names were not for them to comprehend but for the researchers to use, tools of the scientific trade. Stanley spoke aloud to Moses not because he expected an answer but because after so many years alone in the forest he had begun regularly speaking his mind to the trees. He'd been doing it so long it had become an unbreakable habit, and as a result Stanley rarely kept a private, personal moment to himself. Everything he thought, imagined, believed and hoped for eventually escaped his mouth when he was alone in the bush.

Over the years Stanley's conscious mind had seemed to merge with the forest. His practice of thinking aloud and releasing commentary to the canopy reminded him of only one other person he'd ever known—his old boss, Professor Collymore, who according to the university had suffered a psychological break and had mysteriously disappeared more than seven years ago—and Stanley often wondered if his own behaviour might represent the early stages of a similarly ugly progression, one that would end with his own annihilation. Maria would have had a different take, of course. The word isn't "annihilation," Stanley, but "amalgamation." A joining of your being with the being of the jungle. Yes. These sorts of thoughts both haunted him and cheered him up on his way home every night, especially now that he only ever walked home in the dark.

Stanley went all the way down the Appian Way, which bisected the patch and was the best place to set up shop. He found Jerry and Costanza lazily crossing over, pulling shoots as they went and munching on the fresh ends. He could hear the others behind them. But no Moses. Partway down the trail was the only tree in the patch, a huge Inga that towered above the bamboo. Makeshift ladder rungs had been nailed to its trunk, and Stanley climbed these rungs now to the observation deck, two planks of plywood nailed across a fork in the trunk. He pulled himself up to stand and looked out at his monkeys below. Brown mice inching their way across a bright green shag carpet. He counted eighteen. He counted again: eighteen. Stanley descended, set up his camp chair and opened his notebook.

Let the record show: Moses is gone.

6

THE ISLAND AT ROOSVALLEN IS LONG AND SKINNY and lies at the foot of an idyllic set of rapids. Visiting tourists would always end their days with a swim in those swirling waters, and every year one of them would step on an electric eel and nearly die. It didn't matter how many times this happened, or how many tourists returned to the city with stories of near-death, or how close Benny came to withholding CPR from the latest victim. No one could resist the waters of Roosvallen. When the river was low you could stand atop the boulders overlooking the swimming hole and count hundreds of black eels knotted there, biding their time.

South of the island lay a boulder-strewn stretch of river, where Camp Collymore was located on the eastern shore. South of camp lay Moedervallen, Mother Falls, a mile-long stretch of impassable white-water that signalled the end of human habitation and the beginning of the back country. Moedervallen was sacred to the Maroons.

Petrus picked Stanley up on the beach at five o'clock. On game days Stanley left the monkeys early in order to make it to the island for kickoff, and even though Moses's disappearance worried him, Stanley figured there was nothing he could do about it. His only course of action was to do what he'd been doing for what felt like an eternity: keep his distance, observe everything, write it all down.

As the boat wound its way between the rocks Stanley mentally prepared himself for battle. They reached the island in ten minutes, skipped the usual rounds through the village and made straight for the hill to the airstrip. Up top, Stanley found the Boyz assembled in front of the radio house, arguing over whose turn it was to get the goalposts.

Stan-ley! said Benny.

Fuck you.

Stan-ley! said Raymond.

I spend the whole day in there. One of you go.

Mon-key! yelled Hank, and the Maroons collapsed with laughter.

Hank and Stanley had never liked each other. This was partly due to Hank's ex-wife, a beautiful Hindu woman named Sun who used to visit Hank in the bush twice a month. One night, during a party for the tourists, Sun had managed to fall in love with Stanley just a few hours after meeting him—something about his slim build and wild hair had reminded her of a Hindu god. Hank had never learned of Sun's feelings toward Stanley, though he had suspected Stanley's toward Sun—she wore her long black hair in a braid, just as Maria had done. But Hank's issue with Stanley and vice versa went far deeper than some woman who eventually left them both for an import-export guy up in Trinidad. Their enmity for each other was the pure stuff.

Hey, Hank, said Stanley. I saw your *babun* today.

The laughter stopped. Hank swept a hand over his bald head.

She looked really nice, Stanley continued. I think she's ready for you.

Hank lunged at Stanley but the others got between them before anything could happen. Stanley stumbled backwards and smiled. Today will be a good game.

Hank was rumoured to have about twelve bloods running through his veins. He was descended from every race that had ever lived in the country, whether they were indigenous, part of a conquering force or brought over in the tens of thousands to work the plantations. In a country of proud ethnicities Hank was profoundly mixed—his skin the colour of milk chocolate but his eyes almond-shaped and blue, his nose Roman but his lips round and full, his torso slim but deceptively bound with muscle—and therefore racist jokes about cross-species primate love always hit their mark with him. Stanley had to give credit where it was due, though; Hank's fists were quick, and he was a lot more sensitive than he looked.

As usual, Shike lost the argument about the goalposts. With a loud tooth-suck he raised his hands to the sky and broke into a sprint to the other side of the strip. Eh! yelled Benny after the boy. You forgot this. Benny grabbed his machete by the blade, leaned back and hurled it end-over-end towards Shike. Given the size of Benny's pot-belly, the effort caused him to resemble a pear rocking back and forth on a tabletop. The blade travelled a total of ten feet before skidding into the dirt. More laughter. Shike ran back to pick up the machete and resumed his sprint, diving into the bush from which the airstrip had been cleared decades before. His dreads disappeared into the green a split-second after his gigantic frame did. Minutes later Shike emerged with four thick branches shorn of their leaves and the game began.

The Boyz never picked teams or sides. Whoever had the ball would just boot it straight up into the air and whichever end of the pitch you happened to be standing in at the time would be your end. Hank and Stanley were never on the same team, of course, but Stanley had played with every other Roos Boy and had become well acquainted with each of their strengths and failings on the ball.

Benny couldn't run and never tried to. Instead, he would position himself at the halfway mark and call for the ball. If your pass was perfectly weighted it would allow Benny to act as a wall, the ball bouncing off his immense stomach or ricocheting off one of his chicken legs directly into the path of a teammate. One touch!

One touch! Benny would yell in such instances, as if no one else on the pitch would ever know the pleasures of such immaculate ball control. Benny never took two touches. If your pass to Benny was less than inch-perfect, he would simply let the ball go by him, scream obscenities at you and switch teams.

Raymond, a Maroon in his early forties and the lead vocalist of the Roos Boyz, played the game with his mouth. He would take a few touches here and there, and he wasn't a terrible passer of the ball, relatively speaking. But it was with his voice that he made the most impact. Whenever an attacking player neared the goal with the ball at their feet, Raymond would stop running and begin to sing. There were no lyrics. He would just emit one long note which would rise in volume and pitch the closer the attacker got to the goal. If the player scored, Raymond's voice would crescendo into a screech of excitement, and he would jump onto the scorer's back in celebration regardless of which team he was on. If the player flubbed the chance and missed, Raymond would do exactly the same thing, piggyback included. In other words, Raymond was more like an amnesiac season ticket holder than an actual player, participating in the game as if he were both up in the nosebleeds and storming the pitch.

Shike, Alberto and Frank Lampard were all in their late teens, spectacularly athletic and utterly oblivious to physical risk. This meant that when they competed with you for a ball, the best course of action was simply to move aside and let them crash into somebody else. It didn't help that all three were helplessly in love with hash, and would always smoke right before kickoff. Shike had fetched the goalposts from the forest every single time they'd played football up there. He had long since burned through his short- and long-term memory, which was probably a blessing considering his entire family had been gunned down in front of him during a botched robbery in the capital when he was twelve, but the others knew of his disability and constantly took advantage of it. The only thing Shike could recall with regular certitude was whether or not you had paid him for his weed.

Then there was Hank. Rumour had it that Hank had once played semi-professionally in the capital, and in his teens a Dutch scout had taken notice and offered him a trial at the Ajax academy. This trial came with that most coveted document in the years just after independence: a passport to the Netherlands. Rumour also had it that Hank turned down this offer out of youthful allegiance to his home country, even though the domestic league was just a small-time casino for military men and their arrogant sons, and Hank's home country had never once shown allegiance to anyone of such mongrel lineage. It's possible, of course, that a poorly paid cook and occasional tour guide at a dilapidated tourist lodge in the middle of the Amazonian jungle would have many reasons to start rumours such as these, as well as plenty of time to work on his ball skills. But if there was one thing Stanley had learned about Hank it was that feelings of excommunication ran deep in the man. Hank's every word and action was drenched in resentment.

Hank's play appeared effortless, his touch perfect, his use of open space predatory, and when Hank felt the rare need to pass, the ball would end up on his teammate's foot before they knew they were open. At times it seemed absurd to have a player of Hank's quality take part in these ragtag games on the airstrip. But the deficiencies of the others usually balanced things out, such that Hank's record and therefore Stanley's had about as many losses as wins.

Stanley's side went up two–nil within ten minutes. Frank Lampard and Alberto, in a surprisingly lucid display of collaboration, had combined on the first. The other was scored by Stanley after he'd seized on an errant pass from Raymond. As Raymond had jumped on Stanley's back to celebrate his mistake, Hank had leapt on his teammates.

Shike! You *fukkup*, boy!

Shike, who had played no part in the lapse, looked bemused.

No me. Ray-Ray give way.

Aiiieeee! said Raymond, forcing Stanley to his knees.

Boy! Hank approached Shike, put his arm around the boy's shoulders and muttered a few words. Shike nodded and the two parted.

The next time Hank had possession he went around two players with ease and laid the ball into Shike's path. At first, the pass appeared an uncharacteristically poor one, having led Shike a bit too much. But soon the wisdom of the play became clear; this was a hospital ball. Desmond, the fifty-something radio operator whose only exercise aside from these weekly games was lifting a bottle of *palum* to his mouth and chasing the local jaguar off the airstrip each morning, was the closest player from Stanley's team, so he gave chase. Shike and Desmond arrived at the ball at the very same moment, and the resultant snapping sound echoed against the wall of forest. It was so loud that Petrus called out in shock from his seat in front of the radio house. The lack of blood was a surprise to everyone, but surely a lesser surprise than the splintered shinbone protruding from Desmond's leg. Desmond, to his great credit, managed a few words of prayer to the ancestors before he passed out.

Petrus and a few other onlookers arrived to carry Desmond down to the village. Shike, who would forget the entire incident by sundown, looked contrite. Hank simply stood between his goalposts, saying nothing to no one.

Twenty minutes later the game was tied. Hank scored the first, a glorious solo effort from end to end, and Benny, bless his heart, managed the second—although, in fairness, he'd been bent over picking a *maka* spine out of his foot at the moment of impact and only determined the source of the sting on his ass when Raymond leapt onto his back.

Soon the sun was slipping below the canopy, the *siksi-yuru* had begun to scythe, the macaws were flying multiple sorties home and the next goal would win. Stanley got the ball in his own half, spread it wide to Frank Lampard and made for the opposing goal. Then Hank was at his side, marking him man for man, his fists digging into Stanley's sides. Frank Lampard made it to the goal line and chipped the ball across, and as Stanley prepared to leap and head the ball home Hank grabbed him by the beard, gave a swift yank and buried the point of his elbow into Stanley's left temple.

Stanley's world spun. Dust mouth. Footsteps downfield. Raymond's excited voice. The last thing Stanley remembered was Benny leaning over him.

One touch.

7

Collymore, C. "New World in the New World: Revelation and Magic in a Unique Ecological Niche for the Brown Capuchin Monkey (*C. apella*)." *Nature* 455 (2008): 1279–80.

I freely admit that it is never a good sign when a dispatch from the field begins with a plea for forgiveness. But I know the way your mind works, dear reader, and having read the title of this article—the first of its kind since our editors loosened their kerchiefs and voted to include personal memoir in these distinguished pages—your insides will surely have shrivelled into a tight, unbelieving little ball already. "Revelation and magic? In our most illustrious scientific journal? This Collymore character should be strung up!" But please, dear reader, allow me the benefit of your doubt for just a few short moments before skipping ahead to the "real" science on offer. I promise to keep this brief.

You see, I have discovered a new world.

As you may know, I have spent the last thirty-five years studying the natural history of primate species from both monkey superfamilies, the Ceboidea and the Cercopithecoidea, both Old World and New. I have run the numbers, and by conservative estimates I have spent approximately 400% more time in community with wild monkeys than I have with human beings. I have lived and worked in ecosystems as biologically diverse and geographically far-flung as the Boumba Bek basin in Cameroon, Central Kalimantan on the island of Borneo and the Osa Peninsula in

Costa Rica. Over the years my research has resulted in the development of several new ethological theories pertaining to social organization, cultural transmission and seed dispersal in primates, and the legislated protection of over 15 million hectares of rainforest. In the process, I have also discovered five new species of rodent, twenty-seven new species of tree and innumerable new species of beetle (one of which survives exclusively on the feces of female monkeys in estrus. . . . I like to think of this one as a wee gift for our Creationist friends to grapple with).

It appears that I have also earned a reputation for bravado. I am under the strongest possible impression that this reputation is more a result of the lay public's misapprehension of the earth's wildest places than a function of egomania or a screw coming loose in my noodle. (So I wear sandals in the bush instead of boots; who wants to wear sodden socks all day? And the story about my tracking a jaguar back to its lair is true, I admit, but the blasted feline had stolen one of my notebooks, and I refuse to stand for such insolence.) But again, the benefit of the doubt is entirely yours to distribute as you see fit.

Two years ago, I believed I had documented the intimate unfolding of primate lives in every possible earthly environment. I was also beginning to consider retirement. And then I paid a visit to a remote rainforest north of the Upper Amazon basin, a virgin jungle rumoured to be home to multiple species of monkey. What I found there challenged, and continues to challenge, the very tenets of ecological viability.

Simply put, the forest there should not exist.

How's that for bravado?

Upon first glimpse, the jungle presented like any other. But as my boatman brought me to shore at a small beach halfway down the river called Cariban, and I took my first few exploratory steps into the bush, I sensed that I had found something entirely original and as yet unknown to science, a place literally brimming with scholarly potential. The understory was thicker than any I'd ever seen. Tree trunks grew closer together than they should have, almost as if they shared root systems. Lianas hung down from the canopy not like individual ropes but like entire sets of venetian blinds. And the canopy itself allowed such little light to reach the forest floor that to walk beneath it at the height of the day one could almost have used a flashlight. This jungle was more tangled and snarled and matted and dark than any I'd ever walked in. It became, for me, the new high-water mark for biological fecundity.

I admit now that I felt the uniqueness of this place in my heart long before I had hard evidence for it. But the evidence did come. Preliminary phenology studies revealed a diversity of fruiting trees in an order of magnitude larger than any recorded in the tropics before. Even more surprising, composition and pH-testing demonstrated that the soils underpinning the forest were profoundly rich in life-giving nutrients. This contradicts the conventional wisdom that tropical soils are always nutrient-poor, and that the fecundity of rainforests relies upon the ability of resident flora to adapt novel methods of survival (enter the mycorrhizae, the symbiotic relationships between root-dwelling fungi and plants, a truly ingenious way of overcoming nutrient deficiency).

But no need for friendly fungus in this forest. And did I mention that the trees were dripping with monkeys? Eight species in total, with brown capuchins (my personal favourites) by far the most numerous.

I had discovered a new world for New World monkeys.

After a career spent building a forest of knowledge about our primate friends, this forest represented an entirely clean slate. No monkey we have studied before lives in a place like this. Diet choice, foraging efficiency, activity budgets, social organization, evolutionary genetics, troop paternity, troop movement, the mysteries of traplining, infant motor development, precursory tool use, predation vigilance strategies, especially those directed toward birds of prey . . . the biological questions emanating from this jungle were, and are, limitless. And that's not to mention the botanical, ethnographic and environmental opportunities for study, from canopy structure to photophobic vegetation to bio-prospecting to climate change to the impact of ecotourism as the human and wild worlds collide. Within six months of those soil results, the National Science Foundation, the Leakey Foundation and UNESCO had come on board. Now, with every data point we collect and with every paper we publish, we might as well be writing the natural history of an entirely new primate species.

I must say, there is something spiritually uplifting about having been given this opportunity at this late stage in my career, something that smacks of the mystical and the missionary all at once. As you read this, two of my best field assistants and I will be settling into our new home in this mysterious jungle—for how long, nobody knows. Our research, the best research I will ever do, is about to begin.

So why is the soil in this forest so rich and sustaining? Where do the nutrients come from? It thrills me to say I have no idea, and to be honest I don't really care. I am an ethologist, not an environmental chemist, and I leave those questions to the qualified. The local people here, who are known as the Maroons, believe the forest is so fecund because their ancestors are buried beneath it. This sort of magical thinking is, of course, not exactly my cup of tea, but with no better explanation at hand I can only say that such a benevolent and fertile form of magic is unlikely to obstruct our attempts at serious scientific inquiry. To the contrary, these forests I've stumbled upon and the monkey communities therein represent one of the greatest ethological opportunities since Dr. Goodall disappeared into the jungles of Gombe. Our hope and expectation is that in the coming years the revelations we dutifully collect from our new jungle home will appear in the peer-reviewed pages that follow these admittedly more prosaic ones—the pages to which, I am sure, you scholars and skeptics are desperate to flee as you read these final words.

Revelation and magic, indeed.

Sincerely,
Dr. C. Collymore
Professor Emeritus, at large

8

~

THE TOUCANS HAD BEEN CALLING FOR HOURS when they finally woke Stanley. His last dream was of Raymond perched in a tree high above camp, throwing nuts onto the roof below and yelping in celebration of the rising sun. Opening his eyes, Stanley cringed at the shrill calls and the heat built up in his hammock. The living room was filled with light.

Stanley rolled out and reached for his pants. The blood rushed and he remembered his temple, which had evolved a tender lump where Hank had clocked him. He stood, threw on his clothes, filled his water bottles and grabbed his gear. Part of him knew he was probably rushing for nothing, just another boring day around the bamboo. Another part of him, the stronger part, knew that if he didn't go today he might not go tomorrow, or the day after tomorrow. Routine, said Stanley, admonishing himself as he pulled the door shut behind him. Practice.

Searching for the monkeys had been much easier back when Maria was still on the project. The two would head out together before dawn, and at the bottom of Kawati Top they would split up without a word. One would walk south on Broadway and the other would walk north, and for the next twenty minutes or ninety minutes or four hours they would communicate solely by walkie-talkie. The pair had quickly learned that just because they had left

45

the troop in a particular spot the evening before, this didn't mean they would be anywhere near that spot the next morning. It was as if the monkeys were simian somnambulists, as if the whole troop would regularly sleepwalk together in the middle of the night, and by morning they could be anywhere. The first few times Stanley and Maria went their separate ways at the bottom of Kawati Top, both had been terrified by the prospect—the jungles of Roosvallen are among the oldest, wildest and most diverse ecosystems on earth, and to walk them alone at dawn with nothing more than a machete for protection is to welcome every fear into the trees and every nightmare into the understory. Neither Stanley nor Maria would admit their fear to the other back then, but as they hiked deeper into solitude both would yearn for the crackle of their walkie-talkies, for the disembodied voice of their spouse announcing they had found the monkeys on this or that trail. Meeting up again beneath the troop Stanley and Maria would always embrace, quietly acknowledging the profound loneliness each had just experienced, quietly celebrating that this loneliness had been banished for the day. I love you, Stanley, Maria would say while they hugged. So, so much.

On those rare occasions when they could find no monkeys at all, Stanley would descend into a funk. For him, a day without primates was a waste. He could appreciate the fecundity of the jungle, its essential wildness, but only in terms of how this impacted the monkey populations. How does foraging efficiency change across the seasons here? What impact might this have on group dynamics or territory size? And what small corner of evolutionary theory might these findings help illuminate? Maria, on the contrary, considered the fecundity of the jungle to be the point. By studying the monkeys and learning just how deeply they were embedded in their habitat she would build an incontestable case for conservation, for the continuing protection of this jungle and every living thing within it. So on days when they couldn't find the troop Maria simply shifted her focus to another part of the forest—a phenology census, perhaps, or an interview with Petrus about his knowledge of medicinal plants. Maria knew how tenuous a national conservation regime could be in a country like this: a young democracy born through violence, nestled into a quiet corner of the developing world just north of Amazonia. The more knowledge Maria could tease from this ecosystem, the less likely it would be that a timber company or mining conglomerate would be allowed to worm its way into the halls of power and gain the rights to exploit this place.

Stanley had come to Roosvallen primarily to document the monkeys and to learn from them, but Maria had come here to protect them. Both were gifted young scientists seeking answers to important questions, and for the most part these questions complemented each other. But Maria would frequently tease Stanley about his obsession with the data. Dr. Stanley, she would say in a coquettish voice upon waking in their tent. I must apologize, Dr. Stanley, but I forgot to record the canopy height and troop dispersal of my dreams.

Stanley pushed the memories of Maria to the back of his mind and made straight for the Appian Way. He heard no monkeys there, climbed the Inga to make sure. Nothing. Then he went north, around Jag Junction and down Pancho Villa, where he finally heard something, but in the opposite direction than he'd expected. He found the Longfellows over on Main Street, far to the east of the patch and less than a mile from the furthest reaches of the study site. A number of maripa palms had burst their sheaths and fruited. The whole troop were about sixty-two feet up, hopping back and forth between the crowns of two maripa, squeaking with pleasure and eating their fill.

That, dear sir, is a veritable orgy of conspicuous consumption, said Stanley, imitating Professor Collymore's brogue, which had always made Maria laugh. He dropped his camp chair and opened his notebook to record the first good data in at least a month.

Hungry little bastards. You see, Johan? They should have you impeached. Bamboo just doesn't compare.

Stanley unclipped his walkie-talkie, raised it to his mouth, an absurd but harmless little habit that made him feel less alone.

Stanley here, said Stanley. I know you're not listening anymore, but we've got nuts. Over.

He conducted a headcount, assuming that yesterday had just been an anomaly and that Moses would have grown bored of whatever adventure he'd been having and rejoined the troop. It was rare for a monkey to go missing for longer than a few hours, but it wasn't unheard of. Every few months Stanley would hear the mournful, distant sound of a capuchin lost-call, and he would brace himself for the beautiful response, every monkey in the troop echoing the call and guiding the lost individual back into the fold. But he had heard no lost-calls yesterday or this afternoon, and now when he counted the monkeys he only came up with seventeen, two fewer than normal. Who's missing now? said Stanley. The troop was too high up for him to ID individuals with good certainty, and headcounts were notoriously difficult when the troop were in a feeding frenzy, so Stanley decided to start the workday and wait for the right time to investigate further.

For the next two hours Stanley wrote furiously in his notebook. He recorded which monkeys were together in which tree, who was feeding in the best spots, who each monkey was feeding next to and how many nuts each individual could process per minute. Stanley marked the palms by wrapping orange tape around their trunks and scribbling the date onto it with permanent marker. He collected a few nuts the caps had dropped, arranged them on a blank piece of graph paper, wrote down their Latin name and the date and photographed the exhibit for his files. He fetched from his pack several plastic vials filled with rubbing alcohol and his small trowel and began walking back and forth beneath the monkeys, searching for the telltale smudges of green on the forest floor and wincing every time one of them landed on his head or shoulders. When he found fresh poop he knelt down, scraped some of it into an open vial with the trowel, sealed the lid and wrapped a piece of tape around the seam, again with the date and time written on it. Meanwhile, every fifteen minutes Stanley performed group scans, estimating the elevation and spread of the troop to the nearest foot and performing headcounts, which continually came up two short. He made a note of any co-specifics in the area, like the small white hawks who gorged themselves on insects stirred up by the caps, or the orange-rumped agoutis who scavenged among the dropped stones for leftover morsels, or the troops of squirrel monkeys who sometimes travelled for a week or more with the capuchins, or the yellow-footed tortoises who would occasionally rumble by and sniff the air. Every time one of the monkeys displayed or gave a terrestrial predator alarm or began to play, Stanley marked it down. The beauty of a baseline ecological study was that all information was potential data. One could never tell which solitary happening or collection thereof might provide understanding, insight or even hard-boiled scientific breakthrough. Stanley recorded everything he saw and heard, the whole story of the jungle, just as he'd been trained to do all those years ago and just as he'd done every day since, and as he did so a calm came over him, a feeling he vaguely recognized, something close to virtue, something like a forgetting. He loved this feeling. He started to sing. He sang aloud to the animals and imagined his voice passing into the trunks of nearby trees and rising to their crowns by vascular force.

Maria would be proud, he thought.

Stanley spotted Charlie, the flash of white at the tip of his tail. Hello, Charlie. Hello, little man. Charlie was an especially bold and confident monkey, always willing to roughhouse with the youngsters or pick a fight with a gang of squirrel monkeys or attempt to feed in a high-status position next to Johan, the alpha, a dangerous behaviour that usually resulted in his being violently expelled from whichever tree the monkeys were feeding in. But every bit of trouble Charlie got into resonated with Stanley, more so than the actions and escapades of the other capuchins. Stanley felt it when Johan barked or lunged at Charlie. He had sympathized on those rare occasions over the years when Charlie's mother, Marilyn, had refused him suckle. And every time Charlie lost his balance or stumbled or fell, which the monkey did more often than the others, Stanley experienced a twinge of concern not unlike the worry a father might feel towards his clumsy child.

As he watched Charlie fling himself clear of the palm tree, Stanley thought back to the day he'd first laid eyes on the monkey, the day after Maria had left Camp Collymore. That morning, and for the first time since the monkey project had begun, Stanley had hiked in and found the monkeys by himself. He and Maria had suffered such devastation over the previous few days that he could barely walk straight, and he was still drunk, having spent the night swilling *palum* in his hammock, the sour fermented brew addling his mind as he read and reread the cryptic message Maria had left behind on the kitchen table. But when he spotted the newborn monkey between Marilyn's front legs, saw the upside-down face and tiny eyelids still shut to the world, a sudden sobriety overtook Stanley. Charlie was the first monkey to be born into the troop since the researchers had arrived. The scientific potential of this event was tremendous, as Stanley could now watch a wild monkey develop from birth. But this was not why Charlie was so special. And it wasn't the blotch of white on his tail, either. Stanley had lost everything—his child, his wife and colleague, his mentor, his sense of order in the world. Here in this newborn monkey was something he could hold on to.

9
~

IELD SCIENTISTS OFTEN LOSE TRACK OF THEIR study subjects, especially when they are as mobile as primates, and even Professor Collymore admitted to "misplacing" his animals every now and then. After Stanley and Maria had landed at Pangol International on that day eight years ago, Collymore had taken his new assistants for dinner at an upscale restaurant that claimed to be the only sushi spot on the continent north of the Amazon. Over a boat of defrosted sashimi, Professor Collymore shared one of his most embarrassing flubs in the field. It was his first assistantship, in Manú National Park in Peru, and he'd been tracking a troop of brown capuchins on the far eastern border of the reserve when the monkeys ran into another troop of about the same size. Chaos descended upon the forest, and as the alpha males shook the trees and shrieked at each other, and as monkeys fled in every direction, Collymore raced through the understory, trying desperately to keep track of his study troop while recording as much of the rare encounter behaviour as he could.

The canopy was a cloud of panicking animals, said Collymore. Their movements seemed completely and utterly random. I like to say I witnessed Brownian Capuchin Motion that day.

The encounter only lasted fifteen minutes, but when the bedlam was over Collymore found himself lost. There were monkeys above him, and he was pretty sure they were his study troop, but he was now a long way off-trail. He'd forgotten his compass that morning and therefore had no idea which direction camp was.

So, what do you think I did next? asked Collymore, eyeing his new apprentices.

You stayed with your monkeys, said Maria.

Always stay with the monkeys, said Stanley.

Exactly right. I remained with the troop. I was sure that soon enough they would circle back to familiar territory and I would stumble upon my trails.

Collymore started to laugh.

Small problem, he continued. These were not my monkeys.

Holy fuck, said Maria.

As you say, my dear. The very thing we live in fear of. My monkeys had given me the slip. Really quite the pickle.

Somehow, amidst the melee, Collymore had mistaken the alpha of the other troop for his own, and now he was lost on the Peruvian border with Bolivia, hitching his ride to a troop he knew nothing about and that could very easily lead him into oblivion.

I was out there for five days, said Collymore.

No, said Stanley.

Everyone thought I was dead. They'd already sent word home. Ruined my first marriage, if we're being forthright.

But five days?

That was the last time I ever wore boots in the field. Five days in socks and my feet were carpaccio.

How did you get back? asked Maria.

My plan worked, eventually. The monkeys did circle back. They spent the next four weeks at war with my study troop over a particularly rich stand of fig trees. Vicious battles, those were.

As Collymore described various scenes of simian bloodshed, Stanley tried to imagine how he himself might have survived similar circumstances, lost and alone in an unfamiliar jungle with no supplies but what you happened to be carrying on your back.

He liked to think he would be fine, indeed that he would thrive.

In the middle of the dining room sat a hulking piece of black-ened machinery, a peculiar eyesore that would have been better suited as the decorative focal point of a hip bourbon joint in some post-industrial American city. When Stanley asked Collymore about it, the professor's eyes lit up.

Stanley, my lad. What a wonderful segue you've provided us. War and violence in primates, indeed.

Apparently, the bistro they were eating at had been built atop the ruined foundations of the country's only independent news-paper, *De Vrije Tijd*. The paper had been firebombed back in the late 1980s during the civil war that had raged after independence, and the gargantuan printing press was the only piece of equipment to survive the devastation. Somehow, the paper began publishing again just three weeks later, and according to Collymore, no one had ever been held responsible for the attack. Was it supporters of the rebel Maroons, who had risen up in the western jungles and were threat-ening the capital back then? Or was it just a savvy piece of drama orchestrated by the government to bring a frightened populace into line? Decades later, opinions still differed on the matter.

Diversity and peaceful pluralism, said Collymore, as Stanley and Maria felt the first rumblings of rot in their bellies. That's what this country is known for. All these cultures shipped over by the Dutch and then abandoned here once imperialism became uncouth. And yet somehow, against all their basest instincts, they find a way to get along. Hell, just a hop, skip and a jump from here a synagogue shares its parking lot with a mosque! Collymore laughed again. It's a racist, post-colonial narrative if I've ever heard one. Don't be fooled, my dears. I've worked in too many developing nations to believe the marketing hype of a young democracy and their outmoded schol-ars. Like every country, this place was forged through violence and suffering. Believe me, strife is never far from the surface here.

10

~

By four thirty Stanley was exhausted. The sun was dropping, the Longfellows had ravaged six palm trees since noon and they showed little sign of stopping. You won't sleep where you shit, he said. You've got to move sooner or later. He went back through his notes from the day to see if he could deduce which monkey had joined Moses in going AWOL. He was reasonably certain that he had seen Beatrix, Wacky, Costanza, Jerry, Holyfield, Martina and Denzel. Add the unmistakable Johan to the list, and the ancient Lucy, and that was about half the troop accounted for.

Wait, thought Stanley. I saw Lucy. But where is Agnes?

Stanley stood, raised his glasses and scanned the troop one by one. He would be able to tell Agnes apart, just as he'd picked out Lucy, because both had become slimmed by old age and moved much slower than the rest. Also, Agnes only had half a tail, which made her distinct from Lucy. He searched for an elderly monkey with a stump-tail among the palms. Twenty minutes later he was still looking.

And then the light flickered.

Stanley dropped his glasses, held his breath, listened. The near-imperceptible shift in daylight had lifted the hairs on his neck. As a trained evolutionary biologist Stanley knew that spontaneous physical reactions like this—sensations that are usually considered vestigial to modern life, like the unconscious raising of one's hackles or the shiver up and down one's spine—were not to be ignored in the wild. Instead they were to be respected for what they were: physiological warning signs. Stanley scanned the canopy, saw nothing unusual. But as he prepared to sit down again he realized his monkeys had gone quiet. No husks rained down. No squeaks of pleasure.

He raised his binoculars, and it began.

West of the palms, in the high canopy of a *kankan* tree, a blackness unfurled. It grew like an ink splotch against the setting sun. As Stanley watched, the black expanded and then shrank, tipped into the air and swooped toward the palms.

No.

One of the Longfellows, probably Johan, barked an alarm call. But it was too late. The blackness smashed into the palm like a mortar, the sheaths exploding on impact, nuts and screaming monkeys raining to the forest floor. Stanley had always been amazed by the capuchin's ability to jump impossible chasms and land comfortably in the next tree over. But now, for the first time, Stanley watched his monkeys flail. They crashed through a liana tangle one by one. A few of them managed to slow their descent but others weren't so lucky. Soon monkeys were thumping to the floor in front of him, and no matter how far they'd fallen they hit the ground running. The barking continued up above, but the rest of the monkeys had stopped screaming and gone eerily quiet. He saw Beatrix with Mignon on her back. He saw Jerry and Costanza, Banana and Denzel. He tried to count but lost track. The monkeys ran silently on all fours towards Stanley, and for a moment he thought they were coming to him for comfort. He knelt down. He prepared to embrace as many as he could. It's okay. It's going to be okay. But the monkeys ran right past him. They crossed Main Street and stole into the bush, in the direction of the bamboo.

Stanley stood, collected himself, trained his glasses back to the crown of the palm. And for the second time in less than a minute he saw something he'd never seen before. Perched on top of a barren nut sheath was a massive figure. It was so large that at first Stanley wasn't sure what he was looking at. But then she swivelled her head and he saw the telltale crown feathers. In the next palm over, Johan was going berserk. With his tail wrapped around a branch he was throwing himself towards the assailant again and again, barking his high-pitched warnings, gnashing his teeth and swatting at her, his hair on end, bravely defending his troop and enabling their escape. But the bird paid Johan no notice. Her eyes black, her beak a charcoal scythe, her white breast swollen to the point of caricature, she exhibited a poise and serenity that under the circumstances horrified Stanley. With a great shrug of her shoulders she spread her wings—eight feet, maybe ten—and leapt from her perch. Stanley caught his breath, but not because of the prodigious wingspan or the renewed ferocity of Johan's display. Stanley watched as the largest and most powerful bird of prey in the Americas swept out of the forest, the limp body of a capuchin monkey clutched in her talons.

WHO WAS THAT? WAS IT CHARLIE? IT COULD have been Charlie.

Stanley ran. He stopped on Pancho Villa for a moment to listen but heard nothing. Johan appeared, his hair still on end. He, too, crept on all fours into the patch. Dusk had fallen. Stanley kept running. He went south, crossed the bog and hit the Voltzberg, where he upped his pace. Vilakazi Street. Downing Street. Fifth Avenue. The Danforth. By the time he reached Hollywood Boulevard he was out of breath. Eight years, said Stanley. Eight years and not one sighting. He was walking now, his leg muscles burning. Who did she get? Who was that? Was there white on the tail? Please don't let it be Charlie. When he reached Kawati Top darkness had set in. He dug in his pack, pulled out his headlamp and connected the dots. That's what happened to Moses. She must have taken Moses, too. As he arrived at the bottom of Ant Hill, Stanley came to the only possible conclusion: his monkeys were under attack.

Instead of climbing the hill Stanley ran to the beach and dropped his pack in the sand. The rush of Moedervallen reached him on the breeze and the night sky to the west was faintly aglow. He pulled his little boat, *Pasensi*, from the reeds, dragged it to shore and pushed it afloat. He climbed in, primed the motor, pulled the cord, and the two-stroke turned over just like it always had. *Pasensi* was creole for "patience," but the boat had been named before anyone had actually captained it. Stanley's motor was locally renowned as the most reliable piece of mechanical equipment at Roosvallen.

From a dry bag Stanley pulled an industrial flashlight. He aimed *Pasensi* into the main flow of the Cariban and as he turned downriver he flipped on the light and searched for the first boulder. There, to the right. Get around it. Get around it! Okay. Where's the next one? There. To the left. Stanley had probably navigated this stretch of river more than two hundred times over the last eight years. He'd done it by moonlight, by flashlight and even by the flicker of tropical lightning. But it was rare for Stanley to pilot himself when the water was this low. It wasn't the boulders he could see that worried him. It was those that lay just below the surface.

Usually the moon made things easier but tonight there was no moon. The evenings had turned overcast lately; the rains would soon arrive. Stanley traversed his route downriver, at times passing so close to shore that the forest seemed to reach for him. He ground his prop twice on hidden stone but each time *Pasensi* remained true. He remembered the last time he'd made this journey in a panic, seven long years ago. Then he put the thought out of his mind. When he cornered the last turn before the island he heard the sound of *kawina* drums. A tour group must have arrived from the city. Beaching his boat between two dugouts Stanley made straight for the pavilion.

Beneath a thatch roof and by the brown glow of a single bulb, Raymond, Benny, Shike and Alberto worked their magic. They shimmied and shook behind the *kawina*, their hands a blur, beads of sweat flying, their voices clattering off one another. On the dance floor Frank Lampard writhed among the tourists, eyeing the young French women and passing bottles of brandy to the young French men. This was the Roos Boyz' job, to show the tourists a good time, to uphold the tenets of leave-no-trace ecotourism while making sure that everyone who visited the jungle felt as though they'd never left the city.

Stanley found Petrus in his usual spot, standing just outside the pavilion in the dark, humming along to the songs. He knew them all. Although the tourists would never have guessed it, the songs the Roos Boyz played were all Maroon spirituals, in some cases revved up or inflected with dance hall or reggae beats but in all cases lyrically accurate. The Roos Boyz were a cover band, but instead of covering international pop stars or Caribbean reggae acts they chose to cover their ancestors. Every song dated back four centuries to the days of the Hundred Years War, when a hand-ful of brave West African slaves had escaped the plantations near the capital and begun returning at night to murder their overseers and help more of their people to freedom. The stories from the Hundred Years War make up the Maroon creation myth, and the Roos Boyz scored a modern soundtrack to their own history when-ever a group of tourists felt like getting wasted.

Stanley approached Petrus. His hands began to shake.

Bas-Pey . . .

Stan-ley? said Petrus. *Fawaka*?

No good.

How *yu* come?

Pasensi.

San?

I need to talk to you.

Okay.

Stanley followed Petrus to his hut, which stood beneath a giant mango tree in the middle of the makeshift village. Petrus pulled on his door and kicked off his flip-flops. Inside he lit his oil lamp, throwing long shadows across his tiny home. He sat down and motioned for Stanley to do the same.

On one of his walls, amongst countless photographs of his many wives and children Petrus had pinned the group photo taken near the beginning of the monkey project, Petrus in the middle, his adoptive family of Western scientists surrounding him, smiles on all of their faces. Stanley leaned closer, peered at his old self, realized he didn't recognize him. The same went for Professor Collymore. And Maria, with her long black hair, her olive skin, her arm around Stanley's waist. Did she still look like herself? Has she been able to forget? When are you coming back? thought Stanley. I've been waiting so, so long.

Stanley had seen this wall many times before but as he looked at it now his eyes welled and he had to look away.

Fawaka, Stan-ley?

He sat up, collected himself.

Moses is dead.

San?

So is Agnes.

No . . .

She got another one today. I'm not sure who. Stanley began to lose his composure. It might have been Charlie.

Except for the annual ceremony in the *kankan* grove Stanley hadn't wept in years. He did now, in great sobs. Petrus sighed, reached out, gripped Stanley's shoulder.

Might not, said Petrus.

I don't know, said Stanley. I don't know.

Suma? Who kill?

Stanley gathered himself, took a breath. An eagle. A harpy eagle.

Petrus leapt from his chair, which tipped and fell noisily against his propane tank. He reached for his front door, pulled it shut and slid the latch. Righting his chair, Petrus pulled the curtain across his small window and turned down his lamp so that it barely cast a light.

He leaned in.

Say again.

A harpy eagle is hunting my monkeys.

Petrus shook his head.

No possible.

I know it's not. We've never seen a harpy here.

Yu should not say this.

Bas-Pey . . .

Yu should not talk like this.

I saw her. I watched her take a monkey.

No possible!

Stanley squinted in the half-light.

What's wrong with you?

Petrus reached for a plank of wood, fingered the designs he'd carved into it. The piece was ready to be painted in the red, blue, yellow and white of the Kwebo people.

Gonini is gone, he said quietly. She is gone long time. She no come back.

Stanley stood up. Okay, Petrus. You're right. I must have imagined a giant bird killing one of my monkeys. Stanley pushed the door. When it didn't open he fiddled with the latch.

Wait, said Petrus.

I need to smoke.

Wait.

Can I smoke in here?

There is no *gonini*.

My friend, I'm telling you, there is.

No. *Yu* must not say this. She is gone.

Who's gone, Petrus? How do you know there isn't a harpy out there?

Bicasi, said Petrus. I killed her in 1988.

12

IN THE OLD BUNKHOUSE AT THE NORTH END OF THE village, as far away as possible from the tourist lodge, Stanley lay in a hammock and set his mind free. Shike, Frank Lampard and Alberto lay in the other hammocks and together they hot-boxed the room with a fierce batch of hash that Shike's contacts had sent with the latest tourist boat. Stanley couldn't see the others through the smoke but he could hear them talking and giggling about the French ladies who had turned them down earlier in the night. Apparently Raymond had won out that evening. Every now and then a hand would appear through the murk holding a bottle of Red Label.

Stan-LEY! said Shike. Why you here so late?

My head hurt, said Stanley.

Hurt more tomorrow, said Frank Lampard.

Kanday, said Stanley. But now I feel nothing.

True, said Shike.

True boy, said Alberto.

Rude boy! said Frank Lampard. The Maroons erupted with laughter.

I know what we do! said Alberto.

San?

We put bullet in Raymond's hammock.

More laughter. Stanley had seen plenty of bullet ants over the years and considered himself extremely lucky to have never been stung by one. Apparently the toxins can make a man's testicles throb for seventy-two hours.

Raymond *gwe*, said Shike. French lady look better in dark.

Apparently Raymond's dalliance had been short-lived; he had already left for his week off in Konkoniston. He knew the river so well that he could easily navigate it by the light of the moon. The Maroons at Roosvallen were all Kwebo, born and bred on the Cariban, and for every three weeks they put in on the island they earned a week of rest with their families downriver in their home villages of Wintigron and Konkoniston. While on leave they would help their mothers clear new garden plots, shield their pre-pubescent sisters from the unwanted advances of newly pubescent boys, and go fishing with their fathers and uncles up one of the great river's many tributaries. Most of the Boyz had become fathers by the age of sixteen, so they all had wives and children to visit with, but in the villages the Boyz enjoyed a measure of prestige from their regular employment with the conservation agency, and this usually bought them some sway with their wives when it came to domestic duties. Upon returning to Roosvallen, though, they would don their uniforms, lace their boots, straighten their ties and become accommodating tour guides, line cooks, custodians and customer service agents to flocks of insufferable Westerners and their children. Sometimes Stanley suspected these late-night hash rituals were the only thing keeping them from bludgeoning one of the countless chubby families disgorged by the bush-planes onto the airstrip every few days.

Hey, Stan-ley, said Shike after a time. Who you vote for?

I don't get to vote.

San? Stan-ley no vote?

Shike, you *fukkup*, said Frank Lampard. Stan-ley no live here.

Saaaaa?

This is not my country. It's yours.

63

No, no, no, no, no, said Shike, his voice rising. This. Is. You. *Oso*. This is where you live.

Where? said Stanley.

The bag of hash appeared in Stanley's face. He rolled another joint.

Eee-lek-shun! hollered Shike. I vote for everybody.

The smoke thickened. Stanley had forgotten there was an election coming. He hated the city and everything in it, politics included.

Monkeys, said Frank Lampard after a time.

Mon-keys! said Alberto.

Hey, Stan-ley, said Shike. Why you look at monkeys?

The Boyz had asked Stanley this question every time they had smoked together, roughly once a week for seven years. They never missed an opportunity to mock his peculiar commitment to the monkeys. The idea that a white man would leave the luxury of the West to chase after a bunch of obnoxious (and, when stewed, delicious) animals completely baffled the Boyz. At first they had assumed there was something unusual about these particular monkeys, but as years passed and events unfolded their suspicions gradually shifted away from the monkeys and towards Stanley himself.

Whenever the Boyz inquired into his motivations, Stanley would give them roughly the same answer: he was studying the monkeys in order to learn from them. But now he gave them a different answer, the one Maria would have given them.

To protect them, he said.

From what? said Shike.

From him! said Frank Lampard.

From us? said Alberto.

From a ghost, said Stanley.

He hadn't let Petrus explain himself earlier. He had just left the old man behind in his hut with his delusions. 1988. Why would he assume a connection between this eagle and the one he supposedly killed more than two decades ago?

Stan-ley! said Frank Lampard. Ghostbuster!

Aiiiii!

The bottle made the rounds.

You are the one who needs protecting, Stan-ley, said Shike.

Stanley opened his eyes.

San?

Pro-tek-shun, said Shike. The jungle tell me. It want to kill you.

Frank Lampard and Alberto laughed. Stanley raised his head, peered through the smoke. His eyes burned.

What are you talking about?

She talk to me, said Shike, blowing a long drag into the air. You are finished, she say. The jungle want you go home.

The Boyz went quiet. Stanley sat up. His head rushed. Smoke swirled. A teaspoon of bile and whisky arrived in his mouth. He swallowed it back.

What the fuck are you talking about?

Silence.

Shike!

Shike waited, then gave up.

Stan-LEY! he said. Scare you, boy!

Frank Lampard and Alberto howled with laughter.

I get you good!

Fuck you, said Stanley.

The jungle south of the mountain, said Shike in a menacing voice. She tell me she hungry. Boy, you *fukkup*!

The hammock-hooks squeaked as the Boyz swung with glee.

Fuck all three of you.

Stanley lay back down, closed his eyes, drifted off. He saw the bird. She looked straight through him. He saw Johan barking, Beatrix falling, Charlie being born. He saw the body of a monkey with its stomach torn open, its viscera splayed, a purple heart on the ground. He saw Maria asleep in a tree, covered over with palm leaves.

He opened his eyes.

What if I did? he said.

San?

What if I did need protection? How would I get it?

Somebody sucked his teeth.

All you have to do is ask, said Shike.

Shike . . . said Frank Lampard.

And who do I ask?

Uh-uh, said Alberto. Shike, no.

One of the hammocks creaked. Feet slapped on the cement floor. A door to one of the bedrooms opened.

Shike, *san* you do? said Alberto.

A rustle of cardboard and plastic. Another hammock creak, more feet on the floor.

Shike! You *fukkup*!

A brief struggle, an angry howl, a body slammed against the wall. Then Shike's enormous head, his dreads a smoking medusa.

I tell you already, Shike whispered. This is you home.

He placed something heavy on Stanley's chest.

You come to the right place.

Stanley took the object, held it up. A beautiful black pistol.

13

PLEASE STAY WITH THE MONKEYS. *THE STORY IS stronger than I am.*

These had been Maria's last words to Stanley, scribbled on a piece of data paper she'd left behind on the kitchen table seven years ago, and even now the message still galled him. He understood the directive, of course; he had obeyed Maria's command and remained behind in the bush. But it was that second sentence: *The story is stronger than I am.* She could have written just about any other phrase, no matter how peculiar, and Stanley would have been less bothered by it. She could have written, *They are not our children*, and he would have seen through the blatancy, because the monkeys *had* become their children, like members of their family. Maria had always thought of them that way. Her love for the troop had been bone-level, furious, and after she became pregnant she redoubled her efforts to protect them.

She could have written, *I will never leave this place*, and again Stanley would have understood the irony. Because she *had* left this place, although her spirit was still here—of course it was, a mother's spirit never strays far from her children—and her things were still here, too, the few possessions she'd left behind in her haste. And Stanley was thinking about her right now, wasn't he, conjuring her and bringing her into the room? And her annual letters, didn't they usher her voice back to Roosvallen, even if he refused to open them, even if they were all eventually filed away with the data?

Sometimes Stanley had an ugly thought: If Maria had loved them like children, how could she have abandoned them? But he knew this was unfair, and whenever he had this thought he quickly quashed it. Maria had more reason than anyone to leave this place. Her child was buried out here, and if it hadn't been for her uncategorical request, and the appearance of Charlie among the Longfellows, Stanley would have left the jungle, too. But sometimes he felt like being cruel and unsympathetic. Sometimes he felt like punishing Maria for leaving those words behind, *The story is stronger than I am*, because aside from the weakness and prevarication of the phrase, those words, when strung together just so, levied a terrible accusation at Stanley. Those words meant that Maria held him responsible for the death of their baby, and this indictment was all the more painful because Stanley knew it was simply impossible.

It's not forgiveness I need, thought Stanley for the thousandth time, as he left camp the next morning with the pistol stashed in his pack. Some sort of mercy, maybe, but certainly not forgiveness.

When Stanley reached Kawati Top it was still dark and everything below was draped in mist. He dropped down into the study site and began searching. Domineestraat. Hollywood Boulevard. The Danforth. Fifth Avenue. Downing Street. Vilakazi Street. Broadway. Every minute or so he would stop and listen, but he heard nothing. Stanley walked through the bog, passed Pancho Villa and veered up Main Street, back to the scene of the crime. The sun was up, the mist had risen. He bushwhacked to the base of the palm tree where he'd seen the bird perched. He searched the ground, for what he wasn't sure. He saw nothing but empty husks and monkey shit. Stanley pulled out his mapping paper, flipped to a fresh page, and placed an X in the appropriate sector. Back on Main Street he went south, crossed the Voltz and into the high forest, where the monkeys had spent every night for the past six weeks.

He criss-crossed the southern region for ninety minutes. No sight nor sound of monkeys. By this point in the morning Stanley would usually have found the troop, but he would also have run into a variety of other wildlife, trumpeter birds or brocket deer or bearded sakis or the local tapir with her young. He came upon a pig root but the mud was dry. It was as if the animals had moved out of the forest overnight. Stanley reached the south-east corner of the site and decided to follow Pikin River, which ran alongside a tributary of the same name that eventually joined the Cariban to the west. This narrow watercourse signalled the southern extent of Stanley's range, but of course the monkeys could move further south from here if they wanted to. Halfway along Pikin River stood two massive trees, one on either bank of the tributary. Their canopies nearly touched fifty-three feet above the water, and these branches served as a bridge for the monkeys whenever they wanted to head further south. Stanley stopped more often now to listen. He faced south and then north. Hopefully the Longfellows were somewhere between here and two miles north of here. If they'd crossed Pikin River they might be gone for days or weeks or months.

By nine o'clock Stanley had been walking for four hours. He decided to head back to the Voltz and regroup, take a look at the map. And that's when he heard the screams, the barking. Stanley raced up Saramaccastraat, stopped and held his breath. The barking came from the east. He turned and sprinted along Yonge Street, his pack bouncing, his camp chair clanging. He stopped again, looked up, and saw Johan high up in an Inga, leaping and clawing at the air. The rest of the monkeys were gone. Stanley raised his glasses, trained them on Johan and slowly moved off him in the direction of his anger. There you are. Stanley's eyes welled, his hands shook. I fucking see you now.

The eagle sat on a heavy branch in the next tree over. Once again, she was the picture of calm. This time, though, the monkeys had all escaped her fury; the bird's talons were empty. Stanley dropped his pack, unzipped the top pouch and pulled out the revolver. It was already loaded; Shike had sold it to him that way. Stanley left his gear on the trail and crept into the bush. He went as slowly as he could. Every few steps he raised his glasses, and every time the bird met his gaze.

For eight years Stanley had been estimating distances in this forest, by eye, to the nearest foot. He had become quite accomplished at this, regularly testing his estimates against a surveyor's wheel, and until now he'd wondered what possible use he would ever find in the real world for such an obscure skill. He figured the bird to be fifty-two feet away. He had fired guns before but he had never shot to kill. He decided thirty feet would be ideal. Johan continued his display and Stanley crept closer. When he was almost to the trunk of the bird's tree, he stopped, looked up, raised the pistol and took aim. She looked directly at Stanley. She revealed nothing. The terrible girth of her breast exceeded that of her tree trunk. This is where Stanley aimed—at the heart, but more importantly at the flight muscles, the immense pectorals that had delivered her into Stanley's forest with such quiet violence. Stanley took a long breath, began to let it out, pulled the trigger.

The blast knocked him backwards. He saw the bark beneath the eagle's feet explode as his ears began to ring. The bird lifted up from her perch, unfurled her colossal wings and wheeled in the air. She pumped three times and drifted out of the trees, gone before the gunshot had completed its round of echoes. Fuck. He looked for Johan. Fuck! He saw the monkey racing north through the canopy. Stanley ran back to the trail, returned the revolver to the top pouch of his pack and gathered his things.

Then he heard voices. They were coming from the direction of the Voltzberg Trail. This could only mean one thing: tourists.

Stanley shouldered his pack, crashed off-trail towards a nearby *kankan* tree. The voices grew louder. Someone was shouting. A man's voice, yelling in creole. Stanley ducked down between the buttress roots. He heard footsteps approaching. They came to a stop on Yonge Street in exactly the spot where Stanley had left the trail.

Hank, it's not what you think, said Frank Lampard.

Shut your mouth, said Hank.

Hank . . . said Alberto.

Both of you. Shut up.

Stanley heard a machete drawn from its sheath. Footsteps off-trail. Snapping twigs. The scrape of a young *maka* frond.

Hank approached Stanley's *kankan*.

Who is shooting a gun in my forest? said Hank quietly, as if the tree might answer him.

His forest? If this is anyone's forest it's mine. Stanley considered standing up and facing Hank. He readied himself. Then he heard a faraway scream.

Hank, said Alberto. The Françoise.

Fuck the Françoise.

But we know who shoot.

San?

It's Stanley. It's only Stanley.

Boy, no time for joke.

No joke, said Alberto. Last night. Stanley took a Glock.

Hank walked back to the trail. Stanley lifted his head, peered over the buttress. Hank stood nose-to-nose with Alberto.

From who? said Hank. When Alberto didn't respond, Hank placed his hand around the boy's neck and raised his machete. Who gave Stanley a gun? Alberto tried to answer but couldn't. Hank pushed him up against the trunk of a palm tree and strengthened his grip.

Hank, said Frank Lampard.

Shut your mouth. I want Alberto to answer. How did Stanley get a gun? Alberto flailed. Why won't you answer me? Why won't he answer me, Frank Lampard? It looks like this boy is keeping secrets.

It was us, said Frank Lampard.

Boy, I want Alberto to answer.

Alberto's flailing slowed.

We gave it to him!

Hank released Alberto, who collapsed to the ground.

It was Shike! said the boy, struggling for breath. Man was flying. We try to stop him.

Hank straightened his uniform, brushed an invisible speck of dirt from his shoulder. You wheeze like a jungle pig, he said. Another tourist screamed. The Françoise need their mothers. When nobody moved, Hank took a step towards Frank Lampard. Direct! Frank Lampard helped Alberto to his feet and dragged him down the trail. Hank sheathed his machete, took one last look into the canopy and followed.

Stanley dropped back out of sight. He looked north through the understory. His vision began to narrow. The buttresses on either side of him closed in. Forgiveness. Soon he could barely see out of his hiding spot. Mercy. Everything went dark.

14

T HAT NIGHT STANLEY WAS IN HIS HAMMOCK WHEN he heard a boat approaching. He figured it was Petrus, who had probably heard about the gun. Stanley stood, unlocked the front door, pushed it open. Then Frank Lampard and Alberto appeared in the rectangle of light cast by the doorway. Both still wore their uniforms. Behind them stood Shike, a few steps out of the light.

Stan-ley, said Frank Lampard.

What is it?

You make problem.

Problem?

Yes. Frank Lampard walked past Stanley into the house. *Bigi* problem.

Alberto followed, closed the door behind him. Shike remained outside. In the full light Stanley could see the marks Hank had left on Alberto's neck. Frank Lampard had a black eye.

What happened to you guys?

Mi sorry, said Alberto.

For what?

Alberto delivered a quick right jab to Stanley's nose. Blood streamed onto his upper lip and into his mouth. Another jab, this time to his left eye. Stanley stumbled backwards, tripped over the hammock, slammed his head into the cement floor. Before he could right himself Alberto was straddling him, his fist raised. Stanley's vision blurred.

This is a national nature reserve, said Frank Lampard from somewhere above. It is illegal to fire a weapon in a national nature reserve.

What the fuck is this?

A warning.

But you gave me the gun!

Alberto's third blow crashed into Stanley's right cheek.

Where is it?

Stanley snorted blood from his nose, spat it out.

I need it.

Alberto raised his fist.

I do! I fucking need it!

The front door creaked. Shike's massive head appeared above Stanley.

I give you for *pro-tek-shun*, boy! Not *ah-greh-shun*!

Shike winced. The boy looked sick. Stanley tried to focus. Shike's left arm was in a makeshift sling. His left hand was wrapped in gauze. The gauze was soaked through with blood.

Shike's thumb was gone.

Stan-ley? said Frank Lampard. Where is the gun?

Jesus Christ, it's in my pack. Top pocket. Jesus! What the hell is going on?

Alberto stood, grabbed Stanley's pack, pulled out the pistol, held it aloft. Stanley reached for the hammock, heaved himself up to sit, put his hand to his nose and moved it side to side. Pain shot through his skull. He heard the bone.

I'm sorry, said Alberto again.

Great, said Stanley. That's just fucking great. What happened to Shike's hand?

But Shike was already gone, halfway down the hill, and without a word the others had followed him. The door slammed shut.

The growl of an outboard motor. The evening zing of the insects.

Stanley pulled himself up to stand. In the kitchen he tore up an old issue of *De Vrije Tijd* and stuck two wads of newsprint into his nostrils. He grabbed the bottle of *palum* and his bag of hash and returned to the hammock. An hour later the rains came to Roosvallen, thundering onto Stanley's roof and splashing through the rust-holes. The bamboo season was over.

THE FRUIT SEASON

I
~

FOR A THIRD OF THE YEAR A RAINFOREST IS A contradiction in terms. The jungle receives not a drop of rain for at least four months, and during this period the bogs dry, the trees harden, life slows and everything dead crumbles to dust. It is as if the number of species jostling for purchase has been cut by half—whether that species is plant, animal or insect, and whether that purchase is sunlight, nutrient, water or flesh. This isn't the case, of course; it only seems that way. A dry-season jungle is not a world in decline but one in expert slumber. And according to Maroon mysticism, when that world awakens the man who craves logic and rational terms is more than simply out of luck. He is the equivalent of an antique, nostalgia on two feet, a dead man.

The rains had stopped by four o'clock and an hour later Anyumara Falls roared with the runoff. Stanley stood listening in the darkness, imagining the waters lapping over the trail as they would in just a few months. He had changed his footwear from hikers to Wellingtons and in his pack was now a collapsible umbrella. Other than these minor adjustments Stanley could do nothing to prepare himself for what was to come. On Kawati Top the usual mist had thickened into a full fog. He flicked on his headlamp and descended into the study site as if into a white tunnel.

Stanley stopped at Hollywood Boulevard. He hadn't found the

monkeys this close to camp in a few years, but he stopped anyway and listened. All around him, the splash and clatter of water falling from the canopy. He felt the drops on his head and shoulders, heard them battering his pack. For the next two hundred mornings or so this would be his early morning soundtrack, a wet cacophony that would continue until midmorning.

Stanley considered walking north on Hollywood, exploring one of the less trammelled portions of his site. He took a few steps up the trail, which was already overgrown and in need of a good machete. *I could spend the whole day on this. I could clear this trail all the way up to the Khao San Road, follow it around to Jag Junction, hack off-trail to the northern terminus of Main Street and keep cutting from there. I can do anything I want,* although as he said these words he turned around and returned to the Voltzberg Trail.

Just past Downing Street he smelled a familiar musk, the unmistakable stench of *Clathrus ruber,* the stinkhorn mushroom. When Stanley had first experienced this foul smell eight years ago, Professor Collymore had lied and told his young prodigy that he was smelling the wet skin of a nearby snake. Stanley had been completely taken by the ruse, and for the next four months whenever he smelled this horrible reek he would stop in his tracks, grip his machete and scan the understory on both sides of the trail. When Maria saw him do this one day she asked Stanley what was wrong. When he explained Maria burst into laughter, took him by the arm and led him off-trail about a hundred yards. Soon they stood in a bed of red stinkhorns, their latticed baskets scattered across the forest floor, the stink of rotten meat thickening the air. The two stood holding their breath, Stanley smiling and shaking his head and Maria snorting with glee.

From the rotten log spanning Treefall Creek, Stanley could see the water had risen and the bog was beginning to form. Just one night of rainfall had etched the outline of the annual depression. The bog had been thirsty, but here and there Stanley's headlamp caused the earth to glisten and the reeds to shine. He flashed his light to the other side of the creek. Near the trailhead of Saramaccastraat his beam revealed a Brazilian tapir. She had grown since Stanley had last seen her. Her cream-coloured face, dark grey body, stumpy tail and prehensile snout reminded him of a children's book he'd once read in which a little girl dreams a jungle full of syncretic creatures. The tapir resembled a cross between a giant pig, a small horse and a miniature rhinoceros, its nose and upper lip fused into a short proboscis like the beginnings of an elephant's trunk. Stanley cast his light from side to side, searched for signs of the tapir's young but saw nothing. As he stepped off the log she wheeled and crashed into the bush.

Although he did not want to, Stanley walked down Saramaccastraat, turned east on Yonge and returned to the place where he'd fired on the harpy. The fog had lifted. He looked up at the branch where she'd been sitting, saw the wound of the bullet. He wished he had been more careful. He wished he had taken better aim. I am just a man, he said. A useless, ignorant, fearful man. Setting down his camp chair he dropped his pack, sat down and raised a finger to his broken nose. He flicked his wrist and bellowed with the pain. Blood began to run. He flicked again and the hurt arced through his skull. Holding his head between his knees, Stanley snorted blood to the forest floor and waited for his mind to ease.

Not only was he powerless to protect his monkeys, Stanley had also been proven spectacularly wrong. He had believed that avian predation was not a threat to these capuchins. He'd published those exact words in the *Journal of Primatology*, spoken them aloud to a conference audience in Beijing—the last conference he would ever attend. In the study's first two years he hadn't spotted a single bird of prey large enough to snag a monkey. In this particular jungle, he'd proudly announced, predation from the skies was not a selective pressure.

Stanley sat for a long while. He let the blood run and only

leaned his head back when he began to feel woozy. Then he heard a splash. Stanley thought he'd misheard, that the wet noise had come from inside his head, but then he heard another splash and another. Somewhere to the south. He shouldered his pack. The rains had changed everything overnight. They'd given new power to the creeks, stirred hives and nests and warrens and burrows, split the light into multitudinous greens. And after a night of downpour, whenever a monkey jumped from one tree to another the sound was like a sudden storm, buckets of water that would have taken weeks to cycle through to the forest floor crashing down from the canopy in an instant.

Stanley found them on Pikin River. They were tracking east, which meant they'd probably slept in one of their usual sites at the bottom of Main Street. Have you no fear? said Stanley, as he reached for his notebook and started his first scan. Surely the bamboo is the safest place to hide from a harpy. He counted sixteen, which meant the bird had failed the day before. Buoyed by this revelation, Stanley set out to find Charlie.

Johan, Beatrix and Mignon were easiest to spot. They were forty-seven feet up, near the front of the troop, Mignon on Beatrix's back, Johan stopping every few seconds to investigate an old termite hive or to dig his hand into a vacant woodpecker hole. Jerry and Costanza were a little lower, picking their way through a stand of *makas*. Wacky was low down, too, licking something— probably leaf-cutter ants—from the liana to which he clung. Charlie? He saw Banana and Suri Rama softly twittering to each other. He found Holyfield and Marilyn. And then he spotted a monkey clumsily splash into Marilyn's tree. The juvenile scrambled for purchase, tumbled through the branches and would have plummeted to the ground had it not been for his prehensile tail, which wrapped itself around one of the lowest branches at the last second as if with a mind of its own. Stanley's skin tingled. Charlie, he said. Thank God.

Charlie! When are you going to learn how to be a monkey?

The appearance of Charlie made Stanley forget, for a few sweet moments, what had happened yesterday and the day before. Through his glasses he watched Charlie swing himself to the trunk, shimmy up to where Marilyn was sitting and leap over his mother with a squeak. Marilyn hardly seemed to notice the youngster. She was busy eating something wriggly from her clasped hand—a locust, perhaps, or a praying mantis. Soon she opened her hand and the remains of the insect slipped from her fingers, and Stanley dropped his glasses, ran to the base of the tree and searched until he came upon the corpse. It had been chewed beyond recognition, but he marked it down in his notebook anyway as some invertebrate or another.

Stanley slipped back into his old routine. He followed the troop north up Saramaccastraat, conducting group scans every fifteen minutes and attempting to identify each individual. He double- and triple-checked his headcounts. Always sixteen. In about an hour he had marked three palm trees, collected two fecal samples and had IDs on every monkey except Dustin and Peanut.

Soon a troop of squirrel monkeys joined the Longfellows from the south. Stanley noted their presence with the short form "SQM" in his notebook. If the capuchins were the smartest monkeys in the forest, the squim were their diametric opposites. Smaller, lighter and with light-grey hair, squirrel monkeys were nervous little creatures, continually squeaking with fear, screaming with surprise or violently squabbling with their troop-mates. The attention span of a squim was like that of a fruit fly, their perpetually jumpy behaviour like a raw and flapping nerve. And as if evolution had a sense of irony, each squim wore bizarre makeup on his face, the hair around his eyes, mouth and snout dyed a muted rainbow that vaguely recalled the visage of a clown.

Ridiculous fucking monkeys, said Stanley, as he performed a rough headcount on the new arrivals. Why am I writing this down?

Stanley couldn't even tell the squim apart, except for the few who were missing chunks of their ears, digits from their hands or who had pink gashes running along their torsos. To Stanley, in comparison to the capuchins the squim were vicious, low-life parasites, eating whatever morsels the caps passed over, snatching at insects the caps stirred up and then proceeding to fight ferociously for a two-bite cockroach or a slippery worm. By Stanley's estimation even the bearded saki carried himself with greater dignity among the primates of Roosvallen than the squirrel monkey did.

Maria had also found the squim annoying, but in typical fashion had been able to appreciate their essential role. She'd thought of them as the stockbrokers of the forest, fighting over scraps and capitalizing on the hard work of others.

For the next four hours, Stanley followed the Longfellows and squim north to Avenida Maravilloso, east along Avenida and then north on Main Street to the Voltzberg. If the events of the past few days hadn't occurred, Stanley would never have guessed at them. Nothing in the monkeys' behaviour suggested they were being hunted from the skies. Maybe it's over. Maybe the gunshot was enough to permanently scare her off. As the sun began to drop and the monkeys settled in to forage at another stand of palm trees, Stanley allowed himself to consider the notion that the bird was gone, his monkeys were safe, and he was the one who had made it so.

He raised his glasses, counted the monkeys again: sixteen. He looked long and hard for Dustin and Peanut. The light was beginning to fade. A group of howlers began barking somewhere to the west. And just as Stanley considered calling it a day he saw a fuzzy-butt scramble up and over a palm sheath and leap onto Martina's back.

Peanut. Hello, Peanut.

As upsetting as it was to think of Dustin being lifted from the forest and his corpse being picked clean, this was the scenario Stanley had quietly been hoping for. At least Martina hadn't lost both of her young.

2

~

FOR THE NEXT WEEK THE LONGFELLOWS AVOIDED the bamboo altogether. Instead they took Stanley on a tour to the furthest reaches of his site, places he hadn't been in months. The caps were in search of fruit trees that would soon release their bounty, and unfortunately the squirrel monkeys tagged along for the ride. They visited the lowland swamps of the northeast, looped through the rolling hills near Kawati Top and traced the route of the old Lolopasi, the slim corridor where Maroon boat makers used to roll the mighty trees they'd felled back to the river, a bare strip through the forest that now served as the site's northernmost boundary. The monkeys passed through some of Stanley's favourite haunts. They picked their way through the field of black basalt boulders in the southeast, home to a labyrinth of rainforest caves that Kwebo children were taught to fear. According to local legend, the great swarms of bats that poured forth from those grottos every evening were not the caves' only inhabitants. The caps circled the curious grove of *kankans* adjacent to the black boulders, the trees that grew so close together their buttresses nearly touched, an odd display of botanical community from a sacred and exceedingly antisocial species. The monkeys even left the site for an hour or two each day, leaving Stanley with no choice but to hack off-trail after them, tying flags of pink tape to saplings as he went so he'd be able to find his way back, and so he could slash and christen these new trails if the monkeys regularly returned to them.

Throughout these explorations the South American menagerie presented itself in all order of sound, scent and hue. The capybara had returned to Anyumara Falls; Stanley tiptoed around her and her young most mornings. He routinely caught the startled eyes of red brocket deer in the beam of his headlamp, heard the high-pitched peeps of the red-handed tamarin in the trees and stood transfixed by the iridescent cerulean flicker of the morpho butterfly. Many of the more fallow trails were scarred by the stench and disorder of jungle pigs, or pingoes. The caracara birds greeted Stanley on Kawati Top morning and night. Late one afternoon, as Stanley sat munching a handful of cassava flour, a family of bush dogs—three pups and their mother—crept across the trail not ten feet away from him, something he'd only seen once before in all his years at Roosvallen.

One morning, just north of Jag Junction, Stanley came across the eviscerated carcass of an orange-rumped agouti, its organs gone, its rib cage licked clean by a fastidious tongue. Meanwhile, pre-dawn hikes were now punctuated by the snakes that rose up like glistened whips at the side of the trail. One morning he counted eight by the time he'd reached Hollywood Boulevard, each at least five feet long.

The rains came almost every night, and although the late afternoon storms had not yet begun the nocturnal downpours were still harbingers of difficult times. Once the rains had arrived Stanley lived in perpetual damp. The wet got into everything: the hammocks, the data binders, the library, the rice, the flour, the mattresses back when he and Maria had slept in one of the bedrooms. It came in on the air and poured down from the holes in the roof. Stanley had grown weary of fixing the holes a good five years ago now, so instead he deployed a regiment of pots, pans and buckets throughout Camp Collymore for a good portion of the year.

The rising humidity meant Stanley arrived home every night so soaked with his own sweat that his shirt, pants and socks were suctioned to his body. No matter how long he left them on the line his clothes would never dry, so every morning he'd have to don matching sets of stinking, rotting apparel. In less than a week Stanley could feel the preliminary burn of the fungal infection that flared up every year at this time, a scourge he was uniquely susceptible to. Professor Collymore and Maria had never showed symptoms and neither had the Maroons. It would begin with a red mottling on the undersides of his arms, and over the months the spots would develop into a full-blown rash and spread to every tender region of his body. Petrus had experimented with a variety of botanical poultices over the years for Stanley, and last season's brew had been the most effective by far. But still, no pharmaceutical, whether all-natural or synthetic, had ever been able to fully combat the problem.

The rains more than invaded Stanley's life; they infected it. In a few weeks the waters of the Cariban would rise above his beach and begin their inexorable climb up Ant Hill. This meant he would no longer be able to bathe in the river at night. Stanley would have to use the shower house, a rickety shack that smelled like piss no matter how much bleach he poured down its drain. And by using the shower house Stanley would deplete his water tank more quickly, forcing him to pump water more often, a ghastly task that still made him shiver with apprehension. The water pipe stretched down the steep hill at the backside of camp, and as the river rose Stanley would have to climb down and wade into the murk, feeling for the end of the PVC with his foot and then diving under to bring it up. All this would take place on a slope that for six months of the year was above water and therefore teemed with insectivorous life. Stanley always wondered at the slithering, skittering masses that made this particular hillside their home. He imagined them evolving gills to go along with their lungs, and every time he put his foot down he risked being stung, bitten, scraped or slashed by a thousand quivering demons. The slope was also ideal habitat for the anaconda—dappled by the sun for much of the day, a smorgasbord of animals climbing up and down the hill to drink, bathe or angle for food.

In almost every way, the rains made life unbearable for Stanley. But somehow, amidst all he had to endure, Stanley had come to love the wet season. At first he simply relished the change, the sense of there being a season to things. But as the years passed Stanley came around to the philosophical position of the Maroons, that the rains represented not just change but transformation. To change seasonally is to revisit a previous form and condition. But to transform is to become something you have never been, and this requires much more dramatic events. Transformation first requires a ritual cleansing of one's self and surroundings, a purge of all that went before. In recent years and especially now, Stanley subscribed wholeheartedly to the notion that the rains delivered exactly this sort of revolution to his forest.

He was, of course, a trained primatologist, and he knew that rain in the tropics causes a great nutrient runoff, the raw materials of life being drained from the topsoil and lost forever into the black-water rivers and streams; Stanley knew the wet season was a time of impoverishment as much as a time of awakening. But wasn't this forest different? Hadn't Professor Collymore already proven that the soil in *this* forest was rich in life-giving nutrients all year-round? What better time for transformation than a period racked by paradox? Maria, for one, would appreciate this line of thinking.

And Stanley had one more reason to see the world this way. The rains began a week ago. The bird had not attacked since. The forest has been cleansed, he thought. The forest has been saved.

3

~

EIGHT DAYS HAD PASSED WHEN STANLEY CAME home to find Petrus waiting for him. The man carried a small rucksack.

Stan-ley. *Fawaka?*

Everything good. *Fawaka nanga yu?* Stanley pulled open the door. You want to come in? He asked Petrus inside every time he visited, and the Maroon almost never accepted the invitation. This time, though, Petrus nodded. Good. Come. I'll cook for you. Stanley flipped on the lights, removed his boots and dropped his gear while Petrus walked through to the kitchen and sat at the table.

Where have you been?

City, said Petrus.

How'd you get there?

Françoise.

Did you vote?

No.

The presidential election was in less than a month. For the first time since democracy had arrived more than thirty years ago, officials had set up early polling stations for the Maroons who lived in the bush and rarely visited the city. Maroons make up nearly 25 percent of the population, but in the previous election only 8 percent of those with clan affiliations had actually voted. So far, Petrus's people had barely registered on the electoral map.

But Bas-Pey, this is your chance to change things, to really have your say. If you don't vote, the government will just do what it wants.

Petrus looked up at Stanley, who had come to stand in the kitchen doorway. The two held each other's gaze for five, ten seconds. Stanley was the first to break, grinning widely and then dissolving with laughter.

So you've been gone this long?

Ay.

How's Paulette?

Good.

Make anymore babies?

Petrus had five wives. Two lived in the city, the others lived in villages on the Cariban, the Santimaka and the Martelijne, and at any given moment at least two of them were expecting. The man had sired more than twenty-five children across all five Maroon tribes. If it wasn't for the egalitarianism of Petrus's seed, or so went the joke on the island, the clans would have gone to war long ago.

No, said Petrus flatly, forgoing his usual giggle at the joke. Stanley pulled off his sodden shirt and joined the man in the kitchen. On the table in front of Petrus sat two bottles of Parbo.

Hey, shit, yes. Stanley hadn't been to the city in at least six months. Good timing, too. We have reason to celebrate.

Not for party.

Okay, no party. But something to toast. Something to drink to.

Petrus reached out and placed his hands around the bottles.

Not for us.

What do you mean?

We must go outside.

It took Stanley a few moments to understand. It had been a very long time since the two of them had gone outside with a bottle.

No. Bas-Pey, we don't need to go outside.

Ai. We do.

First you tell me I'm wrong, that what I saw didn't happen. And now you want to go outside?

Yes.

So now you believe me about the eagle?

Petrus thought for a moment.

Yes.

Then what was that bullshit about 1988? What changed your mind? Did you see her?

No.

Well what, then?

Petrus looked at Stanley.

I trust *yu*, he said.

You trust me. Fine. It's about time. Well listen to this. I'm happy to report we don't need to worry anymore, or waste any more beer. Bas-Pey, I scared her off. *Gonini* is gone.

Petrus looked quickly around the kitchen, gripped the bottles tighter.

No *taki* name.

Bas-Pey, it's over.

No, it's not.

She's gone. I'm telling you.

Stan-ley, she's still here. *Yu* have headlamp?

No. Fuck that. It's been more than a week.

Stanley snatched one of the bottles. Holding it by the base he leaned the mouth against the edge of the table and brought a fist down on the glass. The cap popped off. Warm beer foamed out.

May your wings command you to the furthest reaches of Hades! said Stanley, raising the *jugo* to his lips.

Petrus leapt from his seat and wrestled the bottle from Stanley before he could take a sip.

Hey!

Yu think *mi* old man.

I'm just having some fun.

Yu think *mi* know nothing.

Bas-Pey, come on.

Yu think she is gone. Petrus took the other *jugo* from the table. Do not be so stupid. He unlatched the side door and walked into the night.

Stanley licked the beer from his fingers. It appeared his friend was losing his grip. Stanley grabbed two headlamps from the cubbies. He found Petrus standing in the dark, in front of the only palm tree on Ant Hill.

Petrus flipped on his light, illuminating the bottles that lay scattered at the base of the tree. They were all empty. Some had toppled over. Most had been there for at least seven years, one of them for eight. Petrus knelt down and righted the bottles.

I'm sorry, said Stanley. I just never come back here anymore.

You should.

I've been busy. Meetings, deadlines, putting the kids to bed. You know how it is.

Once the bottles were all upright Petrus pushed himself up to a crouch, reached for the open *jugo*. He began to speak, but not to Stanley; he spoke to the array of bottles beneath him. He used a language Stanley had never heard before. It had a similar sing-song rhythm to *taki-taki* but the vocabulary was new. Petrus spoke softly, and as he did he poured the contents of the *jugo* over the others. Once every bottle had been splashed with beer, Petrus poured some into his hand and rubbed it across his face, over his head. Then, continuing to speak, he reached for the *jugo* behind him.

Stanley took the bottle without thinking. It had been a long time, but he'd done this so often back then that the actions were burned into his muscle memory. He poured himself a handful of beer and rubbed it into his cheeks, his forehead, his beard. Then he took another handful and rubbed it into his hair. The smell of the hops triggered the memory, and as he handed back the *jugo* and Petrus continued his chant Stanley crouched down, closed his eyes and fought to keep the recollection at bay. Not now, said Stanley. Not now. He and Petrus in the dark. The bottle and the tree. Maria locked in the bedroom with the body of their boy. Stanley battled, held his breath. Then he remembered the technique he'd learned years ago. He flicked his nose. Nothing happened, so he gave a twist. The pain arrived. Yes, said Stanley. He fell back.

The memory left him but was replaced by an earlier one, the location the same but the scenario joyous. He, Maria and Professor Collymore standing behind Petrus in the dark. Camp Collymore just a set of blueprints, the top of Ant Hill still forested, a makeshift campground amidst the trees, the monkey project a dream about to transform. Petrus sprinkling beer over the ground at the base of the palm, requesting the forest spirits to watch over these visitors from another world and to bless the site of their future research station. Petrus passed the *jugo* to Maria, who laughed as she splashed her face with beer. Stanley followed, then Professor Collymore. Petrus spoke for another few minutes, placed the empty bottle on the ground and stood. He looked exhausted. The ceremony was over. Petrus went back to his boat, leaving the foreigners to spend the rest of the evening drinking *palum* with twists of lime, smoking a potent strain of hash and eventually collapsing into their tents.

Stanley remembered what Maria had said that night as she'd slipped off. While Petrus had been chanting she'd been praying, too, but for something other than protection. A private benediction. A shift in the world within her. The next morning, and for the only time, the monkeys found them. They came sweeping over the top of Ant Hill and bolted at the first sign of humans.

Petrus stood, flipped off his light and helped Stanley from the ground.

She is still here, said Petrus.

Who says? The bottles?

Petrus sucked his teeth.

Yu do not believe.

I'm not Maria, Bas-Pey. This shit doesn't work on me. And anyway, I told you, I scared the bird off.

Yu must believe.

Bullshit.

Yu must.

Bullshit, Petrus.

Count your monkeys tomorrow. *Yu* will see.

4

~

HIKING OUT THE NEXT MORNING STANLEY SPOT-
ted a rainbow boa wrapped around the base of a stone
near Anyumara Falls. He had never seen one before so
he dimmed his light and inched closer. The snake was
magnificent, all shades of orange and rust, its head a smouldering
arrow. What are you doing out so late? Are you not aware the sun
is on her way? Stanley reached out and pressed his fingertip to the
snake's skin. The creature gripped itself around the stone a few
inches tighter. Petrus had once told Stanley that snakes were either
beautiful or wise, but never both. When Stanley asked how to tell
the difference, Petrus laughed and asked how Stanley had ever managed to get a woman into his hammock. Beauty, said Petrus, makes
people do crazy things. Wisdom makes people think crazy things.

Stanley had always felt great affection for Petrus—if it hadn't
been for him, the researchers might have starved in their first few
months at Roosvallen. But Stanley had long ago grown tired of the
old man's so-called wisdom. The Maroon could enchant the tourists with his traditional thatched hut, his wood carvings, his belief
in the forest spirits; his repertoire had certainly done a number on
Maria, that's for sure. But that shit didn't fool Stanley, especially
now that his monkeys were under threat. This is where I live. I
spend more time in the forest than Petrus does. If there's a spirit
who haunts this jungle you're looking at him.

Stanley found the Longfellows north of the bamboo and immediately started a headcount. It was still dark. His first count was twelve. Fifteen minutes later he saw fifteen. And fifteen minutes after that Stanley counted sixteen monkeys.

Stanley here, said Stanley into his walkie-talkie. We have confirmation of full complement. Repeat: full complement. Recommend silencing old man, with haste. Duct tape over mouth should do it. Over.

The caps headed west along the Yellow Brick Road. The squim were nowhere to be seen. Near the intersection with Hollywood Boulevard a few of the monkeys began whistling and the troop coalesced in the canopy of a large tree. Somebody alert the queen. I believe we have stumbled upon a treasure trove. Stanley dropped his pack and chair as squabbles broke out above. Soon he was caught in a downpour of nearly ripe, half-chewed figs.

The caps fed voraciously for the next three hours. Figs were one of their favourite foods and one of the rarest trees in the forest. Stanley loved it when they found a fruiting fig because it made group scans a lot easier when all the monkeys were in one tree. But depending on the species, Stanley could also scavenge among the dropped fruits for a sugary snack of his own. He only had one rule: if the fruit had more than one bite out of it, he wouldn't eat it. More than one bite meant the fig had been in the monkey's hands a little too long—an arbitrary judgment, Stanley realized, but one that struck a nice balance between going hungry and tasting capuchin urine. Male capuchins occasionally pee on their hands and rub the pee into their hair. It's called urine washing, and they do it most often when solicited for sex by females or when confronted with aggression from another monkey. Stanley would forgo his snacking altogether, of course, if the troop ever stumbled upon a ripe fig when one of the females was in heat.

Just before noon Stanley heard voices from the south. He smiled. Shouldering his pack he performed one more headcount—

sixteen—and started down Hollywood Boulevard at pace. He slipped over to Fifth Avenue and then Vilakazi Street as he went. He needed to get ahead of the tourists in order to hide. As Stanley approached the Voltzberg he scanned for an appropriate spot. To his left, a tangle of lianas had recently collapsed to the forest floor. He went off-trail and slipped inside the snarl of vines, found a comfortable spot to crouch. He could see out to the Voltz but no one would be able to see in.

Moments later, Shike appeared. He held his machete in his right hand. His left was wrapped in bandaging. Behind him walked a group of six tourists, three men and three women.

Couples, thought Stanley. Couples are always fun.

'Scuse me, said the man behind Shike. Am I hearin' you correct? You're sayin' somewhere out here there's a bunch of college kids buried?

Ai, said Shike.

Well I for one find that darn hard to believe.

Babe, said one of the women. If he's sayin' it, he's sayin' it.

Darlene, please. You believed that old fart last night sayin' that stuff about that Schumacher guy, murdering his whole posse, et cetera, et cetera. I mean, let's get real.

Camp Schumacher, said Shike. Haunted place. We'll be there in three hours.

I just don't know, said the man.

Oh, Roger, said Darlene. I like those old stories.

'Course you do, honey, said Roger. 'Course you do.

Stanley waited until Shike was ten yards from his position in the lianas. Then he began the sound, a cross between the call of a bird and the roar of a cat—*woah! woah! woah!* The tourists turned in Stanley's direction. Shike slowed but did not stop.

What in goddamn hell is that? said Roger.

Babe? said Darlene.

Hey, com-pad-ray? What's that there hollerin'?

Shike stopped but didn't turn around.

Nothing.

Stanley paused. Nothing? "Nothing" wasn't in the script. Shike was supposed to say, I don't know, thereby raising the dramatic stakes and laying the foundation for psychological mayhem. "Nothing" was no help at all. Stanley made the call again, louder this time—*woah! woah! woah!* The tourists came together on the trail.

That sure as shit don't sound like nothin', said another man.

Jesus H. Christ, said another woman.

I told you, babe. I told you this wasn't safe.

Stanley felt a momentary twinge of love for this woman.

Darlene, honey. It's gonna be fine.

It's a frog, said Shike.

A frog?

You see, honey?

A tree frog. Beautiful. Tiny.

What the hell is he doing? A tree frog? He was supposed to investigate. Stanley decided to skip ahead. He increased the frequency and pitch of his call—*woah!woah!woah!woah!*

We got frogs back home, but they don't sound nothin' like those sons a bitches.

How many is that, anyway?

It's a whole family, said Shike. They like to sing together.

Oh, said Darlene. Like in a choir.

Ai.

Well, gaw-lee . . . isn't that the sweetest thing you ever heard? A choir of tree frogs.

I told you, didn't I, Darlene? I told you.

Stanley stopped shouting. As Shike passed, he looked directly at Stanley's hiding spot, pointed his machete and mouthed the words *fuck you.* The Americans kept on walking.

Stanley began extricating himself from the lianas. It wasn't enough to crack my nose for no reason. Now you've ruined one of my sole outlets for creative expression. Then he heard more voices coming down the trail. Frank Lampard and Alberto appeared. They carried a wooden crate between them.

Whenever a group of tourists wanted to stay at the Voltzberg for two nights instead of one, the Boyz had to lug this ungainly crate filled with extra supplies. They complained, argued and fought over whose turn it was to carry the crate every time, so in a rare display of enlightened management Benny had set up a rotating schedule to keep things fair. Shike, of course, hadn't carried the crate once since Benny had instituted the new protocol, because if there was one thing Benny loved more than his reputation for fairness it was smoking copious bags of hash without paying for them.

Stanley wasn't about to let them get away without delivering a parting shot. He cycled through his library of pranks, eliminated from contention the ones he had recently performed. He watched the Boyz approach and saw significant strain on their faces. Don't worry, assholes. Only three more hours to go. Then Alberto caught his foot on a root and stumbled. He recovered, but in his effort to right the ship, he'd caused Frank Lampard to lose his balance. The crate began to roll and yaw. Boy! said Frank Lampard. What you do? The Boyz threw themselves clear of the handles and leapt out of the way. The crate smashed into a boulder and came to a rest on its side, its lid askew, its contents splayed across the trail.

Stanley muffled his laughter as bottles of cooking oil, cans of beans and *jugos* of Parbo clattered to the ground. A sack of rice had punctured and was now emptying itself. Countless rolls of toilet paper bounced down the trail. But Stanley stopped laughing when he saw what else had appeared from inside the crate.

Shit! said Frank Lampard, scanning up and down the trail to make sure no one had seen. Boy. Clean up. Fast. Alberto reached for the *jugos. Fukkup!* Not the beer!

Sitting atop the mountain of supplies was a tangle of firearms. Stanley saw Kalashnikovs, submachine guns and many pistols like the one Shike had given him. Frank Lampard righted the crate while Alberto gathered the guns. They repacked the weapons on the crate bottom and covered them up with the toilet paper, the cans, the beer. Nobody knows this, said Frank Lampard. Hank will kill us. Frank Lampard drew his hand across his throat, and Alberto nodded. With the contents stowed and the lid back in place, the Boyz counted to three, jerked the handles back to their shoulders and continued down the trail.

5

STANLEY REMAINED IN THE LIANA TANGLE TO SORT
through his thoughts. Whose guns were those? Maybe the
Americans had brought an arsenal with them. Does the
Second Amendment count when you're travelling? But
no, the Americans had only just arrived, and Shike had given him
that pistol more than a week ago. The French were here then,
but Stanley couldn't imagine the French were responsible. Maybe
the Germans, but not the French. But why would tourists need
weapons like these? Stanley thought for a moment. Then it hit
him. Roosvallen was a world-famous nature reserve teeming with
exotic wildlife. Hunting was strictly prohibited, but perhaps the
Boyz had decided to capitalize on the well-known fact that within
every group of ecotourists was hidden at least one outdoorsman of
a different nature, the sort of person who would gladly pay tens of
thousands to take potshots at a wild jaguar or spider monkey with
an automatic weapon. Perhaps the Boyz had stumbled upon an
easy way to supplement their meagre wages.

Stanley returned to Hollywood Boulevard and went north.
The fig tree was empty so he continued along the Yellow Brick
Road. He walked for twenty minutes, and just as he was beginning
to think the monkeys had given him the slip he found them moving through dense forest towards the rolling hills of Kawati. They
were going fast—traplining between ripe trees, Stanley figured.

More fruit up ahead. Then he conducted a headcount and was forced to revise this theory.

Fifteen.

Stanley raced ahead of the troop and began gathering IDs. Johan, Beatrix, Mignon, Wacky, Denzel, Marilyn. Where was Charlie? Charlie! There, lurching through the tree behind Marilyn. Okay, who else? Peanut and Banana. Suri Rama and Athena. Martina, Lucy and Holyfield. Jerry and . . . wait, where's Costanza?

Stanley ran ahead again, did another headcount. Fifteen. He performed his IDs. Everyone but Costanza. His knees buckled. He crouched, then sat down on the Yellow Brick Road. He unclipped his walkie-talkie, raised it to his mouth, then pitched the radio into the understory.

6

~

O N HIS WAY HOME, AS HE BEGAN THE LONG CLIMB to Kawati Top in the dark, Stanley heard something that made him stop and cast the beam of his headlamp into the trees. It sounded like a bird chirping. If he'd heard it during the day he wouldn't have given it a second thought, but Stanley knew of only a few birds that would vocalize once the sun had set, and this sounded like none of them. He swept his light from side to side across the understory, rising gradually as he went, and there, midway to the canopy he saw a smudge of white suspended in the darkness. He narrowed his beam and the white resolved into two distinctly lunate shapes, silvery beacons in the dark. He took a few steps off-trail to get a better look and the chirping started again, growing louder as he approached, and finally the figure snapped into focus: a white-faced saki monkey, its small body covered in glossy black hair, its long fingers curled around its perch, its face lit by a shock of bright white hair and delineated by a black muzzle, making the monkey's head appear in the dark like two crescent moons.

Two-Moons, said Stanley. Where have you been all these years?

The chirping continued.

You're up late.

More chirping.

Let me get this off you.

Stanley flipped off his light and the moons vanished.

How's that?

The chirping stopped. A rustle of leaves, a soft splash. Stanley flipped on his light but the saki was gone.

7
~

S TANLEY FOUND A DELIVERY WAITING FOR HIM ON
his front step: a sack of rice, a bag of flour, a crate of rum,
two dozen cans of beans and four cardboard boxes overflowing with fruits and vegetables. The delivery was so late
that Stanley had stopped expecting it weeks ago, and now that it
was here the inevitable anticipation outweighed his anger at the
lateness. Wout would have planned it this way. He would have
delayed the shipment further once he'd realized he'd forgotten
about him again. This pissed Stanley off, even as he flipped on the
lights and rushed the boxes inside.

The fruit and veg had probably been fresh when the boxes had
been packed but now they were beginning to smell. The okra, toma-
toes and Brazilian bananas were rotten so Stanley threw them into
the bush. A few eggplant and bundles of string beans were still edible,
but only the *pampelmoes* and oranges appeared to have weathered the
journey well. Stanley knifed a finger into one of the *pampelmoes* and
searched for the letter. He found it in the bottom of the flour bag,
along with three half-melted bars of Belgian chocolate.

My dearest Stanley,

*All apologies for the delay. The balance has been tipped lately by a
number of unforeseen developments. I must say I am continually*

aggrieved that whenever life becomes unmanageable, our man in the bush is the first to drop from my radar. You must take this as a compliment, dear Stanley. When things go wonky, my unconscious immediately relieves itself of my responsibilities to you . . . surely this must mean I consider you my most capable of charges, yah?

As always, the money continues to flow, so please do not concern yourself with that.

Happy monkeying,
Wout deWitt

PS Petrus asked us to send you the toy. Are you taking up hobbies now? Perhaps boredom has finally gotten the better of you. You really should visit us in the city more often, Stanley. Many believe nature will soothe all wounds, when in point of fact the opposite is true.

Stanley searched among the cardboard and plastic bags. He found nothing resembling a toy. He retraced his steps to the front door and went outside. In the glow of the solar lights he saw the missing freight leaning up against the house—a longbow and a quiver of arrows.

8

~

THE FIRST FEW MONTHS OF THE MONKEY PROJECT had been plagued with problems. Field stations are difficult to establish under the best of circumstances, and Roosvallen, while an idyllic location, was far from ideal. Flights from the city were prohibitively expensive so all building materials had to be procured in the capital and transported three hours west along the coastal highway to the mouth of the Cariban. From there everything had to be loaded into dugout canoes and shipped six hours south. This would have been a relatively straightforward proposition during much of the year, but Stanley, Maria and Professor Collymore had arrived during the height of the dry season. Collymore, who for a field scientist was peculiarly averse to living in a tent, was adamant that the building not be delayed by something so pedestrian as a low river. This meant the shipments of timber, cement and tools from the capital took twice as long as usual, as Petrus and Raymond had to weave their boats through a labyrinth of exposed boulders on their way south. They lost only one shipment out of more than fifty to capsize, a credit to the skill of the Maroon boatmen but a disastrous outcome for the station nonetheless, as among the cargo in that one particular shipment were the levels. These had been flown in from Georgetown due to a shortage of construction supplies in the capital, and without them the foundations of Camp Collymore could not be poured. Stanley still recalled how Collymore had reacted when informed of the unfortunate accident. He didn't fly into a rage or lambaste Raymond for his mistake. Instead, Collymore turned an impressive shade of pink and said nothing at all. Later that night, as Stanley and Maria sat on the beach watching the lightning, they heard a great crash from atop Ant Hill. Rushing back they found their commander-in-chief bedding down by the firepit. All right, then? said Collymore. All's well, I trust? The next morning they found his demolished tent suspended ten feet off the ground, the poles lodged in a twist of lianas.

Sustenance posed another challenge. Upon first arriving in the city Collymore had approached three different grocery purveyors for assistance, but no matter how much money he offered them none would agree to send regular shipments into the bush. The store owners had presented a curious unified front against the foreigner, and with little time Collymore had been forced to strike a deal with one of the tour companies, an exorbitant arrangement that soon fell apart. The provisions were supposed to arrive once a week but only came twice the first month and once the next.

The researchers were already putting in long days searching for monkey troops, hiking, hacking and tagging their way through thick rainforest for eight or nine hours at a time. As their food supplies diminished Stanley and Maria began to feel strange. When they woke in the morning they both had funny tastes in their mouths, and although they were still diligent about their work both felt woozy and a little drunk while out in the wild. They began noticing changes to each other's physiques, too. I suppose you'll be asking for vacation pay, too? said Collymore when Stanley mentioned his and his wife's hunger. But the next day Collymore announced he'd be hopping a flight back to the city to sort out the supply problem once and for all.

With Collymore gone, Stanley and Maria took their first day off in more than six weeks. They would have slept until noon had they not been woken by the buzz of an approaching outboard. They crawled out of their tent to find Petrus standing next to the abandoned, half-finished foundations of their future home. Apparently, the Boyz had also decided to take the day off when they realized the professor was gone.

Petrus carried a long wooden bow and a handful of arrows. The arrows were unadorned and might have been mistaken for sticks, but the bow was magnificent, painted in the primary colours that Stanley and Maria would soon come to know as the colours of the Kwebo people, Petrus's tribe among the Maroons. When he saw the researchers he smiled.

Glok, glok.

Morgoe, Bas-Pey, said Maria. *Fawaka?*

Alasani bun. Fawaka nanga yu?

A bun. Wi sribi langa tim.

Petrus giggled and so did Maria. Stanley hadn't been as quick to learn *taki-taki* so Maria usually spoke first with the Maroons. She had picked up the basics of the language in just four weeks, right down to the honorific "Bas" that should always be spoken, along with the first syllable of the name, when addressing an elder. Petrus was also good with languages. Within six months of the start of the monkey project he could speak passable English.

Petrus had something to show Stanley and Maria. They followed him down the hill to the little beach and then along the shore. They arrived at a field of boulders, where Petrus climbed onto one of the rocks, unslung his bow and nocked one of the arrows. Ten feet below a small eddy had formed at the river's edge. Petrus pulled back on the string, aimed into the eddy, and waited. He stood completely still for at least a minute. Posing like this, motionless in his starched conservation agency uniform, Petrus reminded Stanley of a statue he'd once seen in a European museum, the archetype of the holy archer or some such thing. Without a word, Petrus fired his arrow into the water. It pierced the surface with no sound. A few seconds later a massive fish bobbed to the surface, the arrow lodged between its gills.

Yu wani fisi?

Yes! said Maria, unable to contain her excitement. I mean, *Ai! Fisi! Grantani fi yu.*

Isn't this a nature reserve? said Stanley. Are we allowed to fish?

The Maroons are. They can't hunt game but they can fish.

Petrus stayed on the rock for a half-hour. He shot nine fish and only missed once. Stanley cleaned the dead while Petrus hunted, the first of many practical collaborations between the men. Back at camp, Petrus pulled from his pocket a small bottle of crushed and dried hot peppers, something he called *fon-fon pep-ray*, and sprinkled a pinch onto the skin of each animal. Then he fried the fish in a skillet, and soon Stanley and Maria were wolfing their first good meal in almost two months.

For the next five days, Petrus took the pair to the fishing hole every morning. Stanley and Maria tried their hands from atop the boulder, and soon they were both shooting fairly well, killing more often than not. By noon each day Petrus was on his way back to the island and Stanley and Maria were back at camp, satiated and ready to strap on their gear for a long afternoon of stumbling through the forest in search of monkeys.

Professor Collymore was away for a week, and when he finally squeezed onto a tourist flight back to Roosvallen he returned to a reinvigorated research team. Stanley and Maria barely seemed to register the news that Collymore had found a solution to their supply issue.

Through a contact at the customs office the professor had been put in touch with one of the most influential Dutch families in the country, the DeWitts. Wout deWitt was the founding publisher of *De Vrije Tijd*, the country's sole independent broadsheet. In the late eighties, as the civil war had raged and his printing presses had been bombed, he decided to diversify his holdings by entering the commercial distribution market, becoming among other things the sole distributor for Coca-Cola and Mars north of the Amazon. Wout put his son in charge of the confectionery business, and in a few short years the DeWitts had become one of the richest families in the Guianas.

Collymore had been granted a rare appointment with Wout deWitt in his offices on the Waterkant. The building was one of the first mansions built by the plantation owners in the early 1700s. It overlooked the old ports on the country's largest river, where the slave ships used to weigh anchor to unload their human cargo. As Collymore would later report to Stanley and Maria, Wout deWitt was over six and a half feet tall with broad shoulders, large hands and impeccable taste in suits. Although nearing eighty years he carried himself ramrod straight, towering over the professor as if posture alone were the secret to success.

DeWitt had agreed to help the professor before he'd even sat down.

Science is most important, yah? DeWitt had said as he shook Collymore's hand. We must encourage remote exploration of this little country of ours. In this day and age, as I understand it, your work is the work of the divine, is it not?

Wout had promised to organize biweekly grocery shipments to Roosvallen. He had also offered to siphon Collymore's grant money through one of his business accounts, a simple favour that saved the project thousands in taxes and tariffs in the first year alone.

Collymore was overjoyed upon his return to Roosvallen, and he found his team in similar good humour. The project's future looked bright. Soon the foundations of the building were finished, and although the provisions began arriving exactly as scheduled Stanley and Maria continued to fish on their days off. Both became expert shots with a bow.

9

STANLEY BROUGHT THE BOW AND QUIVER INSIDE. He lit a joint and with a permanent marker drew the outline of a bird with its wings spread on the inside of the front door. Stepping away from his drawing Stanley counted out twenty-five paces, bringing him to the threshold of the kitchen. He took a long drag and then another, stared at the image of the bird at the other end of the room.

He finished his joint and hefted the bow in his left hand. It was made from a superlight material, aluminum or fibreglass. The entire surface was painted charcoal grey. The riser was long, the limb tips were reinforced and the grip was like a sponge, adapting to each individual finger as they wrapped into position. This longbow put Petrus's homemade one to shame—nearly weightless, constructed with precision, military grade.

Stanley pulled an arrow from the quiver and nocked it. Raising his left hand to his eye-line he pulled back on the cable, felt a familiar warmth pass through his right shoulder and along his left arm. When the fletching passed his ear, Stanley held it there for a moment, testing his own strength. Then he aimed, exhaled and let fly.

His first shot missed by at least a foot, high and to the right. His next missed by a similar distance to the left. Stanley fired all twelve arrows into his door and only hit the bird twice, once in the wingtip and once in the foot. He returned to the door and pulled the arrows out, leaving twelve little holes behind. The arrowheads were made of brushed steel and showed no sign of wear.

Stanley practiced all night. When his lights died he shot by headlamp. When the batteries in his headlamp died he replaced them with fresh ones. When there were no more batteries he lit candles. The night passed quickly. It was only when his door became a solar system, sparkling with countless pinpricks of sunlight, that he realized he wasn't going to get any sleep and that he was, in fact, late for work. He packed his gear, changed his clothes and hiked out, the bow slung over his shoulder and the quiver tied across the front of his pack.

He found the monkeys in the northeast, on the edge of the swamps. They were whistling with pleasure and the forest floor was littered with the oblong, yellow fruit of a *Pouteria* tree. Stanley dropped his camp chair but left his notebook in his pack. Instead of beginning the first group scan of the day he only conducted a headcount. Fifteen. He counted again and got the same number. He counted a third time just to make sure. Then while the monkeys fed Stanley nocked an arrow, raised his bow and took aim at the trunk of the monkeys' tree.

He practiced like this for several days, at night against his door and by day against whatever fruit tree the monkeys had found. He slept very little. He conducted no science, collected no data other than headcounts. He didn't even write them down. The monkey project was on hiatus until he had dealt with the bird once and for all. By the fourth day Stanley had doubled his distances and was hitting his mark nine times out of ten. In order to simulate real-life situations he began aiming at innocent bystanders, trapping nearby squirrel monkeys or white hawks or morpho butterflies in his bow sights and pretending to fire. Agouti, boom. Kinkajou, boom. Trumpeters, boom boom boom. By doing this he grew accustomed to moving targets, challenging foliage and varying qualities of light. His eye came into line just as it had when he and Maria had shot fish together in the eddy. He had stopped fishing after Maria had left and only now did he realize he missed it, missed the feeling of quiet power, standing over a pool of unsuspecting animals and firing arrows into their world like alien ships. He was a hunter. So was Maria. Maybe they had always been hunters.

Petrus visited one night and although he didn't come inside he appeared to have forgiven Stanley for doubting him. He had brought some fish as a peace offering. When he saw the holes in the front door he giggled, but Stanley could tell the old man was impressed with how seriously he was taking his work with the bow. Stanley felt proud of himself, at least in the eyes of his only friend. He did not like the conclusion Petrus would probably have drawn from those holes in the door, which was that Stanley had conceded to Petrus's pocketbook wisdom and would now believe everything the old man told him. But as with all friendships there was no need for full disclosure between the men. They could each believe what they wished about the other, as long as when the chips were down each knew where the other stood. They didn't speak of the bird until Petrus took his leave. As he was about to descend Ant Hill he turned and told Stanley to bring a flask of *palum* with him into the bush. It is very important, said Petrus. Do not forget this. Stanley thanked Petrus for the fish. When the man was gone Stanley fetched a bottle of *palum* from beneath the kitchen counter, filled one of his steel flasks and stowed it in his pack. He then poured a couple shots of the sour brew for himself and drank them down as the rains clattered onto his roof.

10

TWO DAYS LATER, STANLEY WAS SITTING WITH the monkeys in the open forest of the southwest when he spotted a yellow-footed tortoise beneath their tree. It was grazing on dropped fruits in the methodical way only a tortoise can. It stretched its head from its shell, gummed a piece of fruit from the forest floor, raised its head to level and slowly began to chew. Each piece required two or three minutes of processing, after which the animal would swallow in elderly fashion, the peristalsis of its neck muscles visible to Stanley from where he sat. Then the tortoise would stretch its head down again and repeat the process.

Watching the tortoise proved meditative and soon Stanley was transfixed. At one point the reptile took a break from feasting, raised its head and looked right at him. Stanley took this as an invitation. Tell us your secret, he said to the tortoise. What do you know that we don't? You impress me with your precision, your painstakingness, your home on your back. Stanley might have been watching the animal for fifteen minutes and it might have been three hours. He only snapped out of his reverie when his monkeys began to scream.

The harpy was perched high above in a cloak of dappled sunlight. Monkeys rained down and Johan displayed from the next tree over. Stanley leapt up and raised his glasses. She had been successful this time; she clutched another young monkey in her talons. You're fucking dead. He dropped his glasses and picked up his bow. I'm going to fucking kill you. He nocked an arrow and took aim. Monkeys scrambled through the understory, swept past his feet. He ignored their wailings, took a deep breath and let it out slowly. He did this again and let fly.

The arrow sailed a few feet wide of the bird. Stanley felt the recriminations arise in him but the bird hadn't noticed the attack. He allowed himself no time to think and nocked another arrow. He pulled back on the cable, closed his eyes. He saw a white shape against the blackness, a fish or a bird or a tree, he wasn't sure. A woman, perhaps. He opened his eyes, renewed his aim and released the arrow with his breath.

The missile plunged into the bird's massive breast and stuck there. The momentum caused her to tip backwards off her perch. She flailed her wings, tried to wrap them around the branch as a panicking human might their hands, but to no avail. The monkey dropped from her talons and plummeted to the forest floor. Moments later the bird followed.

Stanley reached for his walkie-talkie but it wasn't there. Then he raced to the foot of the tree. He found the monkey first. It was Banana. Her eyes were open. Her limbs quivered as if she were a sleeping puppy. Stanley knelt down and put his hand on her little torso, felt for some sign. Ever since he'd arrived in Roosvallen he had longed to touch one of the monkeys, if only for a moment. He'd had plenty of opportunities over the years, and of course he had never dared. Now he wished he had. You invented the sleeping nest, said Stanley, his tears slipping off Banana's hair. I can feel you, little lady. I know you're still here. But soon Banana's hands and feet stopped twitching and nothing stirred beneath his touch. Stanley stood, dropped his pack next to her and went searching for the bird.

She wasn't hard to find. He found her splayed in the underbrush, one of her wings snagged on a liana and spread wide. In this pose she appeared menacing still, one wing raised as if to strike, her crested head and gunmetal beak held upright by the tension. She appeared to be looking straight at Stanley; she reminded him of another statue he'd seen somewhere, or perhaps a painting. He approached, unsure if she was alive or dead. Her body was so much larger than he'd expected, his arrow protruding from her breast like a long toothpick. A bloodstain had begun to form where the arrow had gone in, pooling bright red against her white feathers. Stanley nudged the fletching on the arrow with his bow. Nothing. He did this a few times, then poked the bird's gigantic breast with one of his limb tips. She didn't move.

11

HE BURIED BANANA FIRST. WITH HIS TROWEL HE dug a hole at the foot of the tree she had fallen from and placed her tiny body inside it. He wept as he covered her up. Here lies Banana. We were being lazy when we named her. We hope she can forgive us. Stanley pulled out the flask and sprinkled a few drops of *palum* onto the grave. Rest in peace, little lady. Go find Moses and Agnes and Dustin and Costanza and tell them we say hi. Your family is safe now and so are you.

Stanley took a few swigs from the flask and returned to the body of the harpy. Gripping the end of the arrow that had killed her he dragged the bird's body through the underbrush. He reached Pikin River and turned right onto the trail, headed for the southwest corner of his site. The corpse probably weighed thirty pounds but the arrow was strong and did not snap or even bend. This is the day of my unburdening, thought Stanley, as he yanked on the dead animal and quickened his pace.

Soon the trail emerged onto the peculiar stand of *kankan* trees, their buttresses butting up against one another, their open crowns allowing the sun to shine through to the forest floor. He could hear the river nearby. Stanley heaved the bird to the foot of one of the largest trees he could find and then went searching through the stand. It took him fifteen minutes to find his son's grave. The bottles had all been bleached by the sun. A few had tipped over so

Stanley bent low to right them. He usually came here only once a year, but this felt like the right moment to return. He remained at the foot of the *kankan* for a half-hour, saying nothing but considering the bottles and trying to remember when he had placed each one. The heliconia bracts that he had placed here a few weeks ago had lost their colour and begun to rot.

He returned to the bird and began digging a hole with his trowel, not too far away from his boy but far enough. He chose a spot between the two highest buttresses, a place that would only see sunlight for an hour a day. I return you to the shadows, said Stanley as he dug. When the hole was finished he gripped the arrow still stuck in the bird, placed his foot against her breast and pulled. The arrow squelched from her body, bringing with it another flood of blood. He collapsed each wing with his foot and kicked the body into the hole. He stared down at the harpy, refusing to acknowledge her astonishing beauty. She was stunning, miraculous, a creation even in death. He shovelled the dirt back over her and when he was done he pulled out the flask and poured *palum* over the earth, sanctifying all.

12

AN HOUR LATER STANLEY HAD FINISHED THE FLASK of *palum* and was on his way home. The sun was high but as he walked he spotted many animals. He was too drunk to find this strange and instead it made him very happy. He saw two agoutis in the southern hills, spooked the tapir again up on the Voltzberg and almost stepped on a fer-de-lance coiled in sunlight on the trail. He heard but did not see the tamarins as he stopped to take a piss, the screaming pihas screamed from every direction and the howlers had been howling to the east since Stanley had decided to call it a day. As the trumpeters skittered onto the trail ahead of him he began to feel like the Pied Piper, and when he reached Kawati Top and his world had really begun to tilt he called back to the caracara birds with a song of his own. He serenaded the falcons and when he was finished the birds went quiet but the rest of the forest rejoined. Meet me at the house! he called out. We will celebrate together! On Ant Hill the leaf-cutter ants had worn a stripe into the ground with their marching.

In the kitchen he searched the pantry for more *palum*. He took the bottle outside, set up his camp chair, stripped off his clothes and sat drinking in the sun. He hadn't seen his body in full light for a long time, and as he drank he pondered his slim legs, the pale skin beneath the hair on his chest, the lean muscles of his arms. I am not much, he said, laughing. He remembered *Pasensi* and decided to visit the island, tell Petrus what he'd done, say hello to the Boyz and try to patch things up with them as best he could. His mind wandered down the hill and pulled the boat from the reeds but his body didn't move from his seat. He drank half the bottle with river water but then became lazy and drank it straight. At four o'clock he stood to dance. He stumbled and whirled across the clearing, barefoot and naked with the bottle in his hand, crashing to the ground a number of times and nearly pitching himself into the trash pit. I am a hunter, he thought as he ditched and spun. I am a hunter and a father. At dusk Stanley walked down to the beach and waded into the river. The minnows nipped at his sides and rain began to fall. He knelt down in the water so only his nose was above the surface. He watched the raindrops explode into bubbles and float away.

When the thunder came he dragged himself back up the hill. Halfway home his light caught something in the trees, two crescent moons suspended. He heard the chirping and smiled. Two-Moons, you got the invitation, said Stanley. I'm glad you could come. Join me. I'll pour you a drink.

Stanley climbed into his hammock with the bottle. He had celebrated many breakthroughs over the years but only one other achievement came close to this one and he remembered it now. It was four months into the project and he and Maria had spent many weeks chasing the same troop of capuchins through the bush. Collymore had told them it would only take a few days to habituate a troop but apparently the professor's experiences in Brazil, Peru and Bolivia were not so easily applied to the forests of Roosvallen. During these weeks the two had bushwhacked and tagged many of the main trails that exist today, and on their days off they would return to these faint pathways to clear them properly and give them names. The rains hadn't come yet and the monkeys were spending a lot of time in the bamboo, so one of the first trails they had finished was the Appian Way. And it was while they were sitting on the Appian Way and bitching about Collymore that they experienced their first communion.

It began with one of the fuzzy-butts. She hadn't noticed the researchers, and as she swept towards the edge of the trail Maria had sucked in her breath with anticipation. This was the closest they'd ever been to the monkeys. Unfortunately, the sound spooked the monkey and she screamed, leapt back to where she'd come from and dropped deeper into the bamboo. She wrapped her arms around herself, shivering with fear and continuing to holler. Oh, I'm sorry, little lady, Maria whispered. I'm sorry. Maria looked at Stanley with her eyebrows raised, her mouth wide. He smiled and mouthed the words *Don't worry*, then raised a finger to his lips. They watched as an adult female emerged next to the terrified youngster. The little one leapt onto her mother's back with a yelp and then immediately calmed. As the female crossed over within a few feet of Stanley's head he saw that the monkey riding piggyback wore a silent fear-face, her small teeth bared and the flashes above her eyes flickering up and down. Her mother, though, seemed perfectly content at the proximity of the researchers. As the two monkeys disappeared into the thickness Maria reached out, grabbed Stanley's hand and squeezed. This was monumental. This was a certified breakthrough.

Soon they were surrounded by monkeys, either crossing the trail or perching at its edge to pluck and nibble fresh shoots. Only one other youngster caused a scene when he saw Stanley and Maria; none of the others seemed to care that they were there. Many months of hard work had finally begun to pay off. Stanley and Maria had nearly achieved what every field scientist struggles and yearns for: complete and utter insignificance in the lives of their wild subjects. In no time the data would begin to flow, papers would go to press and grant money would pour in. When the alpha crossed over they could not believe how huge he was—built like a tank, square head and jaws, the base of his tail as thick as Stanley's wrist. A real fighter. Maria suggested they name him Johan, after the country's first president, and Stanley thought this fitting.

That night they'd celebrated by downing two bottles of *palum* with Collymore. But as the night had worn on the professor's mood had changed from one of elation to heightened anxiety. We're onto them now, he said eventually, standing from his camp chair and then stumbling to his knees. They know it, too, and they will do everything in their power to stop us. Collymore pulled himself up to stand, unzipped his pants and began to urinate. Stanley and Maria were too drunk to protest. Especially that curassow, Collymore continued. With her long neck and beady little eyes. Can't be trusted. And that tapir, too. Probably watching us right now, that gigantic tramp. When he'd finished he dropped his pants, pulled off his field shirt and started down the hill naked. Stanley and Maria considered following but instead retired to their bedroom, where they made love in the clumsy fashion of college kids.

In his hammock now Stanley gave in and allowed the memory to overwhelm him. To believe in the sacred was, for him, the mark of lazy thinking and superstition, and the fact that one moment in his life might be elevated, through mere biological timing, to the penthouse suite of significance always brought a chill to Stanley's bones. As the statistician would say, one piece of data is no data at all. And without a good data-set there can never be significance. But that evening when their boss had lost his purchase and splashed into the river was the evening Stanley and Maria had conceived their first and only child together, and everything that followed that night—the good, the bad and the catastrophic—was no reason to deny the sanctity of it. Stanley had long struggled with this knowledge. Now he felt capable of shouldering it. I am a father and a hunter, he said, worthy of mercy, as he slipped off to dream of a long swim down the Cariban.

13

I F TOUCANS WERE PEOPLE, THOUGHT STANLEY UPON
waking, they'd be muzzled and institutionalized. Many indigenous peoples considered the bird a conduit between this
world and that of the ancestors, but Stanley figured that was
bullshit, a bedtime story for children. The ancestors would never
have chosen such an ill-proportioned and incessantly annoying
medium through which to communicate the finer nuances of the
afterlife.

Stanley pulled the clipboard from his pack and dragged himself
to the data table. He flipped the latest binder to the last page and
opened the rings. From the clipboard he pulled the map he had
been keeping of the harpy sightings and slipped it into place in the
binder. With this simple act Stanley relegated the events of recent
weeks to the benevolent cauldron of science, as was his prerogative
and responsibility. Everything that had happened to him since the
bird had first attacked was now, officially and exclusively, data—
observations that could be set free from their emotional context
and mined for their intellectual significance. Closing the binder,
Stanley felt a great weight lift. He stood and walked down to the
beach, which was now half-submerged by the rising water. He
plunged in and felt the cold begin to battle his hangover.

Stanley was late to work, but he figured the monkeys would
understand. He found them in the far east just south of the Voltz,

devouring the contents of a *Spondias mombin* tree. The fruits were bright yellow and about the size of a plum, with a large seed in the centre. The monkeys loved them because they were so juicy, and they could strip the sugary flesh in about four seconds. This meant that to stand beneath an entire troop in a fruiting *Spondias* was to risk repeated concussions from the storm of stones falling to the forest floor.

Stanley kept his distance and dropped his gear. Here in the high forest the screaming piha birds were abundant—*pi pi-haaaaa, pi pi-haaaaa*—and Stanley heard at least four separate calls while he organized himself and began his first group scan. He performed a headcount and tried not to smile when he reached fifteen. The monkeys were in a tight spread, no more than twenty yards across, and the troop was approximately thirty yards high. There were no squim but he did spot the white hawk. An agouti prowled below for half-finished fruits. Stanley marked everything down every fifteen minutes like a diligent and reliable professional. The calm of work arrived, that great forgetting, and when it did he wandered beneath the *Spondias* tree and risked augmenting his headache with every step. He crouched to collect two fecal samples, one male and one female, and when he was clear of the bombardment he taped and labelled the vials. He felt the monkeys were happy to see him. I have earned this, he said, shoving the poop samples into his pack and imagining what Johan or Beatrix would say to him if they could. I'm sure they know what I have done.

Two hours later the caps had moved over the Voltz and down to the mid-canopy, where a few nuts remained in the palms. While the subordinate animals ate their fill the juveniles and fuzzy-butts dropped to the ground and raced rambunctiously through the underbrush. Stanley set up his chair and watched them, laughed at their stumbles, their squeaks of pleasure, their screams of fright. Play is not only a sign of intelligence in animals, Stanley knew, it is also one of the methods by which a primate society builds, tests and strengthens its bonds. These youngsters were putting themselves through an examination, learning who their friends were and how far they could be pushed, and Stanley loved to watch the games unfold. At one point, Charlie slipped quietly down from a *maka* and surprised Peanut and Denzel from above. The fuzzy-butts leapt and twittered, ran straight towards Stanley and hid behind him. Still in his seat, Stanley ducked down, tried to make himself as small as possible. Charlie! he whispered. They're right behind me! Although they rarely admit it, field primatologists play favourites, just as fathers do.

The monkeys played for a little while more. Then all at once they stopped roughhousing and went quiet. The change in behaviour was so abrupt that Stanley thought it was another trick, that the monkeys were now teaming up to surprise another unsuspecting troop-mate. But nothing happened. Each youngster stood perfectly still, their ears perked, as if someone had blown a whistle only they could hear. When Stanley saw Charlie raise his eyes to the canopy, the only monkey to do so, he felt a shiver pass into his neck. Although he wanted to follow Charlie's gaze he couldn't. Time passed. It might have been seconds or minutes. None of the monkeys moved. Then a thought occurred to Stanley: the palm husks were no longer dropping from above. This realization caused his throat to constrict and his mouth to go dry.

Johan began to bark.

Before Stanley could move the youngsters had swept past him and disappeared into the brush. He stood and looked up in time to see the subordinates freefalling from the palms, Holyfield and Wacky and Lucy and Marilyn, a cloud of brown bodies whirling through the understory. Stanley couldn't see Johan; he was somewhere to the east of the stand. But the alpha's alarm barks seemed different this time, not just louder and higher pitched but frantic, hysterical, as if he were attempting to render his threats in a more violent and persuasive language. Stanley ran through the palms, raised his glasses to the canopy and spotted Johan high up in the crown of a *Cecropia*. This time he was displaying at something in his own tree, only higher up. Stanley trained his glasses on the branches above the monkey. There, just a few feet up, a huge bird was perched. Its back was turned but Stanley was sure of the species—no other bird in the forest even approached the size of a harpy eagle.

Stanley's skin went cold. His hands shook and his feet went numb. He nearly toppled over. Goddamn you, he said, bending over and leaning his hand against a nearby trunk. Goddamn you! His glasses swung from his neck as he struggled to comprehend what he'd seen. She must have had a mate, he said finally. This must be the fucking male! But Stanley knew that male harpies are smaller than females, while this bird looked exactly the same size as the one he had put an arrow through the day before. Could this be another female? The second sighting in the history of the monkey project, both within a few weeks of one another? It's possible, said Stanley. It's unfathomable, but it's possible. Johan continued displaying, his voice cracking with the effort, the rains from the night before splashing down with his every lunge at the bird. Exhaustion of a kind Stanley had never experienced crept into his bones and seeped into his mind. Maria had been right, he thought. Nothing is ever fucking over. Nothing will ever come to an end in this godforsaken place.

Stanley pushed himself back to stand, raised his glasses and took another look at the bird. The harpy had turned to face Johan, and now Stanley could see its impassive face, its black eyes, its hooked beak—the all-too-familiar features of the world's most powerful bird of prey. To his great relief Stanley saw that her talons were empty. But now he could see the harpy's massive chest, and what Stanley observed amid the white plumage of her breast was so devastating, so impossible to reconcile, that once he had confirmed it by adjusting his focus and blinking a few times his legs gave way and he collapsed like a ditched marionette. A ringing filled his ears. A fever swept his torso and a wave of vomit arrived. He turned his head to let it out.

On the bird's white breast, a bright red bloodstain.

JUNGLE COMMANDO

I
~

STANLEY LAY IN THE DAMP SHADE. HE THOUGHT OF nothing, as if a door had swung shut inside his mind. His eyes were open but they did not register. A platoon of leaf-cutters wound their way around his body and an orange-rumped agouti appeared on the trail but Stanley did not stir. He only came to when a familiar call echoed through the trees.

Pi pi-haaaa.

Stanley lifted his head. He opened his mouth, tested his jaw, saw the pile of vomit and began to laugh. He laughed long and hard, which caused a splitting pain to knife through his skull. His cheeks wet with tears, the birds screaming above him, the agouti hopping off-trail at the commotion. Another wave of bile arose in his throat and he stopped laughing to let it out. Then he sat up, scanned the underbrush for monkeys and looked to the trees.

The Longfellows and the eagle were gone.

Pi pi-haaaa. Pi pi-haaaa.

Stanley heaved himself up to stand, leaned against the trunk of a palm. The blood rushed from his head. He smelled the sick at his feet and laughed again but the laughing soon turned to weeping and he closed his eyes to the dizziness. He felt his way back to his pack half-blind. He shouldered it and started down the trail after the screaming pihas. The birds led him across the Voltz and all the way south to Pikin River. The tributary was high, which meant the afternoon storms had arrived in the hinterland and would soon descend on Roosvallen. Stanley heard the birds to the west so he took the trail. He stopped a few times to see if he could spot one of them in the trees, but every time he raised his glasses he heard them again, and every time it came from somewhere further down the trail.

Soon Stanley felt the sun warm his face and the understory open up around him. He had reached the *kankan* grove. He walked with purpose between the buttresses, searching for one of the largest trees in the stand. When he found it, a gigantic and familiar specimen, he peered into the shadows between its two highest buttresses. He saw nothing, no sign of turmoil, so he dropped his gear and began digging with his hands.

I put you in the ground.

The earth told him everything he needed to know but he continued to dig until he'd opened a hole three feet deep.

Pi pi-haaaa.

This must be the wrong tree.

He chose another set of buttresses and began digging. He found nothing so he chose another tree, and then another.

Pi pi-haaaa. Pi pi-haaaa.

He scraped at the earth like an armadillo. With each handful of dirt he felt sure he was getting closer to finding what he was looking for, but with each new hole he felt something wither inside him and something else come alive. After the fifth tree and the fifth hole Stanley began to wonder how long it would take him to dig up every buttress in the grove, how many secrets he might reveal in doing so. He laughed at the thought and then began crying again.

Pi pi-haaaa! Pi pi-haaaa! Pi pi-haaaa!

Stanley looked up from his work. He stumbled through the stand and came upon the tree with the eight bottles at its base. His boy's grave. One of the *jugos* had tipped over so he knelt down to right it. His hand shook, the bottles clattered, and the words Maria had left him with seven years ago thundered through his mind: *The story is stronger than I am.*

A great apprehension came over Stanley. He recalled burying his boy at the foot of this tree. He recalled the birth, which had also been a death.

If this is possible, he thought, so is everything else.

Stanley listened for the birds again but only heard the river. Rising slowly he gathered his gear and left the grove. Up Domineestraat, to the summit of Kawati and then down from the hills and past Anyumara Falls, the screaming pihas did not follow and he saw no other animals on his way home. Back at camp he flipped on the radio receiver and was amazed to see its dash light up after so many years of disuse. When Benny answered, Stanley told him there was an emergency at Camp Collymore, and that he needed to see Petrus right away.

2

SOON STANLEY HEARD A BOAT ON THE RIVER. HE opened his front door and saw Petrus appear at the bottom of Ant Hill. When the old man reached the top he saw Stanley and smiled at him.

Stan-ley. *Fawaka?* Benny say—

Come inside, Bas-Pey.

Petrus went through to the kitchen. Stanley detected a strange calm in the man, a measure of peacefulness one wouldn't expect in someone responding to an emergency in the middle of a neotropical wilderness. Petrus sat at the kitchen table. Stanley poured a few drops of pineapple *stroop* into a cup, filled the cup from the tap and handed it to Petrus. The old man chugged the syrupy drink and sighed with satisfaction.

Stanley sat opposite him. He did not cry but he couldn't speak. Petrus refused to fill the silence. When Stanley had gathered himself he felt a sudden anger towards his friend.

I killed the harpy. I shot her through and buried her.

Petrus said nothing.

Stanley felt the fever flush his neck.

Did you hear me? I killed her. I put her in the ground.

Ai, said Petrus, shifting in his seat. Good.

Stanley looked hard at Petrus. The old man avoided his gaze.

No. Not good. Spectacular.

Ai. Okay.

Stanley watched Petrus carefully.

We should celebrate. We should take a bottle outside. We should give thanks.

The old man's face dropped.

No? said Stanley. You don't think so?

If you *wani.*

If I want to? That's strange, Bas-Pey. You are the one who usually gives our breakthroughs to the forest. I've always thought we deserve a little more credit. Stanley pushed himself up from the table. But now I'm game. Did you bring a bottle? I haven't had a drink all day but I promise to leave it alone. I promise to leave it for them.

Fuck you, said Petrus.

Stanley had never heard Petrus swear.

Sit down.

I killed her. I put her in the fucking ground.

Sit.

You knew she would come back.

No, said Petrus, fingering his cup. I did not know.

Yes, you did.

No. I hope.

You hoped?

No *ferstan. Yu* no understand.

Why did you send me the bow?

Silence.

Bas-Pey . . .

Petrus picked up his cup and placed it on the table in front of Stanley.

Gonini can be killed, he said. But if *yu* don't believe, she will not die.

Then Petrus told Stanley a story.

3

PETRUS USED TO BE JUST LIKE STANLEY. HE USED to be a non-believer, a young man convinced of what he knew and confident in his abilities. He'd been born in the mid-1950s in the village of Konkoniston, among the Kwebo here on the Cariban, and he'd spent his childhood learning about the forest and living within its bounds. But as a teen Petrus had grown restless. He'd seen the boatloads of white tourists heading past his village to Roosvallen, which had opened for tourism in 1961 and had quickly become a mecca for tropical bird-watchers. For a curious boy these boats and their cargo were compelling. The evidence they provided—and here Petrus took great pains to put his story in terms of *evidence*, as he was sure Stanley would understand him better—the evidence these boats and their pale emissaries provided was of a world beyond this river and these trees, and the proof was simply too persuasive for young Petrus to ignore. At sixteen he didn't even say goodbye to his mother, his father or his three sisters. He just flagged down a tour boat that was returning to the north and hopped aboard.

For the next thirteen years Petrus lived in the capital. He ran with a gang of tough young Maroons, all of whom had either fallen out of favour or out of love with village life. He slept on the streets for the first few months then crashed with various accomplices and brothers-in-arms. He played the casinos and sold drugs on

Saramaccastraat, mostly just weed, but when a boat fresh from Holland would inject its wares into the markets and dime-stores he would sometimes deal harder things. Soon he had learned to live off the junkies, idiots and tourists who populated the Old Town, just as he'd learned to live off the forest as a child.

Then he got a girl pregnant, Lenore, a Djuba Maroon from the Martelijne region. Then he got another girl pregnant, a Pasamakan named Shannon. Soon, dealing drugs wasn't enough so he started pulling scams and a few heists. The biggest scheme, a robbery of a Chinese jeweller up on Maagdenstraat, had been compromised from the beginning and nearly got him killed. It was just a few days after that, while Petrus was laying low in the brothels of the city's north end, that a strange opportunity presented itself.

Petrus met a businessman, an expat from Holland, who was looking to hire someone to do a job in the bush. I want you to kill a bird, he'd said. You can find her in the jungles of Roosvallen.

The businessman said the job would last two weeks, maybe three, and he would pay Petrus more than he could earn in two years running hard on the streets. The year was 1988. Petrus had five children and he was sure he couldn't stomach another heist. He hadn't been back to the Cariban region for more than a decade, and while he didn't miss his village or his family he also knew he wouldn't miss the city if he left it for a while. Rumours had been swirling for months that a rebel force was mounting in the jungles of the east, and that a full-scale civil war was looming. Tensions in the capital were high.

But this hadn't stopped the tourists. Hundreds of people, mostly Europeans, were flying into the capital via Amsterdam or Curaçao every week, hopping aboard the old military transports that had been retrofitted by entrepreneurial locals and then bee-lining for one of the many jungle camps that had sprung up in the interior. They came to lose themselves on the northern edge of South America and to hike an untouched rainforest, to experience

Maroon culture and to listen to the old stories, the one about that European explorer who had lost his mind and bludgeoned his entire entourage, the one about Ayano, the first slave to escape the plantations four hundred years ago, the man who claimed the rivers for his people. Most importantly, though, the tourists came to spot wild animals. Exotic birds like the scarlet ibis, the capuchinbird and the Guianan cock-of-the-rock had been the country's original calling card. But soon word had spread that these forests, and especially the forests of Roosvallen, were teeming with monkeys, eight species in all. It was this fact, transmitted across the globe, that brought ecotourism in the country to a new high.

Everyone wants to see the monkeys, the businessman had told Petrus. And now an eagle was hunting them.

In the past month, five different tour groups had returned to the capital with tales of horror and outrage. In all cases their stories were identical. They'd been hiking the Voltzberg when they'd come upon a troop of monkeys. Thrilled by their good fortune, the tourists had stopped and raised their binoculars. That's when the sunlight flickered, a massive shape descended from the skies and the monkeys went berserk. In each case, the *gonini* had remained in the trees long after the monkeys had disappeared, and in each case she had been successful in her hunt. As the tourists watched, the bird had torn open the stomach cavity of a young monkey and begun to feed.

Petrus left for the Cariban the next day. He was so focused on his task that he hardly noticed when the boat passed his old village. He could not afford a gun, and the businessman refused to give him one—this was a nature reserve, after all. But Petrus knew how to make a bow and he knew how to use one. Arriving in Roosvallen, he asked the boatman to drop him north of the island, on a small beach on the eastern shore. Two decades later, Professor Collymore would arrive on this same beach and plant his flag for science.

Petrus set up a makeshift camp on top of the hill where Camp Collymore now sits. He hunted the *gonini* for ten days. He figured the best way to track her was to follow the monkeys, so in a strange way Petrus, not Collymore, became the first human to systematically follow wild primates at Roosvallen. Petrus witnessed four attacks in those ten days. During the first three he fired many arrows but failed to hit his target. On the fourth he was successful. His arrow plunged into the *gonini*'s massive breast and knocked her from her perch. He didn't bother burying the animal. He just pulled his arrow free from her body and made his way back to camp.

The next morning, Petrus woke feeling happier than he had in years. The boatman wouldn't return for another few days, and Petrus had so enjoyed his time in the bush that he decided to go to work anyway, to find the troop and spend his remaining days in the jungle beneath them. The monkeys had begun to accept Petrus into their world. They no longer bolted, shook branches or gave alarm calls when he found them in the morning. His experiences of living by the rhythms of the forest, coupled with the fact that he had, in a way, acted as the monkeys' saviour, gave Petrus the sense that he had arrived at an important juncture in his life, that after so long searching for a place that felt like home he had finally found somewhere he could lay claim to. One day, thought Petrus, I will look back on this jungle as the site of my greatest accomplishment.

That morning, Petrus heard the monkeys before he found them. They were screaming somewhere to the southeast of the bamboo, and he could hear the alarm barks of the alpha male. He arrived to a familiar scene—monkeys scurrying on all fours, the alpha lunging at something in a neighbouring tree—and when he located the cause of the upset Petrus dropped to his knees and a fever passed through him. She had come back. The bird he had killed the previous day was alive and continuing her hunt. He knew it by the bloodstain on her breast.

If Petrus had told the thugs, hoodlums and petty criminals he ran with back in the city what he'd just witnessed they would have done more than just laugh at him. They would have beaten him senseless. In the city, superstition wasn't just a sign of a weak mind; it could get you killed. But Petrus had seen what he had seen, and after uttering a prayer that hadn't escaped his mouth since childhood he devised a new plan of attack. He would search for the bird's nest and destroy it. He would not leave the rainforest until he had done so.

But how does one locate the nest of an eagle in a forest as dense as Roosvallen? His task was like trying to find an ant in a termite mound. Petrus began to pray, once a day at first and then every morning, noon and night. Please, he would say, appealing to the forest spirits, the same ones he'd shuddered in fear of as a youngster back in Konkoniston. Please. Soon Petrus was uttering entreaties into the trees on an almost continual basis, whenever it occurred to him, using phrasings he had learned by rote as a child. Between prayers he spoke his thoughts, hopes and fears into the air, and a few days into his search Petrus was holding nothing back from the jungle. He felt at the time that he was losing himself, that he was shrinking into nothingness all alone out there in the bush. But now Petrus had the wisdom to realize that by emptying his mind into the forest he had actually forged a connection to the place that had only made him expand and flourish. His body may have thinned from day after day of arduous hiking and his conscious mind may have begged him to give up, but in a very short period of time his awareness had resolved to such a fine point, like a beam of light, that the more helpless he felt in his quest the more powerful he became in his mind and body. Again, if he had tried to explain these phenomena to his boys back in the city they would have shut him up for good. But out here, all alone, Petrus knew that what he was learning and feeling originated from a place of benevolence and that it was his duty to embrace it.

It took him ten days to find the nest. He'd been wandering west along Pikin River and had come upon a strange complex of basalt boulders, three stories high amongst the trees. And there, in the crown of a gigantic *kankan* that seemed anchored to nothing but rock he spotted a great mass. It was not made of mere twigs and leaves; the nest was constructed from mature branches which had been woven together, some of them six inches thick, giving the nest the architecture of a fortress.

Petrus scrambled up the lowest boulder and picked his way over to the base of the tree. He could not climb it—its lower trunk was bare of branches and its bark was as slippery as polished stone—so he knelt down on the basalt and began his appeals to the spirits. He prayed all day and when the sun dropped he continued into the night. Sun-up, sundown, Petrus implored the force he had felt growing inside of him to emerge, once and for all, and help him complete his task.

It was just before dawn on the third day when his prayers were answered. He heard a loud boom in the distance. He looked up, pushed his aching legs to stand, and listened. Another boom, a terrible blast, this one closer in. Petrus gathered his things and scrambled back down to the forest floor as another explosion let loose, this one so close he could feel the heat. He ran. As he did he looked over his shoulder and saw that everything behind him was now on fire. The flames licked at his feet and singed the back of his head. He leapt into Pikin River to ease the burns but soon the waters began to roil and bubble. If he hadn't dragged himself out of there he would have been boiled alive.

The fires burned for three days. When they finally abated Petrus crept back to the boulders through a newly sunlit and dev-astated jungle. Every tree for a square mile to the north had been reduced to a soot-covered toothpick, and the basalt of the boulders had turned black from the conflagration. There was no sign of the tree that had held the *gonini* nest. Standing there in the blinding sun, surrounded by a post-apocalyptic rainforest, Petrus had many questions. The only thing he could be sure of was this: the spirits had descended and destroyed the *gonini* nest with a black fire.

With his mission accomplished Petrus could have gone back to the city, collected his money and started a new life of relative opulence. Instead he decided to stay in Roosvallen. He swam over to the island in the middle of the Cariban and built himself a hut beneath a mango tree, just downhill from the abandoned airstrip. For the next few years he lived entirely alone in the bush, a solitude that lasted until 1991 when a plane laden with Germans arrived. Over the next two years a small village of huts and tourist lodges sprouted up around his modest home, and in 1994 Petrus was hired by the national conservation agency to run the Roosvallen tourism operation, which was burgeoning once again. He did so until 2008, when he handed things over to Benny. Then he retired, choosing to stay on at Roosvallen, his only real home, as a volunteer tour guide. Petrus never saw the *gonini* again.

4
~

MORE *STROOP*, SAID PETRUS.

Stanley hadn't said a word during Petrus's story and it took him a moment to realize the old man had finished. Stanley refilled the cup and handed it back. His mind had been slowly twisted by the tale but also set free, like a liana climbing in slow spirals to the canopy and then finally reaching the sun.

Who was he?

Suma?

The businessman.

Holland man.

Did he pay you?

Ai. He give my wives. For my children.

Petrus the hustler.

Ai.

Petrus smiled. It was the same smile he had given Stanley a thousand times before, but now Stanley could detect a hint of condescension concealed within that smile, and a thought occurred to him.

The Hundred Years War, said Stanley, the thought evolving into a partial memory, a memory he'd thought he'd lost until now.

Petrus stopped smiling.

San?

The old stories, Bas-Pey.

Ai.

There was something about an eagle, wasn't there?

Mi no sabi.

Stanley watched the old man, felt the memory fade as quickly as it had arrived.

There was something, said Stanley.

Did *yu* hear my story? said Petrus.

Yes, Bas-Pey. But you didn't explain the most important part. How does she come back to life?

Not important.

What?

There is only one thing now. Find her nest and destroy it.

But if we knew how, we could stop it from happening again.

Find her nest. Then she will stop.

How do I follow a bird, Bas-Pey?

Pay attention.

But I can't even see the sky the forest is so thick. Her nest could be twenty miles in any direction.

Petrus drank down his *stroop* and repeated himself.

Pay attention.

The buzz of an approaching outboard drifted into Camp Collymore. Petrus stood and took his cup to the sink.

Yu must pay attention, Stan-ley.

I'll ask the Boyz to help.

No. Petrus turned, wiped his hands on his shirt, straightened his tie. No one can know. If *yu* talk, she will know.

Stanley rolled his eyes. But before he could accuse Petrus of muttering absurdities—how would a bird know who he'd spoken to?—the image of a young Petrus hurling himself into Pikin River to escape a holy conflagration kept him quiet.

Stanley walked Petrus to the door, flipped on the solar lights. As

Petrus stepped into the night Hank and Frank Lampard appeared at the top of Ant Hill.

Stan-ley, said Hank.

The pair entered the halo of light. Both wore cut-off jeans and no shirts.

What do you want?

Benny say you have emergency.

It was nothing.

Can't be nothing. Hank smiled. You haven't used your radio in seven years.

The fever that had been rising in Stanley swept his extremities. He felt lighter, quicker, capable of many things. Hank knew what had made Stanley use the radio seven years ago. Stanley stepped down to the ground but Petrus moved to block him.

Hank, said the old man. Remember last week, when *yu* penis on fire? Remember I make better with medicine?

Frank Lampard burst out laughing. Hank just stared at Petrus.

Yu and Stanley fucked the same tourist, said Petrus. He had to come home early from work.

Old man, said Hank. Be careful.

Watch your mouth, said Stanley.

Boy, said Petrus to Frank Lampard. Take boss home. Put him in bed.

The solar lights flickered. Insects hummed from the roof of Camp Collymore. Something heavy splashed into the river behind camp.

Bas-Pey, said Hank. Have you voted yet?

Ai.

Stanley smiled.

Good, said Hank. It's the only way to be a man in this country now. Problem is, Bas-Pey, you built your home on a gold mine. We all did. And after the election, after your man loses, believe me, they're coming for it.

Who's *they?* said Stanley. The tourists? This is a nature reserve, you fucking *babun*.

Hank ignored Stanley, kept his eyes on Petrus.

I stop infection, said Petrus finally.

Ai, said Hank. Me, too.

Hank and Frank Lampard turned and started down the hill. As they did the lights glinted off something tucked into the back of Hank's pants. A pistol, similar to the one Shike had given Stanley.

Stan-ley, called Hank. We'll see you later.

Can't fucking wait.

Once the Boyz had started their motor and pushed off, Petrus followed them down into the darkness. Pay attention, he reminded Stanley as he left. And if you need to, pray.

5

S TANLEY SHOOK ALL NIGHT. HE DREAMED OF A
great rustling, a canopy of white sails, and while he slept his
fever built. He woke long before dawn, soaked and shivering in the dark, his hammock swinging. This sickness,
whatever it was, had begun to feel like an irreparable condition,
almost like a fate, and although Stanley still had sufficient use of his
faculties to remember what he believed about fatalism—nothing
more than a fear response to an overwhelming challenge—he
also knew that he was, once again, on the verge of vomiting, and
that his brain felt as if it was expanding inside his skull. Stanley
had begun to wonder if this was malaria or dengue, something
he had caught from the jungle, an illness symbolic of his increasingly blood-level involvement with this place, an infection Petrus
wouldn't be able to touch.

The last time he'd had malaria was almost eight years ago.
Maria had sat by his bedside for five days while he sweated it out,
and that's when she'd told him the stories of the Hundred Years
War, the old bedtime tales about courageous slaves who escaped
their bonds and disappeared into the jungles four hundred years
ago, about the brave few who returned to the plantations in the
dead of night to whisk more of their people to freedom—the rebels
who would later become known as the Maroons. Petrus had told
Maria these stories in his own language, and she had done her best

to translate them into English for Stanley. He couldn't remember the details—those five days were now a single hallucination in his memory—but he was sure there had been something about a bird. The only thing he could recall with real precision from those days was the relief he had felt when it turned out he didn't have dengue.

As Stanley continued to shake in the darkness he considered the implications of what he'd seen and heard in the last twenty-four hours, and for only the second time since he'd arrived in this forest his perception of the jungle shifted with the force of a toppling tree. Everything was possible now. The college kids who were burned alive. The curse of Camp Schumacher. The beast in the boulder cave that Maroon children were taught to fear. The Hundred Years War, the creation myth of the Maroons. Perhaps even Stanley's involvement in his own child's death, unbearable as that was to consider. Rolling out of his hammock and replaying Petrus's tale in his mind Stanley realized the forest of science he'd been living in for so long—the place he'd been reducing to Latin etymologies and GPS coordinates and quantifiable data-points for eight years now—was also a forest of stories.

He pulled on his gear and left Camp Collymore. The waters of Anyumara Falls now partly submerged the trail, and with the increase in volume the rapid had lost some of its thunder, the pool below having risen to meet the descending waters. Partway to Kawati Top, with the falls in the distance, Stanley thought he heard human voices coming from the direction of camp. He stopped and listened. The voices were high-pitched and seemed to be repeating the same thing over and over. The sound was too faint for Stanley to make out, and it wasn't until he had moved on and dropped down into the study site that he determined their source. Must have been the toucans. Something about the distance, the falls, the hills between us must have made them sound human.

Treefall Creek was now a bog, and as Stanley approached the rotten log he realized it was time to cut handholds for the bridge.

He drew his machete and walked off-trail, hacked down eight saplings and sheared their branches. Returning to the creek Stanley thrust the saplings into the swamp on either side of the log, creating a makeshift set of supports that would stop most tourists, but certainly not all of them, from plunging into the mud below. Stanley tested his engineering by crossing the log himself. He found the saplings to be firm and well spaced. Then, as he stepped off the log, he felt eyes on him. Up ahead stood the Brazilian tapir.

Stanley took a few quiet steps towards the animal. She appeared to be looking straight at him and she didn't move as he approached. He was now less than ten feet away, the closest he'd ever come to the charming, storybook creature. Stanley stopped walking. His mind raced. Where is your child? I always see you two together, but lately . . . What happened to him? Surely he isn't old enough yet to strike out on his own. The tapir continued to stare at Stanley, and for the next few minutes he silently returned the look. Maybe you don't know? Is that possible? Stanley considered this idea. It's conceivable that a young animal who has yet to be weaned may simply go missing out here without explanation, without its mother knowing what happened to it. But it seems highly unlikely. A wild mother doesn't send her son off into the world and spend the rest of the day praying for his safe return. A wild mother never leaves her child's side. Surely nothing can happen to the young out here without a mother knowing the details.

It was this thought that made Stanley's throat tighten. The tapir stomped her front foot lightly on the trail and Stanley took another step towards her. Do you know what happened? At the sound of his voice the tapir turned and smashed into the understory.

An hour later Stanley found the monkeys up near Jag Junction on the edge of the lowland swamp. Instead of performing his usual headcount he walked the length and breadth of the troop, searching for Charlie. He saw Johan taking a nap, his torso flat against a high branch, his arms and legs dangling lazily down. He saw

Martina and Lucy next to each other in a tangle of lianas, Lucy picking bugs, ticks and chiggers from Martina's midsection. He saw Wacky bashing a nut in the fork of a large Inga. Once again, nothing in the monkeys' behaviour suggested they were under threat, but this time Stanley knew to remain vigilant. Charlie? Where are you, little man? Stanley walked back and forth, squelching through the swamp, wearing a trail through the mud as if through a foot of snow. Charlie?

He eventually found Charlie back at Jag Junction, rough-housing with the youngsters. Stanley spotted him when a squeal of excitement rang out and three monkeys tumbled to the forest floor: Charlie, Suri Rama and Peanut. As the two females ran off and Charlie chased after them, Stanley felt relief for two reasons. First, Charlie was alive. Second, Peanut appeared no worse off for having lost Banana, her favourite playmate. Stanley watched Charlie bound after the others. The monkey leapt through the fronds of a low *maka* palm in hot pursuit but miscalculated his jump and wedged himself deep inside the crown, with only his rear end hanging out the back. A moment later, Charlie burst free in an explosion of detritus, but surely not without a *maka* spine or three lodged somewhere on his person. Sometime later, during a late-afternoon grooming session, Marilyn would have to pull those spines from her youngster's skin.

Stanley opened his camp chair and sat down beneath the troop. Petrus had told him to pay attention, but what the hell did that mean? Stanley had been paying attention to these monkeys, these trees and trails, for more than eight years now. What would he need to change about himself in order to follow Petrus's command? Soon, an orange-rumped agouti appeared not five feet away from Stanley. The animal hadn't noticed the man, but when Stanley turned to look a shiver of terror went through the rodent. The agouti hunched down, raised the rust-coloured fur on his rear end and began thumping the ground with one of his hind legs. For such a small animal, the agouti could sound one hell of an alarm. Stanley didn't move. Slowly the fur on the agouti's hindquarters dropped and his rear end lowered. The animal gave one last thump with his foot, sat back on his haunches and began nibbling a fruit he'd found on the ground.

The monkeys were drifting west of the swamps so Stanley repositioned his chair. Pay attention. Stanley decided he would have to wait for the bird to attack again. Much as this plan filled him with dread he had no other choice. He would wait for her and then track her somehow. He would need to get up high. I should climb. I need to get as high as I can before she returns.

Stanley walked beneath the monkeys, looking for the ideal tree to climb. He had once been told that a single square mile of rain-forest might contain up to one thousand species of tree, and only now that he was being choosy did the meaning of this trivia sink in. His first thought was to climb a *kankan*; that would give him the ultimate view of the bird's flight path. But the trunk of a *kankan* is far too slippery, and the lowest branches are in the crown, a good fifty feet up. In fact, most of the trees surrounding Stanley were just trunks at ground level with no branches, and those that did have low branches had trunks that were too young and flimsy to support his weight. This was, however, a liana forest; the under-story was thicketed with woody vines. Stanley arrived at a robust liana that turned a hairpin a few feet off the ground and stretched forty-six feet up. He gripped the vine with both hands, gave it a couple of pulls. Strong and steady. Once he was sure he hadn't disturbed a phalanx of bullet ants Stanley leapt onto the liana and began shimmying up it.

He made it twenty-two feet off the ground before taking a break. He looked below and saw the agouti sitting directly beneath the liana. The rodent was looking straight up at Stanley, a half-eaten piece of fruit in his forepaws. Stanley shimmied up another few feet and then looked down again. The agouti hadn't moved.

Stanley guessed he had about forty-nine more feet to go before the canopy began. The higher he climbed the more the liana swung, and whenever he stopped climbing the vine swept him slowly back and forth through the air. The first few times this happened he felt like a circus performer. But at about thirty feet Stanley began to feel utterly ridiculous. *What am I going to do when I get up there, just sit down next to Johan and wait? And what happens when the monkeys start to move, or when the eagle attacks? Am I just going to leap through the trees?* He looked down again. The agouti was still watching him, but now the animal was also munching his fruit. *Okay, I get it.* He took a few deep breaths and began shimmying back down to the ground.

Back in his camp chair, Stanley watched his monkeys and became even more convinced of the futility of his goal. *Pay attention. Pay attention.* Petrus's command seemed designed to make a man go wild with hopelessness. *How long will I have to wait? And how should I entertain myself until the moment comes?* He made a resolution. *I will watch my monkeys as I always have. There's nothing else I can do.*

Then he heard a familiar thumping from up the trail. Stanley looked around for the agouti but the rodent was gone. The thumping got louder, which caused one of the juvenile monkeys above to emit a high-pitched alarm. Stanley stood and took a quick scan of the troop. He observed no fear behaviour, no monkeys dropping from the trees. The thumping continued. Satisfied that his monkeys weren't in danger Stanley grabbed his gear and walked up the trail to investigate. He found the agouti fifty-one feet away in the middle of the trail. When Stanley appeared the rodent stopped thumping, turned and hopped further up-trail, towards the junction with the Yellow Brick Road. The agouti took the corner, disappearing from view. Stanley heard the thumping again so he took the corner and followed.

6

~

MARIA HAD ALWAYS CONSIDERED THE CUTTING of new trails to be a sacred act. Not only did she and Stanley slaughter a menagerie of botanical wonders with every pass of their machetes, they also opened up new areas of the understory in a forest that had been otherwise impenetrable for tens of thousands of years. The significance of this was never lost on Maria, and so every time they completed a new trail she made Stanley perform a modest ceremony with her to honour the new pathway and the many lives that had been sacrificed in its creation. Stanley would stand at one end of the trail while Maria would stand at the other, and the two would alternate lines from her favourite stanza of "Kéramos," Henry Wadsworth Longfellow's great lyric poem, on their walkie-talkies:

> *Turn, turn, my wheel! All things must change*
> *To something new, to something strange;*
> *Nothing that is can pause or stay;*
> *The moon will wax, the moon will wane,*
> *The mist and cloud will turn to rain,*
> *The rain to mist and cloud again,*
> *To-morrow be to-day.*

Sometimes the new trail would be so long that once they were finished it would take them ten minutes to meet each other in the middle. By walking the trail together and by connecting the two ends with their voices Maria felt they had woven the new path into the tapestry they had already cut into the jungle, and that by doing so their presence in the forest gained an additional measure of virtue. Over time, Stanley came to appreciate this sentiment because although they never spoke of it, as young scientists Stanley and Maria felt guided by virtue back then. They wouldn't have been able to name the feeling or identify the time and place where they first acquired it, but with their questions in hand and grant money pouring in and a troop of wild monkeys at their disposal they both felt secure in their righteousness, that they themselves had uncovered a good, reliable trail.

In his latter months at Roosvallen Professor Collymore adopted a somewhat different christening process for new trails. Whenever Stanley or Maria would arrive home and announce that another had been cut, Collymore made it his priority to hike out the next day to defecate at the new trailhead. Christ almighty! he would say upon returning to camp, chastising no one in particular as he sat at the table and sketched the new trail onto the system map. We must claim every inch for ourselves!

That was around the time Collymore started speaking with the animals. To spend a day in the bush with the professor now was to witness a surreal pantomime of one-sided conversations, debates and quarrels. Collymore hardly spoke to his field assistants anymore, preferring to while away the hours nitpicking the monkeys, castigating the agoutis and consoling the occasional armadillo. Fight back? he would say, as he raced after a troop of bearded sakis. Fight back against what? Your shackles are imaginary, you foolish creatures. And besides, the bush is too thick. You wouldn't stand a chance.

Collymore's delusions hewed closely to a single theme: animal revolution, an uprising of evolutionary proportions. It was as if the writings of Kipling, Orwell and Conrad had simultaneously infected his mind. Everywhere the professor looked he saw evidence of a coming rebellion: the seasonal hatching of the termite nests, the gradual rise of the Cariban up Ant Hill, the manic squabbles of the squirrel monkeys, many of which turned bloody. Every happening in the forest was suddenly ripe with menace. She's coming back, he would say, over and over on their way home every night—she's coming back!—and whenever Stanley or Maria would ask who he was referring to the professor wouldn't have an answer. They refuse to tell me, he would say, blaming his ignorance on a pair of tight-lipped caracara birds or a secretive herd of pingoes. They don't think I can handle the knowledge. But she's coming back. The animals swear it, and I can bloody well guarantee she'll use our own trails to strike.

Then one day Collymore became convinced the animals were speaking to him in verse, and for the next few weeks the professor acted as if he were the conduit of a new form of literature, the poetry of the animal kingdom. When the trio would return to camp at night, Collymore would rush to the data table and spend the rest of the evening scribbling madly, transcribing the poems of the animals. Gorchenski was right! he hollered one night as he wrote. This is where the great man was leading us, God rest his soul. This is the meaning behind the data.

On their days off, Stanley and Maria would read Collymore's latest notations in the data binders with a mixture of mirth and concern. One was a simple rhyming couplet about an anaconda who had eaten too much:

The mound in my belly is much too big
I should not have eaten that jungle pig

Another spoke of a baby bird who could not fly:

*A baby bird who cannot yet fly will crash to the ground in the
   blink of an eye.
A baby bird with two broken wings will certainly make a big
   mess of things.
A baby bird with too much mass will come to a halt in a forest
   of glass.
A baby bird who cannot be saved will come to a rest in a baby
   bird's grave.*

Maria's favourite was a quatrain about the red-handed tamarins:

*They told us to paint with our fingers
They told us to paint or we're dead
We painted and then did not linger
That's why our hands are still red*

But while Collymore slipped further and further from reality,
Stanley and Maria knew their boss's suspicion around the trail system was at least partially based in reality. Hardly a day passed when
they didn't find evidence that the animals were indeed using their
trails. The piles of scat, clumps of fur and corpses of small prey
scattered throughout their site every morning proved that every
time they cut a new trail they were indeed opening up not just
a new pathway but a new frontier, and yet another route back to
Camp Collymore.

This idea took on new meaning for Stanley now, as he followed
the agouti along the Yellow Brick Road on a winding tour of the
Kawati Hills. The monkeys rarely came up into the highlands so
Stanley hadn't visited these trails for more than a year. The paths
were in terrible disrepair. While the agouti could hop past any
obstacle, Stanley had to machete a detour around countless toppled lianas and at least three massive tree-falls. He was a deft hand
with the blade and he made quick work of the bush, but Stanley

soon grew weary with the effort. His fever had dropped earlier but now returned with a vengeance. He began to feel woozy. He followed his guide in a mild delirium, his legs aching, a fire burning in his shoulder. Hours passed. His mind slipped back to cutting trails with Maria, to cutting off-trail with Professor Collymore, but before any particular memories could take shape he smelled something awful.

Stanley slowed, blinked a few times. He was deep in the hills. The agouti had hopped off-trail and was rooting around in the understory, his front legs a blur. A cloud of detritus rose up behind the animal as he quarried a large pile of rotting vegetation. The smell that had awoken Stanley intensified: musk, rotten fish, sour mash. When the agouti stopped digging it hopped away, and Stanley left the trail to inspect the hole.

Nestled into the gooey leaves and black earth were the decomposing remains of an animal. In life the creature had probably been about three times the size of the agouti, but now its torso was nothing more than a partial rib cage and a few tattered strands of hide. The animal's head was mostly intact, and when Stanley bent low to inspect the unfortunate animal's skull he saw the short proboscis and quickly understood whose grave he was peering into. With a stick he flipped over a piece of hide; the vague pattern of stripes was all the confirmation he required. Stanley felt a wave of sadness pass through him. He peered into the mid-canopy above, thirty-seven feet of dense lianas through which the sun could barely pass. He stayed with the corpse for a minute more before the smell drove him away.

This is nothing. This body could not have been delivered here by a bird. This has been a goddamn waste of my time. But Stanley knew that the sadness and coincidence of his little discovery would stay with him even if he had reached a resounding dead end in his search. Stanley returned to the trail, and as he did his scholarly training kicked in. Many animals are known to grieve: elephants, chimpanzees, dogs and cats, baboons, even rabbits and goats. But what about tapirs?

A wind blew through the hills, bringing down a shower of debris. Stanley watched a dead epiphyte drift lazily down from the canopy, a jungle tumbleweed, and the possibility that Maria had been right all those years ago crept back into Stanley's mind. Thunder cracked and the skies opened. A torrent of water bashed through the foliage and Stanley looked up, closed his eyes, let the cold splash his face.

I was a parent once, too, he thought. I will deliver the terrible news myself.

7
~

THE RAINS CONTINUED ALL AFTERNOON AND ONLY
relented at dusk. When Stanley arrived back at camp he
found the river had risen by six feet. His beach was now
submerged and the waters lapped against *Pasensi*'s hull.
Stanley removed his sodden clothes and waded into the water,
curled his toes into the sand, knelt down and braced himself as
he slipped beneath the surface. He imagined the heat in his body
dissipating into the river, warming the eddies at the base of the
boulders, bringing schools of minnows to the surface, lifting steam
from the sacred rapids of Moedervallen to the south. After the
shock of the cold a warmth enveloped Stanley, the combustion
of his body winning out against an unfathomable volume of rain.
Years ago he used to hike out to Moedervallen after a big storm,
wade into her white water, lie down and then fight the current with
every muscle. The river would always win, pushing Stanley off balance and sweeping him downstream like a fallen palm husk. But
the more often he struggled against the flow of the Cariban the
stronger he became, and he visited the rapids often back then, considered this new fitness regime to be yogic in nature, with benefits
for the body but also for the mind. Now, with this fever smouldering inside him, Stanley realized the error of his thinking back
then, and felt once again like the husk of some discarded fruit. If he
were to step off this sunken beach it would be a difficult ride and

there is no telling where he might end up: the Caribbean Sea, the shores of Grenada, some tidewater marsh off Georgetown where the mosquitoes are the size of quarters and the mud comes all the way from Manaus.

Stanley untied the boat from its mooring and pulled it partway up the hill. Gathering his clothes he heard a faint rumble of thunder and realized this would be one of the last times he would bathe in the river this season. At the top of Ant Hill he pushed open the door to the shower house for the first time in four months. A posse of six- and eight-legged creatures skittered to the corners and the stench of urine made Stanley cough. In the near-darkness he could see the floor was coated in a malevolent black mould.

Flipping on the lights in the main building Stanley observed that a few of the buckets had overflowed and spilled their catchment. The resulting flood had gathered the corpses and constituent parts of the dead—the forewings, abdomens, mandibles and tails that had accumulated in the corners of the living room over the years—and spread them across the floor. Stanley dug in the hammock for his only set of dry clothes and found them to be moist but he put them on anyway. He emptied the buckets out the side door and walked through to the kitchen. He lifted the lid of the rice bucket, retrieved the scoop and found that a small proportion of the grains were discoloured and wriggling. He took the scoop to the table and picked through the grains, separating the protein from the starch. Then he searched through the bag of onions and garlic for the least mouldy specimens and chopped them. After sweeping the pebbles of rat shit from the stovetop he set the wok on one of the burners and poured in some oil. Then the lights flickered and dimmed. Stanley turned on his headlamp, walked to the power panel and flipped off the switch.

Stanley could handle the mould and the infiltration of animals and the fact that it would be months now before his solar lights would hold a full charge. None of these privations even registered with him, so accustomed was he to welcoming the rains and the rodents into his home; these minor disturbances provided further contour to his life in the jungle, just as the swollen waters of Moedervallen used to provide shape to his muscles and his mind. But when Stanley began filling the rice pot with water the tap sputtered and gasped, sediment poured forth, and he raised the pot above his head and brought it crashing down upon the copper tap. He did this three times, swearing aloud with each downward thrust, and then he threw the pot at the opposite wall, showering the kitchen with rice. Tomorrow he would have to descend the backside of Ant Hill to pump water, a difficult task when the river was low and a repulsive one now that the Cariban had topped her banks. Fuck! Stanley stomped through the kitchen. Fuck! Fuck! Fuck! Who was he kidding? The rainy season had not provided what he'd most wanted. The forest may have been transformed but it had not been cleansed. Not only had the bird returned, it had been resurrected. The promise of the fruit season was null and void.

He thought of Charlie, wondered what the monkey was doing or thinking or dreaming about. Stanley had always found it odd that the researchers went home every night, that they left the troop alone for at least ten hours every evening, a period of time in which any and all forms of drama could play out. Wouldn't field researchers fulfill their stated mission more sincerely by never actually leaving the sides of their study subjects?

Stanley retrieved a fresh bottle of *palum* and a clean glass from beneath the kitchen counter. He sat at the table, pushed aside the rice scoop and poured out a large measure of rum. As he reached for the drink he detected movement next to his glass, and leaning in he watched the pile of tiny brown maggots he had picked from the rice, thirty or forty of them writhing together. Stanley watched them struggle, the circumference of their little gathering expanding as individual larvae tumbled from the top of the pile like people from the roof of a burning building. After observing them for a while Stanley reached out and plucked a fallen maggot from the table, held it between his thumb and index finger, brought it close to his eye. He wondered if the young insect could sense the heat growing in Stanley's body, if the fever might pass through his fingers and elicit some ancient mechanism in the bug. What would it be like to witness metamorphosis first-hand, indeed to trigger it? What kind of winged beast might emerge? Would it be hideous or beautiful? Would it sting the very being that had given it life? Stanley reached for his rum and brought the maggot to hover over the glass. You would eat me if I were dead, he said, releasing the maggot and watching it sink into the greasy liquid. Pushing himself up from the table Stanley raised the glass and tipped its contents into his mouth.

He began preparations. From the Rubbermaid beneath the clotheslines he pulled his sleeping bag, his oversized orange tarpaulin, his waterproof expedition pack and hefted these items into the kitchen. Flipping the lids of the waterproof bins he rummaged for anything edible—a box of three-year-old protein bars, four bags of biscuit bread, a jar of peanut butter, two pounds of peanuts, instant-noodle packages, a handful of sugar crystal packets, a bag of cassava flour—and piled these on the floor next to his pack. From the cubbies he pulled a tin pot, a camp stove, butane canisters, every battery he could find, two extra-large water bottles and the emergency medical kit. From the lockbox he retrieved three vials of anti-venom and the last remaining ferrocerium fire-starter, a panic whistle attached to its lanyard.

Stanley poured himself another rum and began packing. When he was finished he sat on the front stoop in the darkness sharpening his machete. He spent a long time on the blade and when the knife was ready he sheathed it and strapped it to the outside of his pack. Stanley rolled up the orange tarp, tied it to the top of the pack and then lifted the whole kit onto his shoulders. He tested the weight and balance. It would be a tough first couple of days but he'd soon adjust to the burden.

He unravelled his hammock, placed the *palum* within arm's reach and slipped into bed. Then the rains returned, the buckets began to clink and Stanley had one last thought. He walked to the cubbies in the dark and felt for the pile of old towels. He rolled up four of them and wedged them into the space at the bottom of each bedroom door, the doors he hadn't opened in seven years. The buckets would surely overflow before his return.

8

~

S TANLEY LEFT CAMP COLLYMORE BEFORE DAWN.
He pulled the latch across the front door, walked down
Ant Hill, found *Pasensi* now bobbing among the trees and
knew he was making the right decision. Everything he
would need to survive in the forest he carried on his back. He'd
even remembered to pour himself a few flasks of *palum*, partly to
make the first few nights in the bush bearable and partly because
he was sure that one day soon he would need to sanctify another
grave. As he veered east onto the Voltzberg and heard the rum-
bling of Anyumara Falls Stanley had the strange sense that the next
time he would lay eyes on Camp Collymore the entire building
would be submerged. He imagined the river growing so massive
in his absence that everything he'd ever possessed or coveted at
Roosvallen would be swept downriver to the sea. This was the direction he had once yearned to travel, in the days following his boy's
death when all Stanley wanted to do was the easy thing, but as time
passed he'd convinced himself that the jungle was the only home
he deserved. Bending down to fill his water bottles beneath the
falls, Stanley said goodbye to his beach, his kitchen, his hammock.

Down in the bog new ferns had sprouted, their emerald fronds
tracing the old banks of Treefall Creek. Beneath the rotten log
the swamp had filled and Stanley's handholds were now so solid
they might have been sunk in concrete. As he crossed he noticed a

fresh depression in the mud below and winced as he imagined the unfortunate tourist slipping on the tree trunk earlier that morning and plummeting into the mire. Stepping off the other side Stanley heard monkeys splashing to the east and instinctively picked up his pace, but then, arriving at the tapir's usual spot, he remembered the job he had to do.

Stanley calmed his breath and listened. After a minute or two he thought he could make out the hollow whoosh of the tapir's breath, so he crept into the understory. A few feet from the trail he squeezed himself through a thicket of lianas, getting stuck a couple of times because he hadn't bothered to remove his pack. Once he was free of the creepers he stopped to listen again, and now the tapir's breath was so loud he felt uneasy that he couldn't see her. Surely she could smell him. He had better get down to business.

How does one speak to a wild animal? He'd done it before, uttered threats and curses and even words of love in the direction of his monkeys, and every now and then a snake or a butterfly or a capybara would elicit a small snippet of one-sided conversation. But this was different. Now he had something important to say. He thought of Collymore. Perhaps everything the old man had uttered into the trees had actually carried real consequence and was not, as Stanley had assumed, merely the signs and symbols of the unhinged. Perhaps the professor had learned something about the forest, much as Stanley had learned the day before, and all he'd been trying to do was communicate this new-found education. Bullshit. Stanley surprised himself with the volume of his voice, and before another thought could occur a great smashing arose not ten feet away and the tapir burst through the foliage. The animal charged, its short proboscis curled down over its mouth, its thick, ungulate legs churning like massive pistons. Stanley turned to run, but as he ducked into the thicket the top of his pack struck a particularly woody vine, sending him crashing backwards to the forest floor. The tapir pounded past, its hooves inches from Stanley's head. He cried out from shock and then pain as he had landed awkwardly, his knee twisted beneath him. Now that he was on the ground he learned the real power of the Brazilian tapir, the creature long gone but the earth still thundering.

Stanley grimaced as he swung his leg out from under him. He reached for a nearby liana to pull himself to his feet but the vine gave way, showering Stanley with rotting debris. Spitting insects from his mouth he hurriedly checked his body for bullet ants. Instead he found that his torso was writhing with ticks, the tiny arachnids scrambling across his field shirt, searching for blood. Stanley had forgotten his duct tape so he worked quickly, picking each tick from the fabric and, more out of tradition than need, tearing their abdomens in half. Ten minutes passed before he'd rid himself of the infestation. He checked one last time for bullet ants and then struggled to his knees. He crawled through the thicket and back to the Voltzberg, pushed himself to his feet and limped a few steps down-trail after his monkeys.

Then he heard voices. Stanley stopped, listened, muttered a quiet curse and stumbled into the understory again. He hid in a stand of heliconia on the other side of the trail. Peering back through the fronds he saw the Boyz round the corner at Hollywood Boulevard, a few hundred feet up-trail. Hank led the way, machete in hand, followed by Frank Lampard and Alberto, who carried the wooden crate between them. As he watched them cross Treefall Creek, Stanley wondered if those weapons he'd seen a few days ago had been a one-time venture or a matter of course. Perhaps Hank had heard about their little mishap and felt the need to provide an escort. Or perhaps this was nothing more than a delivery of canned meat, fry oil and shit rag for the tourists who'd passed through earlier.

Stanley's pranking days were over, so he made no preparations and resolved to let them pass. But as the Boyz neared his position Stanley spotted something on the other side of the trail that made his stomach drop. Hanging there a few feet off the ground, lodged in the lianas he had crawled through minutes before, was his heavy-duty orange tarpaulin. Stanley frantically patted the top of his pack and felt only the loose straps. The tarp glimmered in the morning sun like a blooming heliconia.

Stanley closed his eyes. He did not allow himself an outburst like he had the previous evening. He reached a hand to his nose but it had healed, so he dug his thumbnail into his wrist instead. This is no time to self-destruct, he said, twisting open the skin. He sat with the pain for ten seconds. Then he opened his eyes and gazing softly at the trail he concluded that nothing untoward would happen here. Hank would see nothing and continue down the trail. Frank Lampard would be too concerned with his footing to look up. Alberto would be so high that a glimmer of orange in the understory wouldn't register as an anomaly. A cloud would pass before the sun. Stanley knew these things would occur. In fact, they were already in the past, so powerful was his control over the angry territory of his mind, a skill he had honed many years before. Unfortunately, Stanley was only able to predict the human variables. Alberto had indeed smoked a good deal of hash before setting out that morning. But as he passed the tarp, a beam of sunshine slipped through the foliage and illuminated the vinyl with such intensity that the material seemed to emit a light of its own.

Hank, said Alberto.

San?

Looku.

Hank turned, followed Alberto's gaze.

Naai mi, he said. Fucking Canadians.

Frank Lampard and Alberto lowered the crate from their shoulders. Alberto walked off-trail, pulled the tarp from the thicket, folded it and placed it on top of the crate. Then the Boyz lifted it back to their shoulders.

Slow and easy, said Hank. Like she's your first wife.

The three continued down the Voltz. Once they were out of sight Stanley limped back to the trail, considered his options. Without a tarpaulin it would be difficult but not impossible to overnight in the bush. He could pull together a shelter of heliconia fronds each night and reconcile himself to the imperfection. He could also simply return to camp each evening, pump water and use the bathhouse and cook infested rice until the rains abated. He quickly dismissed this idea, however, not because of the inconveniences but because he had made the decision to leave Camp Collymore, and ever since he had pulled the latch across the door that morning he had felt a wave of virtue rising inside him, a sense that he was getting closer to a solution to his predicaments. To turn back now would be to capitulate to the very forces he had allied himself against. His third option, of course, was to follow the Boyz all the way to the foot of the Voltzberg, keep hidden until the moment presented itself and then steal his tarpaulin back. At first this seemed the unlikeliest scenario, as he felt compelled to get back to his monkeys and his search for the eagle's nest. But as he imagined tracking the Boyz and turning the tables on those assholes without them even knowing it, Stanley warmed to the idea. It would only take a few hours. He could make it back before sunset, find the Longfellows as they were bedding down, set up shop and spend the next few days awaiting the next attack.

Stanley heard the monkeys splashing up ahead, the twitters of the juveniles, the *ke-junks* of a troop on the move. Then he heard a rustling above him, looked up and saw Two-Moons, the white-faced saki. I know. But I'll be back before you know it. Stanley hefted his pack and crouched a few times, testing his swollen knee.

9

BACK WHEN THE MONKEY PROJECT WAS STILL A going concern, Stanley and Maria would walk to the Voltzberg Mountain once a week. Every Sunday they would rise an hour earlier than usual and stumble down to the trailhead in the pitch black. Maria would set her stopwatch, perform a short countdown, and the two would begin walking east, away from the river, in a trancelike state. They walked as slowly as possible—three miles an hour, as prescribed by the scientific literature—and they took great care to cushion their footfalls. The pair wouldn't speak for the entirety of the trek. When they did need to communicate they used hand signals, and if one of them tripped or sneezed or laughed aloud at something that had bubbled up from their unconscious they stopped mid-stride until the disturbance had passed. If something in one of their packs began to rattle or if one of them needed to pee, Maria paused her watch and whomever had screwed up their packing technique or water intake would rectify the situation. At all times, Stanley and Maria kept their eyes on the forest and their ears perked for the slightest sound of an animal. When they saw or heard something—a red brocket deer, a herd of pingoes, a troop of bearded sakis causing havoc somewhere off-trail—they stopped to gather as much information as they could (species, estimated number, rough direction of travel) and then continued silently on their way. The

Voltzberg Trail extends seven miles into the Roosvallen rain-forest, five miles deeper than the study site does. The path leads into the literal wild, a teeming jungle devoid of human habitation where it seemed anything was possible, and the night before these weekly hikes Stanley and Maria would be giddy with anticipation. The pair had seen their first puma on one of these walks, the whis-kered phantom slinking across the trail not ten feet ahead of them. On another, Maria had spotted a twenty-foot anaconda splayed among the stilt roots of a palm tree, a lump the size of a wild boar distorting its midsection.

But walking the Voltz was more than just an adventurous break from the monkey project. Each hike was a line-transect census, a meticulously controlled survey of the flora and fauna at Roosvallen. Over time and taken together, the data from these surveys would provide an estimate of the volume and distribution of animal life in the larger forest. The pair took their role in these measure-ments very seriously. Every time they crossed the threshold of their study site and entered the wider jungle, Stanley and Maria felt like Renaissance cartographers, journeying into the unknown on behalf of an ignorant world.

It was all training for this moment, thought Stanley, as he followed Hank, Frank Lampard and Alberto along the Voltz. In twenty minutes the Boyz had reached the eastern edge of the study site, Asgard Stream, a trickle of a creek in the dry season but now a muddy mess. Stanley heard them splash across and began to feel faintly nervous. He arrived at the stream a minute later, crept through it, and on the other side he turned to face his study site and realized he hadn't left in seven years. After Maria left Stanley had mothballed the line-transect study. His official reasoning was that their methodology required two sets of eyes and ears, and any data he collected by himself would be incompatible with previous censuses. But unofficially Stanley was in no state back then to leave the relatively secure confines of the monkey project, and after a few Sundays had passed unobserved, the bush beyond Asgard Stream ceased to exist for him. Whenever the monkeys came out this far Stanley wouldn't follow them. He would just sit on his camp chair and wait for them to circle back, as if the scientific enterprise shared the limits of his psyche.

Stanley couldn't see the Boyz up ahead but he could hear them talking. The trail was pretty much a straight shot to the mountain, with just a few twists and turns along the way, so he wasn't going to lose them. Even so, his nerves grew worse with every step and he nearly turned back twice. But then he crossed Bedrock Stream and began to recognize the forest: the giant heliconia patch where he and Maria had waited out countless storms; the strange and solitary boulder shaped by the wind and rain into a perfect sphere; the high forest where troops of spider monkeys swept through like gangs of hirsute twelve-year-olds, snapping branches and heaving them like javelins at the intruding pink creatures below. The further into the bush Stanley crept the more memories flooded back, and the more his nerves calmed. He had walked past these trees and through these bogs and across these streams so many times before that he was, in fact, still the owner of this place, its principle inhabitant and therefore its overseer, and just because he hadn't visited in seven years didn't mean he had relinquished title to this forest floor, this understory, this mid-canopy and the crown of every *kankan* for miles. What's more, back at Camp Collymore was a binder containing the data sheets from every Voltzberg hike Stanley had ever taken, and upon these yellow sheets of graph paper were scribbled the scientific title to these lands, a record of who and what lives here and a running insinuation of their roles and relationships—a census of the empire as it was on that day, at that hour, as distilled through his and his wife's expert consideration. Stanley walked faster, lengthening his stride. He was a scientist, something he had forgotten about himself recently, and he still possessed the rights and privileges that came with the designation. Fuck those tourists for thinking they could just waltz in here with their insect repellent and their lightweight Patagonia and their automatic weapons and make themselves at home.

Stanley crossed Wonderland Stream and Neverland Stream and grew angrier every minute. By the time he reached Earthsea Stream he had clenched and unclenched his fists so many times that his fingers ached. Then with little warning the forest brightened, the trail rose in elevation and Stanley emerged, squinting, onto the West Platte, a surreal tabletop of sunbaked granite where a desert microclimate thrived. Here were no trees or vines, no forest at all. Instead the unfiltered sun pressed down, cacti dotted the undulating rock face, and platoons of lizards skittered amongst ground-dwelling orchids, low grasses, pineapple plants and rainwater pools of cerulean sky. All of this was background scenery to the main attraction, the Voltzberg itself, a monolithic granite dome that rose up from the jungle on the far side of the Platte. Stanley always felt a twinge of awe upon emerging from the jungle and laying eyes on the massif, its western face streaked with rivulets of rainwater, its summit shaped like the shoulders of a sitting elephant, its sheer, brutalist architecture at odds with the lavishness of the surrounding rainforest. Seven years since his last pilgrimage and Stanley now found himself paralyzed with veneration, his anger gone, his limbs loose, his mind all but crashing. The memory of his last visit to this place came back to him now, as if he lay drinking *palum* in his hammock. It was only when he spotted the Boyz disappearing into the forest at the foot of the mountain that he snapped out of his reverie, found the old hunting trail along the southern edge of the Platte and made his silent way towards Camp Schumacher.

~

H E AND MARIA HAD COME TO THE MOUNTAIN TO get away from Collymore. The professor's paranoia had become too much to bear, and after the team had witnessed something truly remarkable in the forest one day the old man had lost his grip entirely. It happened late one afternoon as the monkeys were slowly entering the bamboo from the south. Maria was busy identifying them one by one as they swept through the amphitheatre when she noticed Marilyn leaping from branch to branch at high speed. She was hot on the tail of Johan, the alpha. Marilyn was vocalizing in a way Maria had never heard before, a guttural sort of whistling, and as the chase continued through the amphitheatre and along the edge of the bamboo the pitch of Marilyn's vocalizations rose. It sounded to Maria as if the monkey was both desperately frightened and wildly excited. She hollered to her colleagues, and when Stanley and Collymore arrived in the little clearing and took in the scene, Maria saw the professor go white.

That, my dear friends, is the estrus vocalization of *Cebus apella*, said Collymore. They are reproducing. Banging like rabbits, if you will allow me the colloquialism. In short, the monkeys are multiplying. In summary, we're all officially done for.

Stanley and Maria ignored the professor and raced over to the Appian Way. They dumped their gear at the foot of the Inga and climbed together to the observation deck. There they raised their glasses and searched the perimeter of the bamboo for Johan and Marilyn, whose wheezing had turned into an all-out wailing.

There! said Maria. In the fork of that *Cecropia*. You see?

Stanley saw them all right. Johan had mounted Marilyn from behind, his hands on her back, his little waist pumping back and forth. Marilyn looked sickened by the whole procedure. She wore a grimace Stanley had never seen before, her lips pulled so far back that her teeth were bared to the gum line. She frantically scraped at the branch beneath her and leapt in all directions as if trying to escape the very situation she had pursued.

That looks awful, said Maria.

Nothing wrong with a little jungle fever, if you will allow me the colloquialism, said Stanley, drawing a giggle from Maria.

I always figured Johan for a romantic.

This is far from the Ritz, my dear. In summary and in conclusion, this mess here is the bloomin' jungle.

Stanley and Maria knew that copulation between capuchins was a rare thing to witness, as it usually took place away from the troop and—from a researcher's perspective, at least—rather secretively. If they had managed this after just six months of effort at Roosvallen, imagine what they might accomplish in the next five, ten or twenty years. The scientific potential of this place seemed infinite at that moment, and it was for this reason that Stanley reached for Maria's hand as they stood watching Johan and Marilyn across the bamboo. Their lives, their careers, had finally begun, after nearly a decade of toil through higher education.

From that day on, though, Professor Collymore spent every day and most nights slumped at the data table back at camp, flipping through binders of observations, consulting the site map like an actuary and uttering vague threats to anyone who would listen. The morning after Johan and Marilyn's tryst, Stanley and Maria left camp in the dark as usual but Collymore refused to join them.

I'm not stupid, he informed his team as he sipped a mug of hot cocoa. We didn't build these fortifications for nothing. She's coming back, and when she does I'll be ready for her.

Two days later, the professor accused Petrus of sorcery and threatened to report him to officials in the capital because he had cured Stanley of an earache with nothing more than a smouldering plantain shoot. Two days after that, Stanley and Maria returned from the field to find the front door of their home barricaded shut from the inside. They had tried to reason with Collymore through the windows but the old man had refused to let them in, accusing them of smuggling wild animals in their backpacks and of switching allegiances in an almighty struggle only he was aware had commenced. The pair eventually gave up and took *Pasensi* to the island to bunk in one of the tourist lodges, but not before capsizing just above the rapids and barely making it to shore.

While they were on the island that night, Stanley and Maria learned more distressing news. Collymore had apparently been coming to the island every day while his assistants were out with the monkeys, and Benny had heard Collymore on the radio on multiple occasions, cancelling all future grocery shipments and telling Wout the monkey researchers were no longer in need of his assistance and were officially living off the land.

Upon returning to camp the next morning the pair found Collymore standing down by the outhouse, naked but for his gitch, pouring gasoline from the reserve canister onto the trash pit. At his feet was the latest data binder, which contained the complete records of the last four months of monkey research—raw data that had yet to be duplicated. When the professor saw Stanley and Maria crest Ant Hill he quickly pulled a box of matches from his pocket. Evidence! he yelled. We must get rid of the evidence! Stanley raced over and leapt upon the binders before Collymore could set them ablaze, as the trash pit went up with a *whump*. Maria approached Collymore more slowly, speaking softly in an attempt to calm him.

Professor? What have you done with your pants? Professor, why don't we go inside and make some lunch? And it was during this exchange when Maria first noticed Collymore's left leg.

His skin was pale, even for a Scot, but that's not what made Maria's stomach drop. Halfway up Collymore's shin was a grotesque wound. Running vertically up one side of the bone, it looked as if three inches of flesh had been melted by a flame.

Oh, Professor, what have you done to your leg?

Maria knew what she was looking at. She knew that somewhere deep inside his mind Collymore knew, too. Leishmaniasis. Black fever. From the bite of an infected sandfly. If left untreated, leishmaniasis can quickly turn visceral and lay waste to the liver and spleen.

The professor smiled at the tone of concern in Maria's voice, dropped the matchbox and peered down at his leg.

Ah, yes, this, he said. It's remarkable, no? Then he reached down and plunged a finger into the wound. Maria saw the flash of bone.

Here is the proof, said Collymore, showing no sign of pain in spite of the terrible infection. This place is diseased and no one is immune.

Collymore wouldn't let Maria near his leg to treat it, so after locking the remaining data in the safe-box in their bedroom, Stanley and Maria began considering their options. Should they write to Wout and ask him to contact their colleagues at the university? Should they squelch the intimidation they still felt in Collymore's presence for just a few minutes, sit him down and try to talk him into returning home? Should they take him over to the island right now, and risk capsizing *Pasensi* again? Maria suggested they take a day off and walk the Voltz, spend the night at Camp Schumacher, discuss the issue in private. They could ask Petrus to watch over Collymore while they were away. Stanley objected—it was only Thursday, after all, and their census methods required a consistent schedule. But Maria didn't want to conduct a line transect; she wanted to put some distance between themselves and their disturbed employer.

We deserve a little vacation, she'd said, and after a short pause: I need a little vacation.

Something in her tone brought Stanley to attention, so he said nothing more and the two left camp at five o'clock the next morning, their hammocks strapped to their packs. They didn't set their stopwatch and they walked at whatever pace felt natural. Stanley had radioed the island to find out if any tourists were due that day, but no flights or boats were expected. They would have the forest and the mountain completely to themselves.

They emerged onto the West Platte at noon. The summit of the Voltzberg shimmered before them as the sun beat down. Without a word they split up, drew their machetes and began investigating the rock face. Ten minutes later Stanley heard Maria holler, and soon his wife came bounding over a small rise, her arm raised in triumph, a perfectly ripe wild pineapple in her hand. The pair joined the old hunting trail and walked single file towards the foot of the mountain, where they reentered the jungle and hiked another half-mile around the south face until they came to a small clearing. Here on the western bank of a quiet stream were the ramshackle remains of Camp Schumacher: a collapsed log cabin, a stable without a roof, a rickety but reinforced bandstand where tourists could now hang their hammocks. This is where Roosvallen's tour guides had been bringing sightseers for more than a generation, the only suitable spot to set up camp for miles around. Every tourist who had ever visited the Voltzberg had spent a night at Camp Schumacher.

The clearing was strewn with the wrought-iron implements of mid-nineteenth-century exploration: a blackened anvil, inch-thick chains, two wagon axles, a pile of used horseshoes. The great German explorer Ernst Schumacher had once travelled to Amazonia in search of El Dorado, and upon glimpsing the

Voltzberg from his boat on the Cariban he'd concluded that the legendary city of gold was somewhere to be found at the great mountain's foot. The German, who was renowned for his tenuous grip on reality and his fierce temper, searched the jungle south of the mountain for two years. Then one morning he woke with the sun, sharpened his machete and hacked to death his entire entourage—twenty-five porters, guards and learned men, including his esteemed colleague the geologist Franz Voltz, in whose honour the mountain was posthumously named.

At least, that's the story the Boyz liked to tell the tourists.

Upon entering the clearing Stanley and Maria dropped their packs beneath the bandstand, hung their hammocks and bug nets and refilled their water bottles from the stream. It felt good to be back at Camp Schumacher, a place where they had spent many exhilarating nights together since launching the census project, and it felt even better to have put many miles of undisturbed rainforest between them and Collymore. With their home base established Stanley and Maria followed the creek past the hut a few hundred feet into the bush until they reached the southern face of the Voltzberg, and the understory was so thick that the pair couldn't see the mountain until it loomed before them. They found the bottom of the crevice and pulled themselves up into it, using the vegetation that grew on either side as handholds, and Maria went up first with Stanley following close behind, watching for rocks set loose by his wife while paying close attention to where he put his hands. The first time he had climbed the Voltzberg he had slipped on the slick stone and, in his flailing, come within inches of seizing a particularly well-camouflaged bushmaster for purchase. Now, though, the pair were old hands at the ascent, and in fifteen minutes they had cleared the fissure and popped out above the treeline. Here, with the equatorial sun pounding down and an infinite heat rising from the granite, Stanley and Maria trudged upwards without a word. They did not pause to take in the remarkable view. When they needed a break they lay flat against the searing rock surface, because to remain upright on such a steep angle with no forward momentum was to invite disaster, fatal slips and long tumbles into the void. They passed bushes that buzzed with bees. They found two piles of fresh jaguar feces. Finally, after thirty more minutes of toil they rounded the summit and collapsed amidst the field of stone cairns that had been fashioned over the years by countless insipid tourists.

When's the next NSF cut-off? said Maria after a time.

Six weeks.

We could start seeing infants in six months.

Could be sooner.

We need genetics, access to a lab.

We'll get a draft going.

Maria sat up.

He's got to go, she said. He's fucking sick and he's got to go.

Agreed.

Should we talk to Wout?

Maybe.

I'm not saying we should stop. I'm saying we should lance the boil. We have a lot to protect here now. We're going to have young here soon.

I know.

Stanley sat up. He felt a chill as his sweat-soaked shirt peeled away from the rock. Below them in every direction the rainforest spread to the horizon.

You need to start acting like a father, said Maria.

Sweetheart, we'll figure it out.

No. Maria turned to face Stanley. You need to start acting like a father. Like, rehearsing.

Maria's eyes glistened. Stanley stared blankly at her for a moment. Then all came clear.

Holy shit, said Stanley.

You're telling me.

Holy shit!

Maria laughed, began to cry.

Do you have a p-value for me?

Fuck off! said Maria, shoving Stanley, who wrapped his arms around her.

Seriously. What's the p?

Oh, Stanley. P is definitely less than point-oh-five.

So, confidence is high?

Confidence is extremely fucking high, you fucking idiot.

Stanley hugged her tighter. The jungle below slipped out of focus. Somewhere to the south a family of red howlers howled.

I love you, Stanley. So, so much.

~~

11

As Stanley approached Camp Schumacher the rhythms of Jamaican dance hall echoed through the trees. He slipped off the hunting path and felt a sudden yearning for reassurance, good confidence intervals and low *p*-values, proof of statistical significance. Arriving at the south end of the clearing Stanley found himself a suitable hiding spot and took stock. Alberto and Frank Lampard lay on the grass, passing a joint between them and nodding their heads to the music. Shike, who had led the tourists here earlier in the day, lounged in a hammock in the bandstand, absolving himself by filling the structure with an impressive cloud of hash smoke. Hank sat apart from the others on a wooden bench near the firepit, shining his pistol with a rag. The wooden crate sat next to the bandstand, just a few feet from Shike, the orange tarpaulin still folded neatly on top.

Stanley made his way around the edge of the clearing until the bandstand was between him and the rest of camp. From here he could creep onto the site, lift his tarp and retreat to the forest without anyone seeing him. Shike's hammock swayed, his prodigious dreads poking out like the fronds of a pineapple plant. Stanley took a few steps into the clearing, then a few more. Halfway to the bandstand he caught his foot on a stray piece of chain and dropped quickly to the ground, but the music was so loud that Shike didn't stir. Stanley reached the bandstand and began inching towards the crate on his hands and knees. Then, without warning, the music abruptly stopped, plunging Camp Schumacher into silence.

Stanley held his breath. He peered through the latticework at the base of the bandstand and saw Hank walking quickly towards the south end of the clearing, where Stanley had been hiding just a few minutes before. Sluts, said Hank. Stand the fuck up. It's time. Shike's hammock creaked, his gigantic feet slapped to the floor. Frank Lampard and Alberto leapt from the grass and ran straight toward the bandstand. Stanley cowered, inched back a few feet— What should I say? How do I explain this?—but the Boyz stopped a few feet short of him and hefted the crate back to their shoulders. They turned and followed Hank south into the bush. As they disappeared into the trees—with Stanley's tarp still atop the crate— Shike drew his machete with his good hand and cut the air as if warming his muscles.

Stanley rolled onto his back, blew a long breath, gazed past the slope of the bandstand into the sky. He winced as the fever flared. Two birds, maybe they were king vultures, circled high above Camp Schumacher, and he remembered the football game a few weeks after everything had happened all those years ago. Petrus had insisted that Stanley attend, as if returning to the island for a casual game of pickup football would somehow help his mourning. He remembered slipping the ball between Hank's legs for a goal at one point, and Hank chasing him back down the field and yipping at him, saying something that caused Stanley to erupt. Hey, *fuk-kup*, said Hank. Why didn't you go to the city? Stanley had turned, shrieked, landed three punches to Hank's face and two to his belly before the men collapsed in a writhing ball on the ground. I'm going to kill you, said Stanley, kicking his legs and swinging his fists and gnashing his teeth at Hank's neck. I'm going to rip your fucking heart out. And when Hank had gained the upper hand and sat on top of Stanley, his own fists raining down, he said things like, You can't kill me, Stanley, and, Whites need special medicines, and, Maria was the last slave in Roosvallen, and, You're a native son now, Stanley. A native son.

Stanley watched the vultures revolve, wished for such ease down here on the ground. He knew where the Boyz were headed and he did not want to follow, but he also knew he probably would. He thought of heading back down the Voltzberg Trail and away from this haunted camp, back to his monkeys and to finding that nest, but instead he rose without will or intention and slipped from the clearing to the hunting trail.

Heading south he caught up to the Boyz in fifteen minutes. They were nearing the lekking site of the Guianan cock-of-the-rock, a popular spot for die-hard birders. Males of the species, bright orange and with impressive head-crests like those of Roman centurions, gather together at specific sites, or leks, to perform extravagant courtship displays before an audience of choosy females. Stanley had figured this was where the Boyz were headed with their crate full of entertainment. As they approached Stanley hung back, just in case the Canadians were particularly trigger-happy or bad shots, even though they had probably been hunting and exterminating nature since the age of five. But then Stanley spotted one of the bright orange birds, then another and another, and none of them were dancing, and there were no Canadians here, either—all was eerily quiet—and the Boyz had now left the trail and were bushwhacking east. What the fuck is this? Where are you going? Stanley followed, but slowly now. This was virgin territory, the jungle south of the mountain, the place from which Maroon children's stories came fully formed and spitting blood, the burial grounds of the ancestors, the gnashing of beastly teeth. When Stanley saw the Boyz stop and lower the crate to the ground he veered off the path and hid himself between the buttresses of a *kankan* tree. From there he watched as Shike, Alberto and Frank Lampard took up positions around Hank and the crate, machetes dangling from their hands.

For five minutes nothing happened. The men just stood silently, peering into the bush. But then Stanley spotted movement between his position and the Boyz. A tree had begun to move. No, not just one tree, but two trees, cloaked in grey-green lichen, branches like polished stone, sweeping quietly through the understory. Stanley tried to holler a warning but fear had taken hold, and now he couldn't move or speak or take his eyes off the scene. This is it, he thought, his ears beginning to ring. It began with the harpy and now the chasm grows wider. It was all a hallucination. The jungle is fucking walking!

The trees became three trees, then five. Stanley blinked, lost count, felt he might vomit, figured he should celebrate as the jungle around him shifted and swayed. My monkeys are safe and this is the proof. Petrus can go fuck himself with his spirits. The forest is going to swallow them. The forest is going to swallow us all. It's all been in my imagination! But then Hank and the Boyz shuffled closer together and raised their machetes, as if alert to the threat— as if the danger were indeed real—and Stanley's focus finally resolved. He saw the walking trees not as evidence of the psychological break that would explain everything away but for what they actually were: Maroon soldiers, their camouflage matched to the Roosvallen bush, their Kalashnikovs trained on Hank and his meagre party.

12
~~

AN ENORMOUS MAROON EMERGED FROM THE forest of soldiers. The man was easily the largest human Stanley had ever seen, six foot eight and thicker than an Inga. The blotches of his camouflage were the size of stingrays, the submachine gun that dangled from his shoulder looked like a toy, and as the man approached the Boyz Stanley prepared to duck down, to close his eyes and cover his ears, to protect his mind from the imprinting of further violence. But as the man walked past each soldier he tapped their gun barrels, causing them to lower and his men to stand at ease. Now Stanley noticed that the enormous man wore wire-framed glasses and carried a book tucked under his arm. If not for his uniform and the AK, he might have resembled a gigantic librarian.

We have three Luke Skywalkers! said the giant. A few of the soldiers laughed. Can you make light shoot from those things? Frank Lampard, Alberto and Shike looked at Hank, who nodded. The Boyz lowered their blades.

And one Han Solo, said the man, stopping in front of Hank. The clatter of Kalashnikovs as Hank reached back, slowly pulled his pistol from his waistband and handed it to the man.

You have good taste. These are my favourites. I hope you brought more.

Hank stepped aside and the man lifted the crate lid. As he examined the contents, he spoke.

I was raised in the east, Mr. Hank, on the Martelijne among my people, the Djuba. As a child I loved to read, so I became a schoolteacher in my village. I was paid a set amount of money every year by my superiors in the capital. This amount never went up and it never went down, and in return I was expected to dispense the entirety of my knowledge, everything I knew about the world and about living inside it, to my students. And I did so, happily, for many years. But then, Mr. Hank, something changed. I woke up one morning with a question in my mind, a question that burned with the intensity of battery acid. How did my superiors decide what they would pay for everything inside me? How does one put a price on the contents of a man's heart and soul? And that, Mr. Hank, was the revelation. Because there is no answer to that question. There is only weakness in those who think they know. One man cannot buy the heart and soul of another. One may set a price, and the other may accept it, but the transaction will always fail.

The man looked up from the crate.

Mr. Hank, your resourcefulness is something to behold.

Commander Bigaman, said one of the soldiers. Sir, did they bring us any pussy?

The men laughed. Bigaman dropped the rifle he was inspecting, walked over to the soldier who had spoken and pursed his lips thoughtfully. Then, in one motion, he let the book slip from under his arm, swung it through the air and brought the hardcover crashing into the side of the young man's head, just beneath his left ear. Stanley heard the crunch of bone and teeth, saw the soldier lifted from his feet. The man was unconscious by the time he hit the ground.

Ask yourself, said Bigaman, tucking the book back under his arm. Did Ayano ache for women when he cut the reeds? Did his *obiaman* Kwafunu let female flesh come between him and the demands of the *kunus*?

The soldiers said nothing.

It is true, continued Bigaman. Celibacy is an unnatural condition. Until we are finished, this boy's broken mouth is all the pussy we need.

The commander returned to the crate, inspected its contents for a few more minutes and then returned to Hank. Again he pursed his lips, let the book slip into his hand, reached it towards Hank's face. Hank's body quaked but he stood his ground.

Do you know the stories, Mr. Hank?

Ai, mi sabi.

Do not answer me in the language of oppression. The creole is a bastardization of the mother tongue. Do you know the mother tongue?

No, sir.

Then we will use the language of diplomacy, the lingua franca of international politics. Do you know the stories, Mr. Hank?

Yes, Commander, I know the stories.

Who owns this forest?

We do.

No, Mr. Hank. We are only its custodians. Who owns this forest?

Hank thought for a moment. Before he could answer, Bigaman continued.

My mother owns it. Your grandfather owns it. Bigaman gestured at the unconscious soldier. That man's great-uncle owns it.

Yes, Commander.

We have only our ancestors to answer to, Mr. Hank.

Yes.

And how do they pay us back?

They bless us.

Yes, but how? Be specific, son.

They return our loyalty by welcoming us into the soil when we die.

Commander Bigaman lowered his book, stepped back from Hank, shook out his shoulders and craned his colossal neck from side to side.

If this election goes ahead, the oligarchs in the capital will allow the law that protects this country's forests to expire. And when the president's friends in China and Europe and Indonesia make him an offer, as they most certainly will, he will believe it's a fair price. But there is never a fair price, Mr. Hank, not for a people's heart and soul. I know this, my men know this. And we also know that we cannot lose. This is the beauty of the whole operation. Because even if we fail here, now, we will all eventually triumph. When the foreign companies move in, when they begin uprooting these trees and turning over this soil, they will release a rage so punishing that our little uprising here will pale by comparison.

Bigaman brought his palm roughly to Hank's cheek, clapped it three times like a proud father might, cupped the man's chin as if considering his selling price. Then the commander reached into his belt-line and retrieved the pistol he'd confiscated.

I am beginning to think you would take a bullet for us, Mr. Hank, said Bigaman, casually waving the gun in Hank's face. Would you?

Yes. Yes, sir.

Bigaman smiled, flipped the gun in the air, caught it by the barrel and offered it back to Hank.

When do we see you next?

Six days.

Why so long?

The Australians cancelled.

Six days is cutting it close, Mr. Hank. We will be ready to move by then.

There are rumours in the city.

What rumours?

People are scared to come to the bush.

Bigaman stepped back, gave Hank a quizzical look.

And who is telling them to be scared?

Nobody. It's the election. It makes people nervous.

Bigaman laughed. It should make them nervous! His gigantic body shook as he roared, and now his soldiers joined in. It makes me nervous, too! Bigaman backed up amongst his men, gripped the magazine of his submachine gun and chuckled one last time before eliminating the smile from his face.

What about you, Mr. Hank? Does it make you nervous?

No, Commander.

That's good.

Commander Bigaman motioned for two of his men to handle the shipment. The soldiers replaced the lid and lifted the crate to their shoulders, leaving Stanley's tarp unnoticed on the ground.

Walk well, Mr. Hank. We will see you in six days. Now take your Luke Skywalkers and get the fuck out of my mother's jungle.

Stanley ducked down. He heard Hank and the Boyz pass his hiding spot and head north to Camp Schumacher. He heard the soldiers depart in the opposite direction. Stanley didn't move for another five minutes, then poked his head up. Bigaman and his men were gone but Stanley's orange tarp still lay on the forest floor. He stood, let out a long breath, inched his way out from between the buttresses. But then he heard footsteps approaching, and before Stanley could hide again one of Bigaman's soldiers, a skinny boy no older than twelve, returned to the delivery site. The boy's uniform was many sizes too big and he carried his rifle with both hands. Stanley stood motionless as the boy put down his weapon, picked up the tarp, shook it open and threw it over his head. The tarp covered him entirely. The child began to giggle as he romped back and forth through the clearing.

Stanley slipped down between the buttresses and unsheathed his machete.

Sorry, little man. But this is the jungle south of the mountain. No place for a kid.

Stanley gripped the hilt of his blade, raised it in the air and slammed it against the buttress. The boom reverberated through the canopy. He waited for the echo to die down, then struck the wood again. After the third blow he stopped to listen. At first he heard nothing. Then a shriek, frantic rustling, footsteps retreating to the south. Stanley looked up just in time to see his abandoned tarp billowing to the ground.

13

B Y THE TIME STANLEY HAD CROSSED ASGARD
Stream, reentered his study site and begun searching
for the Longfellows, the *siksi-yuru* had been singing for
more than an hour. The sentiment that remained from
his adventure in the jungle south of the mountain had nothing to
do with the discovery that Hank and the Boyz were helping arm
a secret militia, or that the legislation protecting the rainforests
of Roosvallen might be allowed to expire, or that something big
might happen in about a week's time. Instead, what needled him
for the entire hike back from the Voltzberg was a question:

How have I become so accustomed to this place?

All around him such boisterous, vigorous growth. Such wet-
ness and disease. So many fang-like teeth and prehensile tails. So
many greens. Basalt boulders shaped by the rain to look like the
gills of a fish. Epiphytes like splashes of paint in the nooks of black-
and-white trees. Lianas that strangle each other as they reach for
the sun. Orchids evolved to impersonate the sexual partner of a
particular species of wasp. Giant anteaters with tails like feather
dusters, silky anteaters that look like caricatures of themselves,
giant armadillos that are one part kangaroo, one part tank and one
part lunatic imagination. How had Stanley lost track of the jungle's
surrealist foundations? How could he have lost his bearings so? It
took a roughshod group of soldiers dressed as trees and carrying

weapons to remind him that this place had never been moored to the real world in any significant way. He understood the phenomenon of sensory adaptation, the gradual change in responsiveness towards a constant stimulus; the shock of the shower when you first step into it, the eventual forgetting that the water is pummelling you. But what good is a person who forgets his sense of awe, his attention to mystery?

I have grown accustomed to it all. I have allowed my rationality to rationalize everything, which must be an irrational thing. After all, how can a frog two inches long contain enough poison to kill ten men? How can a caterpillar exist whose fur can blister human skin? How can a three-toed sloth only defecate once a week? Even the bright red latticework of the stinkhorn mushroom is a travesty. How can all of this be?

The only culprit Stanley could come up with was: time.

Given time, a human left alone in the wild can learn to accept anything. All he needs is for days and weeks and months to pass—Stanley was walking proof of that. But to live out here and grow accustomed, to adapt oneself to a world in which an ant the size of a human thumbnail can inject a venom so powerful it can cause a man's testicles to throb for three days is, Stanley realized now, a form of madness. No, not just madness, but irrationality, much the worse indictment of the two. And having levelled it Stanley decided the eagle, the *gonini*, was dead.

Yes, he had seen her alive and hunting again. But he had also put an arrow through her chest and buried her. Both of these observations were accurate and true. Only the chronology of events posed an issue. And since the passing of time had already caused more problems than it had solved, Stanley decided to simply ignore it, to eradicate time from his sensory experience. How does one do this? If left alone in a remote rainforest for many years it's surprisingly easy. One simply says, "Time doesn't matter," and it is so.

Time doesn't matter. I resolve to live without time.

He had already done away with the trappings of a human schedule: the mealtimes, the bathing times, the waking times. Now the only rhythm he would follow would be that of the jungle. Stanley removed his wristwatch and tossed it into the understory. Time doesn't matter. He would find the eagle's nest and destroy it. He would tell someone about Bigaman and the rebels. When? What a silly question. After the nest and before it. Time doesn't matter. By Stanley's new estimation he had learned of Hank and the rebels four hours ago, five weeks ago and in about three months. He had learned that something catastrophic would occur in about a week, six months ago and about nine years hence. And he already knew that something disastrous had happened just last week, next month and seven years ago. Wait! yelled Stanley, swooning at the revelation of his new logic. Something catastrophic *did* happen seven years ago. Only time stood in the way of Stanley making perfect sense of his world, so he decided to simply do away with it.

That's the secret of the yellow-footed tortoise, said Stanley, as he took Pancho Villa north towards Jag Junction. The tortoise carries his entire life with him; the only thing he doesn't pack for the journey is time.

The lowland swamps had become a small lake with the rains. Stanley circled them and listened for his monkeys but only heard squim, so soon he was through the Junction again and heading west along Khao San Road. The light was fading, and when he reached the foot of the Kawati Hills and still hadn't found anyone Stanley began preparing himself to spend his first night in the forest alone. Chief among all the rules Professor Collymore had laid out for the researchers eight years ago was that no one was permitted to overnight in the bush. Stanley had always thought this a strange stipulation to make, as the team had already spent more than two months at the beginning of the project living out of tents, waiting for the house to be completed. Would it really be the end of the world if he and Maria camped out in the wild every now and then? Wouldn't it benefit the project to have occasional eyes and ears on the study site at night? But on that first evening in their new home, between rounds of *palum* and poker, Collymore had issued his fiat, along with a warning that anyone who broke this rule would be sent home immediately and disavowed by the university. Back then Stanley had assumed his boss was simply trying to protect his assistants from the jaguar, the puma, the bushmaster and the fer-de-lance, not to mention the anaconda, all of whom come to life once the sun goes down. But now, as Stanley began eyeing *kankan* trees and stands of heliconia for the ideal spot in which to bed down, he knew Collymore had been motivated by a different sort of fear back then, the fear of the scientific aristocracy, the worry that without a roof and four walls between us and our subjects we risk losing our integrity, the virtue we had earned by coming here in the first place. That roof was our first mistake, said Stanley, as he turned south on Hollywood Boulevard. That roof was the beginning of the end. Then he heard a splash to the east, the excited squeal of a fuzzy-butt, and hacking through to Fifth Avenue he found the Longfellows devouring the contents of a *Pourouma* tree.

Stanley managed two headcounts before the light became too poor. He got fifteen both times, and although he'd only been able to ID Johan, by the numbers Stanley knew Charlie was up there somewhere, probably with Marilyn, grabbing a last-minute snack before seeking out a sleeping spot. Soon the monkeys moved out of the *Pourouma* and settled noisily into nearby trees, an occasional squabble here and there, a few fuzzy-butts causing scenes. The monkeys would wake tomorrow with breakfast close at hand.

Once he was sure they were staying put Stanley set about finding himself a spot in the darkness. Ideally he would have built himself a platform to keep him up and off the forest floor but he had neither the energy nor the inclination. Instead he pulled out his headlamp and searched for a suitable set of buttress roots across which to spread his tarp. He found a *kankan* fifty feet to the north and shone his lamp between the two largest roots. He stared into this space for more than a minute, taking in every hue and texture of the leaves and nuts and soil with the knowledge that during the day, camouflage enabled animals to avoid detection, but by night it enabled them to completely disappear. Once he was sure that he had found a vacancy for the evening, Stanley dropped his pack between the roots, unfolded his tarp and fashioned himself a shelter. Then he surveyed the ground with similar attention to detail. No fire ants. No scat. A small, neat pile of empty nut husks. Eight feet up the trunk he spotted a grey tarantula, its hairy forelegs waving in the beam of Stanley's lamp. He let the spider alone.

Stanley pulled a protein bar from his pack. He decided against a fire, which was just as well because the rains soon drove him beneath the tarp. There in his wooden grotto he flashed his lamp, searched for leaks, found none, shoved his pack behind him, shivered, pulled out his poncho, wrapped his arms around himself, closed his eyes and lay back to listen to the storm. Far off, maybe a mile away, a tree that had stood for many human generations gave way to the winds, a snap like the prologue of thunder, a boom that shook the earth.

14

TWO DAYS AFTER RETURNING FROM THEIR PRIVATE trip to the Voltzberg, Stanley and Maria woke at two in the morning to a haunting sound. At first they thought it was just a family of howler monkeys starting up in the trees above camp, but as the sound grew louder and human voices emerged above the din, shouts and hollers and snippets of song that echoed up from the river like voices of the dead, the pair sat up in their bunk and fumbled for their lamps. This was a field scientist's worst nightmare. Boats were approaching from the north, boats filled with animated, uninvited men.

As the first dugout growled into the bottom of Ant Hill, Stanley raced to the electric panel and flipped the switch, but the solar batteries had been drained the night before and would need a full day to recharge. Maria fetched the camp lanterns and searched madly for the matches while Stanley knocked on Collymore's bedroom door. Professor? With no response he tried the door handle but it was locked from the inside. Professor. You need to get up. And that's when the men swept over the top of Ant Hill, their voices carrying through Camp Collymore like a storm gust. They sang a raucous song in *taki-taki*, a call-back tune Stanley recognized from the *kawina* parties on the island, this rendition less celebratory in nature, though, more aggressive, the men atop Ant Hill barking the lyrics, the men still down at the beach returning the bellows of their marauding brothers. From somewhere far-off came the pounding of drums. Then the men poured into the clearing, encircling the building and giving Stanley and Maria the impression that the entire forest was wailing.

Professor! said Stanley again. Get out of bed!

Maria had finally lit the lanterns, but when she'd run to the front door and pushed back the latch she'd found the door wouldn't give. She heard two men grunting with effort on the other side.

They won't let us out. Stanley.

Stanley joined Maria at the front door, turned the handle, threw his shoulder into the wood. Nothing. Stanley tried the side door, found two more men stationed there, the same at the kitchen door. The drums grew louder. They smelled smoke. From the kitchen windows they saw a line of fire spreading around the camp, as if someone had touched a match to a stream of gasoline. By the light of the rising fire they could see the faces of the men, swaying in time to the beat. All of them were painted white and Stanley recognized none of them. These were Maroons, but they were not the Roos Boyz.

Maria aimed the beam of her flashlight through the screening, landing it on individual faces.

I see you, fuckers, she screamed. I fucking see you.

When the kitchen filled with smoke the pair retreated to the camp library.

I'm calling the island, said Maria.

You can't. We don't have power.

How could they let this happen? They're supposed to stop things like this before they happen.

Maybe they're coming. Maybe they're on their way.

Then Collymore's panicked voice rose up.

She's here! he called from his bedroom.

Stanley and Maria caught each other's gaze. Maria's eyes went wide. The chanting outside reached a fevered pitch.

Professor, yelled Stanley. Come out of there.

I told you this would happen! he called back. I told you. She's here! She's here! She's here!

Stanley watched Maria through the thickening haze, saw her face go still, saw tears appear on her cheeks.

Sweetheart, said Stanley. Don't listen to him. It's just a bunch of teenagers.

Maria felt for her belly.

They're drunk, said Stanley. They don't know what they're doing.

Make them stop, Stanley.

They don't want to hurt us. We're just going to have to wait—

Make them stop!

Maria sank to the floor of Camp Collymore, closed her eyes, pulled her knees to her chest. Stanley threw his shoulder into the front door again but to no avail.

Maria, come.

Stanley walked Maria back into their bedroom, lay beside her on the bed as she shook. Slowly, finally, the voices outside began to trail off. The drums retreated down Ant Hill and the boats groaned to life. Stanley could hear the crackle of the dying fire, Collymore's muffled warnings from his bedroom. But just when Stanley thought the party was over and that it might be safe to go outside, he heard a mighty howl followed by a great smashing, as if someone had taken a sledgehammer to a plate of glass.

Petrus arrived at Camp Collymore at sun-up, a rucksack over his shoulder. Instead of knocking on the front door he went straight to the sacred palm tree and began sweeping up the broken bottles. Maria had finally fallen asleep an hour earlier, so when Stanley had heard the old man's outboard he'd crept quietly from their bunk and gone through to the kitchen to make some tea. When he saw Petrus kneeling at the tree he opened the kitchen door and joined him.

Bas-Pey, you don't have to do that.

Petrus didn't look up from his work.

Are you hungry? I'm making *pannenkoeken*.

Petrus sifted the soil through his fingers, making sure to catch every last shard of glass.

Bas-Pey, who were those men? I've never seen them before. We can't have people we don't know coming ashore here.

Once the space was clear of glass, Petrus pulled a new set of empty *jugos* from his pack and began placing them one by one beneath the tree.

We can't have a bunch of drunks wandering into our camp and throwing parties, Bas-Pey. This is a scientific field station, for Christ's sake. I know you're not running Roosvallen anymore, but you have to talk to Benny about this. Last night was fucking unacceptable. Especially now that Maria—

No drunk, said Petrus, pulling a full *jugo* from his pack and cracking it open.

Okay, fine, whatever they were doing—

Petrus sucked his teeth.

Stan-ley. No drugs. No party.

I don't care who they were, Petrus. They are not welcome here.

Now Petrus paused, looked up at Stanley, a look of faint amusement on his face.

What's so funny?

Not welcome.

Bas-Pey, they could have burned the building down.

Stan-ley, said Petrus, his face turning grim. Go now. *Gwe.*

Petrus went back to his bottles. Stanley was about to continue his protest when the old man began chanting and pouring beer over the empty bottles, so he left Petrus to his ministrations and returned to the kitchen. He retrieved the flour and the last carton of eggs and began heating oil in a skillet. Professor Collymore emerged from his bedroom and shuffled wordlessly to the data table. He would sit there for the rest of the morning, half-heartedly inspecting the latest maps of troop movements, as Petrus's melodic voice drifted through camp.

Maria had woken by the time Petrus had finished blessing the tree. The old man had walked the bag of broken bottles down to his boat and then returned to the top of Ant Hill, knocking on the front door as usual, and Maria had let him in. When he stepped inside he pulled Maria into an awkward hug, something he had never done before. Then he explained the events of the previous evening.

Apparently, when Collymore had visited the island two days earlier he had gone straight to the Maroons' ancestral shrine, a roughshod collection of ancient beer bottles at the base of a wooden cross with an old T-shirt nailed across it like a flag. While Petrus, Raymond and Benny had looked on, the professor had closed his eyes and reached out his hands, appearing to prostrate himself before the jungle spirits. But then he had reached down with both hands, unzipped his field pants and pulled out his penis. When Benny realized what the old man was about to do he had run and tackled him to the ground, showing surprising swiftness for such a rotund man, but not before the bottles and the T-shirt and the portal to ancestral lands had been desecrated by Collymore's piss.

Word of the professor's actions had spread quickly downriver, and when the villagers of Wintigron and Konkoniston heard the news they'd immediately convened a council meeting and reached a unanimous decision. The next day, yesterday, five boatloads of Kwebo men had set out for Roosvallen, all of them painted head-to-toe in the white chalk of supplication and all of them growing increasingly incensed as they drew nearer to the site of Collymore's sacrilege.

Why didn't you stop them? said Maria.

We can do nothing when they come, said Petrus.

That's shit, Petrus, said Maria. They tried to burn us alive.

They no hurt you.

They torched the place!

We hear them pass in the dark. But what can we do?

You can protect us, that's what you can do. You can keep your fucking word, Petrus. That's your fucking job.

Collymore started in his seat at the data table. The others had forgotten he was there.

My dear, it is not his fault, said the professor. No one can protect us now. Look here. Look at their movements. Don't you see?

Maria pushed herself up from the table and walked out the kitchen door. As Stanley watched his wife pace the scorched grounds, Petrus informed him that unless something was done about Collymore, the Maroons on the Cariban had voted unanimously to kick the researchers out of Roosvallen.

15

STANLEY WOKE SHIVERING IN HIS GROTTO WITH A tingling in his limbs. In the darkness he ran a finger up his forearm and felt the prickle so he flipped on his light: the undersides of both arms were coming up, nothing yet on his belly, his thighs, his crotch. He had not packed the poultice leftover from last season—it was probably rotten by now anyway—and not in a thousand seasons would he have been able to identify the plants Petrus had used. The only ointment he had was the antibiotic cream in the first-aid kit, and he knew this would offer no relief, so instead he pulled out a flask of *palum*.

The nighttime forest spoke in beeps and murmurs, shouts and whirrings, gurgles and pops—a chorus of dissonant voices laid over a rolling electric hum. Stanley slipped in and out of consciousness. He had stopped scratching but now the heat of the drink or the fever or the wet of the air caused him to tremble through half-dreams of riverboat trips and dazzling sunshine. Drops of rain-water stippled his tarp and became insects pinging his skin. Tree frogs transmogrified into wind instruments, oboes and clarinets. A nocturnal bird took on the eerie wail of a theremin. During the day Stanley's movements and the continual circling of thoughts in his mind muffled the noise of the bush. But half-asleep in the jungle at night, the world around him rejoined.

When he came to again the insects had quit their scything and the birds had gurgled to life. Then a soft *ke-junk*, a muffled squabble, and Stanley wormed his way out from beneath the tarp. Dawn was still an hour away. Mist swirled low through the understory but the air was thick with something else, too, a sourness Stanley knew but had never smelled in such concentration: a night's worth of capuchin shit. He struck camp. Folding his tarp he heard the first splash of the day and knew his monkeys were on the move. They were headed north, passing above him, echoing last night's storm with their leaps. Once he was sure that even the laziest animals like Holyfield and Wacky had joined the troop, he followed. They crossed Khao San Road and the Yellow Brick Road and the sun had risen and the mist was bright. It was almost light enough to begin gathering IDs but the monkeys were moving too fast and it was all Stanley could do to keep up. Then halfway between the Yellow Brick Road and Lolopasi the Longfellows filled the crowns of two fresh *Pourouma* trees and began to feed.

The majority of trails had been cut during this season, the time of year when distant regions that the monkeys usually ignore command their attention. Throughout the forest the *Pourouma* was in full fruit, and the monkeys had navigated their way between these trees with great efficiency, almost a sense of schedule. This ability to trapline was still poorly understood. Was it simply indicative of a good spatial memory combined with a bit of luck, or perhaps the ability to detect ripe fruits from many miles away, some kind of olfactory superpower? Or was the navigational prowess of the troop something that had developed over many years, a knowledge specific to this particular forest, something passed down to subsequent generations like a culture? Under normal circumstances Stanley tended towards the latter theory—he liked the idea of an alpha male learning the ropes as a subordinate—but now, as he dropped his camp chair beneath the *Pourouma* Stanley had the impression that the forest was wired with invisible communication channels, as if the whirrings and buzzings at night were simply the off-gassing of bandwidth, an electrical sigh, and that come morning the network returned to full power with a grand reboot and the monkeys simply tapped into this power.

What does it matter which system of thought I follow now? This is my life. Hands off my life.

By the time the mist had risen he had identified all fifteen monkeys. A little later and with no fanfare the troop slipped out of the *Pourouma* and began traplining east. Stanley hadn't noticed they were on the move until only a few monkeys remained, so he ran north to an unnamed side trail and followed it through to Broadway. The side trail had never been completed and was still flagged with pink tape, and halfway along he hit a tree-fall. It took him ten minutes to forge a way past, and when he finally emerged onto Broadway he stopped to listen but heard nothing. The side trail did not continue so Stanley had two options. He could head north to the Lolopasi, which would give him a straight shot further east, or he could bush-whack from where he stood. He looked north, held his breath, then drew his machete and stepped into the understory.

He found them on La Rambla, north of Jag Junction, just as the clouds opened. Stanley set up his chair and put up his umbrella and sat beneath the *Pourouma*, listened to the seeds and the rain clattering down. At its height the storm blotted out all other sound, and for thirty minutes Stanley felt like the only person for miles— which he was, and which he almost always was, but the realization of which now sunk into him like the tip of a machete. The first time he and Maria had been caught out like this it had been his birthday. They had been searching on opposite sides of the bamboo patch when the storm had hit, and they had hunkered down beneath their umbrellas to wait it out. Without his wife nearby, without the usual soundtrack of the daytime forest to distract him, and with the awful vigour of the storm all around, Stanley had begun to feel perilously alone.

Then his walkie-talkie beeped. Maria's soprano cut through:

Happy birthday to you.
Happy birthday to you.
Happy birthday, dear Stanley.
Happy birthday to you.

From then on they sang through the storms. Sometimes they would be right next to each other, sometimes they would be miles apart, but they would always sing, usually something timeless and poppy, a tune that would stay with them for the rest of the day. Now, waiting out the storm on La Rambla beneath what he hoped was a troop of capuchins and not an empty *Pourouma* tree, Stanley sang a classic, something they had sung together countless times: Neil Diamond's "I'm a Believer"—as performed, of course, by The Monkees.

When the worst of the rain had passed Stanley lowered his umbrella and peered into the canopy. He listened for a splash but the rain was still too loud so he gathered up his things, took a wild guess, and headed north to the Lolopasi.

Stanley lived like this for four days and nights. This was the height of the rainy season, when the storms could last for hours, and he spent most of his energy shivering and singing through the downpours and searching for the troop. The monkeys continued pillaging *Pourouma*, which grew in pockets throughout the site, so the traplining continued. Whenever Stanley had to choose between sticking to the trails or hacking through the bush he chose the latter, and whenever he had to guess where the monkeys had disappeared to he almost always got it right. He had been tracking monkeys through this forest for more than eight years, but only now, as he began using the trails less and less, was he actually *following* the monkeys. I've been going in circles since I got here. My trails are just detours. How could I not have seen this before?

But to bushwhack was to welcome new perils. While rushing through the understory one morning Stanley caught his foot in an abandoned armadillo burrow and collapsed, badly wrenching his ankle. That same afternoon he put his swollen foot down two inches away from an adult fer-de-lance. As he grew accustomed to being off-trail Stanley used his machete less often, preferring to slip past tree-falls and dangling vines and walls of foliage instead of levelling them. But this meant he often had to stop and inspect his body for ticks, spiders and bullet ants. Twice he got stung on the arm by urticacious caterpillars. While clearing himself a sleeping site one evening he sliced down a young *maka* frond with a hornet's nest affixed to its underside. He spotted the writhing black ball just before it blossomed into smoke. He ran, presuming this to be the end, but somehow the stings didn't come.

At night Stanley slept at the foot of the nearest *kankan*. He lit a few meagre fires, sparking the few old bird's nests he could find, but most potential tinder was soaked through and by the end of the day he was so exhausted that all he wanted to do was crawl between the buttresses, pour some *palum* down his throat and shut his eyes. The rains were torrential most nights until three or four, which was usually when Stanley would wake scratching, the rash on his arms spreading to his torso and the insides of his thighs, the fever still steaming his insides. Sometimes the howlers would grunt to life and rattle Stanley's bones. One morning he woke to find he had chosen his spot poorly; his tarp was foul with monkey feces. On another he woke at dawn and the capuchins were long gone. He always found fresh footprints in the mud around his tree—some with hooves, some with claws, some that sank three inches deep. And each time he wriggled from his shelter and pulled himself to stand the trees seemed to waver and shift, just as they'd done in the jungle south of the mountain. Seconds later he would get his bearings, but in this way Stanley began each day with a few short moments of hope.

There were no attacks. Every time he caught up with the troop he conducted a headcount, and aside from an occasional visit from the squim he always counted fifteen monkeys. Whenever it wasn't raining he watched Charlie. The monkey spent most of his time with Marilyn, but on rare occasions he would amble away from his mother toward the periphery of the troop, leaping awkwardly through the mid-canopy or hanging upside down from his tail to play with the fuzzy-butts or sticking his arm deep inside the knots of trees and then squeaking when something stung him on the hand. Stanley kept his eyes on Charlie at all times, especially on these little excursions, and when the monkey would finally grow bored of his adventures he would return to Marilyn's side and Stanley would breathe a little easier.

He ate when they ate, slept where they slept, and whenever the sun would appear he would bask as the monkeys would bask. After three days he was able to predict the rains a good hour before they arrived, and soon he began to feel both entirely woven into the fabric of the forest and deeply, profoundly alone. This confused him. *How can I feel so enveloped one minute and so alone the next?* It used to be that when Stanley spoke his thoughts into the canopy he recognized them as having originated within his own mind. But now he heard these thoughts, these ruminations and recriminations and provocations, and he felt distanced from them, as if an old record player were spinning albums of his monologues somewhere down-trail. *There is someone else out here with me.* He sensed a separation between the self who rigged the tarp every night and the self who wondered aloud at all moments of the day. *Who's there? Who is it?* He did not know.

Then one day around noon Stanley heard something he hadn't heard in more than a year, something that made him cast about for a suitable tree to climb.

16

~

THE MONKEYS WERE IN THE HIGH FOREST ON Saramaccastraat when the pigs swept through. At first the clacking of their tusks had sounded like the preliminary snaps of a tree-fall, and Stanley knew that under such circumstances the best thing to do is to remain calm, attentive and perfectly still. But as the sound grew louder and the forest did not appear to be collapsing some instinct kicked in and Stanley ran. Without dropping his pack he leapt onto the lichenous trunk of a tree and shimmied into the branches just as they surged in from the west. The ground beneath swarmed with hogs, their heads down, their snouts in the mud, an army of hairy rumps and absurd little tails careening into each other and rooting for whichever fruits the monkeys had dropped. As Stanley watched the rampaging swine he remembered the journalist from the *Telegraph*, that bird-like creature who'd visited Camp Collymore in the early days to report on the monkey project, the woman who'd spent the next six months in traction on the coast, her leg bones shattered, her torso pocked with tusk-holes, her spirit and one of her kidneys gone but her love of the wild more stubborn than ever. The article she eventually wrote detailed how the white-lipped peccary, or pingo, travels in herds of up to three hundred strong, holds territories that stretch hundreds of miles, does not back down from anything, and reeks like something cursed or something dead. "Peccary" is a Carib word for an animal that makes many paths through the woods, and for this reason Stanley had always felt a kinship with the pigs. Nonetheless, as they rioted below, snorting and stinking and clacking their jaws like terrestrial piranhas, Stanley hugged his tree as tightly as he could. He peered up at his monkeys, who hardly noticed the commotion. I'm here now, aren't I? Who is holding on to this tree other than me?

And that's when he saw the eagle, perched in the high canopy just south of their position, looking down upon the scene as if she couldn't believe her luck. Stanley's arms went limp. He slid a few feet down the trunk before catching himself. Hey! He pulled himself to stand on the nearest branch, waved his free arm at the bird. Hey! Hey! He pushed and pulled on the trunk with his other arm, got it swaying. He didn't care what he might wake within the tree, an army of bullet ants or a hive of killer bees. He had to warn the troop. Get down! Get down! He made as much noise as he could. He modelled his behaviour on Johan's. But Stanley's voice and the fuss he caused was swallowed by the grunts and rumble of the pingoes below, and the monkeys continued drifting south, lazily picking their way through the mid-canopy, inching closer to the bird. They can't hear me. You can't hear me! Stanley looked down, considered a descent into the pigs. What does it matter now? He hugged the tree and prepared to shimmy down.

Wait. Wait! Stanley returned to his branch. He pulled out the lanyard from beneath his shirt and felt past the ferro stick for the emergency whistle. He found the bird again, fixed his eyes upon her and brought the whistle to his mouth.

At the first blast the pigs bolted; a pulse of swine radiated from the foot of Stanley's tree like the shockwave of a bomb. The vibrations of their stampede travelled up Stanley's tree and into his legs, but he did not look down. He watched the bird. He watched his monkeys. Nothing was happening. He gave another blow on the whistle, longer than the first. The shriek deafened him but still the monkeys did nothing and the bird didn't move. He blew again three times, grimaced as the sound knifed through his skull. What the hell is wrong with you? I'm telling you to get down! He saw Charlie sitting with Marilyn atop a liana tangle, the youngster grooming his mother, the mother half-asleep on her stomach, draped over a thick vine like a stuffed toy. Wake up! Charlie! She's here!

Stanley leapt down from his perch and ran through the understory, giving blasts on his whistle and screaming his warnings. He was right below the troop now, the monkeys no more than forty-two feet above him, and yet they ignored Stanley just as they had been ignoring him for nearly eight years. All of his and Maria's and Professor Collymore's hard work was paying off. No matter what Stanley did, no matter how loud or obnoxious he became, through years of effort he had transformed himself into an inconsequential part of the landscape, a boulder shaped by the wind and rain, and there was no reversing this transformation now, no convincing the monkeys of his significance. He continued to blow on his whistle and felt the loneliness creep in like a fog, cold and thick. Am I even here? He yelled these words into the trees. Can you even see me?

The attack had already happened inside Stanley's head. He could see it all, and for a moment he relaxed knowing that it was inevitable, that it was over. Time doesn't matter. But then he looked up and saw the bird tip into the air and he forgot his agreement with time. She slammed into the tangle of lianas where Charlie and Marilyn had been resting. Monkeys plummeted and the air filled with their screams. Stanley dropped to his knees as he saw the bird pump back up to her perch, a writhing monkey in her talons. She nipped at her prey three times and the monkey went still. Then she threw out her wings and climbed out of the canopy.

The troop was on the ground now and every monkey was racing south. Stanley crashed after them, barrelling through the bush like a tapir. He knew where they were headed and he had to get there first. Otherwise he'd have no way of knowing who the bird had caught and killed, whether it was Charlie or Marilyn, whether this was the end for him or simply another terrible setback. He crossed Avenida Maravilloso, Yonge Street and Abbey Road, and when he emerged onto Pikin River he sensed it was already too late. The creek was higher than he'd ever seen it, the tributary swollen into a raging torrent, its waters flooding west to the Cariban. Stanley crossed the trail and squelched through the swamp to the edge of the river. This was the southernmost boundary of his study site. He leaned out over the water and peered upstream. Sure enough, fifty-three feet above the surface he spotted the last of his monkeys leaping south across the canopy-bridge.

Back on the trail Stanley dropped his pack and sat on top of it. The rush of the river blotted out his thoughts. He watched the ground to his left writhe with millions of tiny black ants. He did not know if they were stingers, and he did not wonder about it; he just watched them undulate, not caring if they came closer and climbed up his boots and into his pants. He was already covered in forest debris from the bushwhack. Surely a tick or ten were already burrowing into his skin. Over the next thirty minutes the ants travelled a total of five feet north and Stanley went nowhere.

Can I cross? It's only ninety-two feet to the other side. The waters are fast, but I could walk east, jump in upstream, kick and let the current float me back. My pack is waterproof. My clothes will dry. I should cross. I'm going to. I'm crossing.

Then he heard a familiar chirping from above. Perched in a tree twenty-nine feet above Stanley sat Two-Moons. The saki was looking directly at him and continued to chirp.

No. I don't care. Stanley stood and searched the ground for something to throw. He found a scattering of rotten nuts and gathered a handful. That's just your fear talking, Two-Moons. I don't hear them. Do you hear them? He threw a nut at the monkey and missed. They sound worse than they are, anyway. It's all just a big show. He threw another nut and hit the tree trunk, but the saki didn't move. It's all a show! Fuck you, Two-Moons. I'm going, I'm crossing, I don't care. I don't fucking hear them! It'll be fine. Stanley missed again with his third attempt, so he gripped the remaining nuts in his hand and threw them all at once. At this, the saki spun and leapt out of its tree.

Stanley shouldered his pack and walked east along Pikin River, past the bottom of Main Street, and then veered off-trail again. As he neared the river's edge and prepared to swim for it, he realized the problem with Two-Moons was that he had never been right and he had never been wrong.

17

STANLEY WAS THE LAST PERSON TO SEE PROFESSOR Collymore alive.

Today you and I will have a little adventure, said the professor, surprising Stanley by joining him one afternoon as he left camp for the monthly phenology transect. I have seen the heart of this place, and it's imperative that you see it, too.

Stanley considered standing up to Collymore, telling him he was no longer welcome in the forest, informing him of the letter he and Maria had sent to Wout requesting the old man's immediate evacuation. But Maria was feeling especially unwell that day—and not just with morning sickness—so he figured a day without the professor around camp might do her some good. Maria had been despondent since the night of the fires—she hadn't been into the field since—and Stanley had doted on her for weeks, trying desperately to lift her mood. He'd brought her fresh heliconia bracts every few days; he'd regaled her with the hijinks of the fuzzy-butts every evening. But nothing Stanley did could rouse Maria from her unease.

So he relented when Collymore appeared behind him on the trail that morning, and he let the old man take the lead. The professor walked with a pronounced limp now, the wound on his shin surely causing him immense pain, but Collymore never complained. He led Stanley along the Voltzberg to the high forest of the southeast. Halfway down Main Street, and without saying a word, the professor veered off-trail. Both men drew their machetes but Collymore was such a wizard with the blade that Stanley hardly had to cut a thing. At first he thought Collymore was leading him at random through the bush. But then he spied the occasional piece of pink tape tied to a liana, the bread crumbs of every primatologist, and imagined an increasingly detached Collymore making this trek alone, muttering his thoughts into the trees, marking his path not through conscious effort but simply through physical habit. Stanley imagined an elderly Collymore shuffling down a long corridor, talking to the walls and affixing pieces of pink tape to every doorknob he passed.

Stanley had cut off-trail many times but never in the eastern region of the site. Aside from the slim corridor of bush made available to tourists by the Voltzberg Trail, the rest of the eastern forest represented an important geographic and psychological division for the researchers: on one side lay the growing order and scientific integrity of the monkey project; on the other, nothing but hundreds of miles of unruly rainforest, steaming rivers and uncharted territories. Bushwhacking here took on an entirely different sentiment, one of caution and restraint as opposed to the usual haphazard slashing, and as Stanley followed his boss further into the unknown he felt increasingly uneasy.

After a half-hour of walking the two reached a small stream; it might have been Bedrock, or Wonderland, Stanley couldn't be sure. Collymore led Stanley to the water's edge, and using his machete to push back the reeds the professor revealed a long, flat stone that formed a good portion of the bank.

There, said Collymore. Look there.

Stanley bent down to examine the stone. On its surface were three parallel indentations, scars that could not have been made by random forces.

What are they?

The best evidence yet that the reckoning is upon us.

The professor dropped to his knees and fingered the smooth marks.

They used to sharpen their axes here.

Who?

The rebels. Four hundred years ago.

Stanley looked closer. It made sense. Although he couldn't remember the details, he knew that Roosvallen had been a central battleground in the Hundred Years War, the ancient struggle for Maroon freedom from the Dutch.

This is an incredible find, said Stanley, his skepticism of the professor receding slightly. But what does it have to do with us?

Collymore looked up from the stone and clenched Stanley's forearm. Don't you see, lad? All this time I thought I was speaking with the animals, I was actually hearing the voices of these people. Collymore pointed to the stone. Something happened to their descendants. Something terrible. And that same something is going to happen to us.

Stanley pulled his arm free, annoyed that he'd once again given Collymore the benefit of the doubt.

Professor, nothing is going to happen to us out here. We're safer than we are in the capital.

Collymore laughed.

You should stop listening to Petrus. That old charlatan would say anything to keep us here. She's coming back. Petrus knows it.

Stanley stood.

Professor, Maria and I are having a baby. We're starting a family out here. And we can't have your bullshit going on when we do.

No, no, no! Collymore scrambled to his feet, grabbed Stanley by the collar, pulled him close. Listen to me. There was a time when everyone listened to me.

Professor, let me go.

You cannot bring a child into these woods.

Professor—

Not here. Not now. I'm telling you. Collymore yanked his protégé to within an inch of his face. She's coming back.

Who is, Professor? Goddamn it. Who is coming back?

The bird.

Stanley stopped struggling, surprised to have received an answer to the question he and Maria had been asking him for months.

What bird?

They tell me she's a bird. That's all they tell me.

Who's they?

I told you.

The animals?

No, lad. You're not listening. The people. These people. Collymore gestured to the sharpening stone. They're the ones I've been speaking with. It's not safe for us here. It's not safe for your child.

Stanley smelled Collymore's rancid breath, the reek of his clothes and hair, the foulness emanating from the rotting wound on his leg. He tried to pull free from Collymore's grasp but the old man was surprisingly strong. Feeling the contents of his stomach rising, Stanley shoved the professor in the chest. Collymore slipped, gave a sharp shout and fell backwards into the stream.

You need to listen to me, Professor. You need medical treatment. You've got leishmaniasis. It's eating your leg. You need to go to the city. That's the fucking truth of it.

Collymore flailed in the shallow water, weighed down by his backpack like an unfortunate tortoise. Stanley reached out a hand but Collymore refused it. Instead, he lay back and let the creek-water rush over him.

This is why we became scientists, isn't it, boyo? he said. There is no more rewarding a feeling, no more spectacular an emotion, than when a man's predictions come true. She's coming back. The only thing we don't know is when.

Stanley bent down and grabbed Collymore by the straps of his backpack.

Get up, Professor.

Leave me be, lad.

Professor, get out of the water.

Stanley wrenched on the straps as hard as he could, but as he did Collymore slipped an arm free and swung hard, catching Stanley in the temple with his fist.

I said leave me be!

The blow was a good one. A gong went off in Stanley's skull and the next few moments took an eternity to pass. Stanley heard a shriek and didn't realize it was his own voice. He pulled the old man half out of the water and held him there, suspended, again their faces inches apart, and he saw a look of horror come over the professor's face, as if the old man had spotted something horrendous in his protégé, or as if he were staring straight through Stanley to something terrible sneaking up behind him. Stanley waited for Collymore to say something. When he remained mute, Stanley threw him back into the stream like a sack of mouldering rice.

Collymore hollered as he splashed into the water. His head whipped back and slammed into the sharpening stone, his eyes fluttered shut and Stanley stumbled back from the stream.

Fuck, said Stanley, feeling for the lump on his temple. Fuck. Professor.

Collymore said nothing.

Let us help you.

Again, Collymore was quiet.

Stanley looked up. The old man was still. A wine-stain drooled from the sharpening stone into the creek.

Stanley scrambled down to Collymore. Professor? Stanley pulled softly on the pack straps again but now Collymore's body hung limp, his lips sagging open. Professor? What's going on? Professor! He felt around to the back of the professor's skull, pulled his hand back slick with blood. He pressed his fingers to Collymore's neck and detected a faint pulse.

Slipping his own pack from his shoulders Stanley rifled inside for something to staunch the bleeding. All he could find was a spare field sock, which he slipped beneath Collymore's head. Then he stood, pulled the walkie-talkie from his belt and raised it to his mouth. What do I say? How do I say this? How much worse can this get? And while he considered how to tell Maria what had happened and where to find them, he looked down at his elderly boss, saw the rivulet of crimson in the water, saw the paleness of his face and the thinness of his legs and the weak angle of his arms and thought he'd never seen anything more miserable in his life.

The first time they had met, Stanley and Maria had knocked on the door of his faculty office as recently married doctoral students, trying to wipe the smiles from their faces as they prepared to meet the legend of Amazonia, the man who had once run with the pingoes, the man who had once tracked a jaguar back to its lair just to retrieve a notebook full of data. The door swung open, nearly sucking them inside, and Collymore bellowed at them. Welcome to the land of opportunity! A giant map of South America was tacked to the wall behind his desk, a small orange flag pinned up near the ceiling, midway along the north coast. A couple, he'd said, his brow knitted as if peering at the pair through binoculars. What a grand idea. A couple will stick by each other no matter what.

The land of opportunity.

Stanley took a deep breath, gazed down at the twisted body of his old mentor, smelled the fires the villagers had lit around Camp Collymore, heard the chanting and the smashing of the offering bottles and recalled how Maria had shaken with fear in the darkness. Then Stanley made a decision that felt like the only rational decision to make.

It would be a terrible thing. It would solve all of their problems at once.

Stanley slowly returned the radio to his belt, hefted his pack, took one last look at the professor and turned to leave. Then he heard a strange chirping from above, almost like a bird. He looked up and saw a white-faced saki, two crescent moons, peering down at the scene.

18

~

AFTER THE MONKEYS HAD CROSSED TO THE SOUTH side of Pikin River, and after deciding to ignore Two-Moons's warnings and to swim across by himself, Stanley pushed off and hugged his pack onto the water. The river was colder and the current more powerful than Stanley had expected, but he was a good kicker and once he was ten feet out the eddies quit pulling on him and everything sped up. He raced down the waterway like a plank of purple-heart timber set loose from a mill, hard and reliable and water-resistant, cleaved from the belly of an amaranth tree. Halfway across and two hundred yards down his legs began to burn, and he nearly lost grip on his pack twice as he crashed into submerged blockades of debris. He could no longer see the small opening in the trees he'd spotted from the opposite shore but he didn't care. He'd land anywhere. He'd make do. From downstream came a curious sound above the water's rush, an intermittent and barely audible squeal, and when Stanley scanned the surface ahead he saw nothing. But something about this sound made him kick harder, and when he heard himself grunt with renewed effort he realized that his body was either about to shut down or exert itself like never before. He heard the sound again, a little louder, an almost electric whine, and then the current dunked him, and when he found air he saw something black bobbing up and down in the water downstream, something black with a flash of white. He was three-quarters of the way across now but the water was too fast for him to make it to shore ahead of this object, which was now two objects, bobbing in opposite rhythm and rushing to meet him. The sound was continuous now, a banshee's wailing or that of a ghoul, the most intimidating sound in the rainforest, even worse than the howlers. He'd heard it twice before and each time it had chilled him, even though he had known its source and he had been nowhere near the river's edge. Now he was being swept headlong towards them, flailing his legs, trying to use them as rudders, the opposite shore no longer a goal, his only mission to avoid a confrontation, a skirmish that could easily turn bloody. Two-Moons had finally been right or wrong about something. The giant river otters of Pikin River were here, and they were angry.

Fifty feet, forty, twenty-five, fifteen. He was almost on top of them when the otters went under. Stanley scanned the surface, gave a great howl as if to summon them, the only form of display available to him under the circumstances, and as he sped through the spot where they'd disappeared he pulled his pack tight to his chest and braced for the collision, the slash and the bite, the smash of a six-foot-long weasel into his hip. He had stopped kicking and flailing. He would float through this moment with a level of self-assuredness that was wholly unearned and that bordered on the absurd, something he had learned in the Ivy League, something Collymore would have called naiveté, something Maria would have called acceptance, something Hank would call strength, something Petrus would call *bribi*, faith, belief. He even closed his eyes. Until one of the otters surfaced just a few feet from him and gave an explosive snort. Stanley hollered at the missile-headed, bewhiskered creature—*lobo de río*, the river wolf, *bigi watra dagu*, large dog of the water. Then all air left Stanley's lungs as its mate surfaced and bared its teeth. Stanley barrel-rolled downstream and began to kick. I'm leaving! I'm leaving! I'm leaving! But he had little impact on what happened next. No matter how confident or naive or accepting or strong or faithful, Stanley was not leaving; he was being made to leave, and he felt the truth of this when he spied the opposite shore again and watched it recede. Pikin River controlled him now. The swollen tributary would decide how fast he would escape and where, exactly, he'd get dumped.

After leaving Collymore unconscious in the creek-bed, Stanley had followed those pieces of pink tape back to Main Street. But as he'd walked he'd torn each marker from its mooring and pocketed it, ensuring that no one would ever find that prospective trail again, that no path would ever lead back to the sharpening stone—that the jungle would swallow the professor, devour him a second time, and no one but Stanley would know.

19

RIVER RAT, HE CAME TO SHORE AT THE FOOT OF A fallen *Cecropia*. The submerged canopy had ensnared Stanley midstream, stopping him from being spat into the Cariban and providing him a makeshift bridge to dry land, but also bruising his thigh with a deep charley horse, the pain of which only reached him as he dragged himself and his pack up the bank. He heard the *siksi-yuru* but had no idea how long they had been scything. Through fifteen feet of bush Stanley came upon a wall of black basalt, a boulder three stories high, and when he walked around this boulder and found another and then another and very few trees, he knew where he was and decided to stay the night. The sun was dropping quickly and his leg was stiffening and his body had begun to quake with cold. There were caves here; he'd never explored them but every Maroon child had, every night when they went to bed, the home of a man-eating jaguar, or so the legends said. Somewhere beneath those stories and between these stones was a labyrinth of low dwellings. As he searched for a passageway he pulled out his headlamp, keeping an eye out for half-dry leaves and old bird's nests, anything that might kindle a flame.

Just as his lamp died he found a crevice wide enough to squeeze through. On the other side he found a pitch-black chamber. Who's here? Anybody here? His voice echoed off the rock, confirming the space was enclosed. Nothing stirred. His light was too weak to reach the walls; the cave might have been the size of an outhouse or it might have been a great hall. Water trickled into the room at his feet but the floor sloped upwards and soon he found a dry patch of ground. Stanley dropped his pack and the handful of brushwood he had found, groped in the dark and found a wall, mercifully, not three feet further on. His thigh ached, his arms shook with the cold and his light had gone out, so he knelt and rifled through his gear for fresh batteries. When he couldn't find them he settled for the case of cotton balls soaked with Vaseline, reached into his sodden shirt for the fire starter, felt the whistle and realized he wouldn't even be able to blow it he was so cold, so depleted by his battle with the river. Making a small depression in the earth, using a rotten shard of hardwood as his base, he piled the remaining junk on top and squeezed three cotton balls in between. Then he leaned forward on his elbows and began striking the ferro stick into the mess. Light. Light. Light. The stick responded, sparks splaying into the pit, *shiff*, *shiff*, *shiff*, his elbows burning, his hips on fire, the cotton balls finally catching and nearly singeing his beard he leaned so close. Now he blew, softly, his throat tightening, and when the debris caught his lungs filled with smoke and he collapsed coughing. He had about three minutes before his fire would die. Stanley felt through his pack again but still couldn't find the batteries. He needed to find something else to burn. He stood and by the faint flicker inched his way along the nearby wall, sweeping his good leg in front of him, the stone beneath his fingertips smooth and then rough and then smooth again. He limped ten feet from the fire and stopped, stared ahead into the darkness, coughed again, cringed as a spasm went through his mid-back and into his belly, felt his way down to the ground for a rest, just a quick one, then I'll get up again, I promise. He shuddered. Charlie might be dead. Charlie is probably dead. And when he lay his head down in the dirt he did not feel the earth beneath his skull but something softer, a fabric or cloth of some kind, and he wondered whether he had conjured this pillow for himself or if this was one of those tricks of hypothermia, a near-religious hallucination of comfort at his moment of greatest peril. He didn't think any more of it, just reached his hand under this strange pillow to prop his head more comfortably for sleep, and when he did he felt the fabric, understood that it was real and that it was very dry, and something about this revelation woke him, reinvigorated his mind. He gripped this new material and pushed himself to his knees and crawled back to the dim glow of his dying fire and draped his imaginary pillow atop the embers.

The glow went out. Stanley felt shame although no one was there to witness his failure. Then the flame caught, the pillow burst to blazing, and Stanley choked again on the smoke.

He stared into the fire, half in amazement and half in frustration, and saw that what he had placed there had been a torn piece of clothing, and although the combustion was fast he could still see remnants of the original item, a stitched pocket, a camouflage pattern, greens and browns and blacks. He also saw that the chamber around him wasn't as empty as he'd first thought. Along the wall to his left was a circle of blackened stones, and beyond this Stanley spotted something even more surreal: a pile of sticks and branches. He crawled over to investigate. The stones encircled a firepit, unused for many years. The stockpile of fuel was blanketed with spiderwebs but was very dry, enough to last at least the night.

Hello? Who's there? Hello?

Stanley stoked his fire until it was raging then peeled off his clothing. The smoke was thick but then rose and left the chamber by a hidden chimney. His boots on hot stones, his socks and pants and shirt draped over sticks to dry, he sat wrapped in his sleeping bag two feet from the flames and inspected the injury on his leg. It was more of an indentation than an open wound, which seemed a miracle, but the bruising had begun in earnest and the leg was stiffening. Stanley pulled out his first-aid kit and wrapped his thigh with a tensor bandage. Then he swallowed three painkillers with a healthy dose of *palum*. The rum stoked his insides and he took another swig, shovelled a handful of cassava flour into his mouth, then a handful of peanuts.

By the new light he took in the full dimensions of his cave. It was a room about the size of the old tourist lodge on the island, dirt floors, concave walls, and a high ceiling of stone. Stanley noted the curious lack of guano on the floor, the lack of detritus in the corners, the general punctiliousness of the room. But it was what he saw on the walls that most unnerved him. A canvas of contorted stick figures, line drawings of humans and animals and forest objects, flickered all the way to the ceiling. They were not painted onto the rock; instead they had been engraved directly into the surface, smooth indentations in the otherwise rough stone. From his seat by the fire Stanley spotted a rainforest menagerie: a coiled snake, an owl in the knot of a tree, a tapir with its young, an army of ants wearing crowns, upside-down monkeys hanging from their tails, a bow and many arrows, a sun and a moon, an undeniably human face contorted with surprise, its mouth a small circle, its hair on end. Three phalluses sprouting from one bulbous sphere. A butterfly with the symbol of infinity for wings. Everywhere Stanley looked the jungle stared back at him in multitudinous forms. Although no expert on petroglyphs he was sure this artwork was not recent. By its burnished quality and animist themes Stanley placed the carvings at least a few thousand years in the past. Then why is this chamber so tidy? And where did that piece of camouflage come from, and this wood? Stanley hugged himself tighter, felt the warmth growing inside his bag. Who's there? Who's in here with me? Lying on his side now, resting his head on his pack, the fire crackling and the animals dancing into the darkness, he felt the answer to that question—Who's in here with me?—but he wasn't able to articulate it. If Maria had been lying there with him, he would have tried to explain that they were not alone, that there was actually someone else in that chamber with them, or at least some*thing* else. But maybe she would have felt it, too, as he felt it now, and this was good enough for him, and when he closed his eyes he heard the hoot of an owl from somewhere beyond the crevice to his cave.

20

WHAT DO YOU MEAN HE DISAPPEARED?
He said he wanted to go on a little adventure.
Where?
The north. Off Lolopasi.
You didn't follow him?
Of course, but I got turned around, and then he was gone.
What do you mean gone? He's an elderly man with a limp, Stanley. How could you lose him?
He was gone. I called for him but he didn't answer. I called a million times, Maria. I searched all fucking afternoon.
Why would he go north?
Why would he go anywhere?
Stanley, how could you leave him?
I lost him, Maria.
But I don't understand how.
Neither do I!
He could die out there.
I know.
He's going to walk until he dies.
I know.
We should radio the island. They need to let the city know. Wout should know he's missing.
With no news from the island neither of them slept that night.

For Maria, every call and whisper of the nocturnal jungle sounded human, and every splash down by the river was a man emerging from a long and perilous journey home. Whenever a nut crashed onto the roof she was sure it was the slam of the front door, and she would rush out of bed into the living room calling out for him. Professor? Professor? When she would return to bed Stanley would wrap his arms around her as she wept. That poor man. To be out there all alone.

Meanwhile, for Stanley every utterance from the forest was an incrimination. He knew that if he told Maria the truth it would spread like a wet-season rash through everything they had built together, everything they were about to embark on. She may not find his story as convincing as he'd hoped, but that was the one he would stick to. It had been an accident, an awful accumulation of random events, something he would live with so that Maria wouldn't have to.

The Boyz arrived at sun-up and formed a search party along the Lolopasi. Even though Collymore had desecrated their shrine, everyone from the island came over to help, Petrus and Hank and Shike and Alberto and Frank Lampard, even Benny, Desmond and two of the cooks from the latest tour group. They spread out from Hollywood Boulevard all the way east to the lowland swamps. They hollered all day long to no avail. When they returned home Maria half-expected to find Collymore perched at the data table, rifling through the binders or using their maps as handkerchiefs or making paper airplanes out of their fledgling careers. When they found camp as empty as they'd left it, and after radioing the island and receiving no further news, Maria went to bed without eating and Stanley lay in his hammock with a bottle of *palum*.

They held vigil on the Lolopasi for two more days. On the third morning Maria stood up from her camp chair and announced she was going to find the monkeys. Stanley followed his wife down Broadway, along the Khao San Road, through the bamboo patch and onto Saramaccastraat. When they found the Longfellows on Avenida Maravilloso, Maria opened her notebook, took the first group scan in more than five days, and the pair settled back into the rhythm of their work.

A week after Collymore disappeared the monkeys did, too. Stanley and Maria watched them leap south, one by one, over the canopy-bridge at Pikin River. They wouldn't see the troop again for more than three weeks. The pair would search the study site every morning, hiking hard until eleven o'clock, but with no monkeys they would have no choice but to retire for the rest of the day. With no data to transcribe and no poop to process and no maps to copy and no fruits to photograph, Stanley and Maria suddenly found themselves with more free time on their hands than they'd had since their undergraduate days. Stanley filled his afternoons by clearing trails, patching the holes in the roof and clearing out the professor's bedroom to make way for a nursery. He smacked and seared the old man's mattress in the sun and boxed up Collymore's belongings to be stored in the attic. Petrus came over every day and between them they fashioned a crib from cast-off pieces of hardwood pilfered from a construction project on the airstrip. Petrus had also sewn a set of curtains for the nursery, the colourful fabric leftover from a marathon *pangi*-making session in Konkoniston and sent upriver by the village women as a gift for the expectant parents.

Meanwhile, Maria was growing bigger by the day. Stanley nicknamed her "the Cariban," she had so blown her banks. Would the Cariban like more beans and rice? Would the Cariban like the last piece of Belgian chocolate? Petrus was convinced Maria was carrying a boy, and after he shared this news with the pair Stanley dropped to his knees, pulled Maria towards him and spoke directly to her belly. Little man, he said. Little monkey. I can't wait to show you the forest.

In those days Maria spent every afternoon at the data table, either reviewing the CVs of prospective field assistants or writing grant proposals or drafting papers or sending missives to her colleagues at the domestic conservation agency and in government, revising her arguments and adorning them with the latest discoveries from the bush—anything she could to get ahead of things, to keep the monkeys at the forefront of decision-makers' minds, to rally the funds and the political support they would need in the years to come. Silence begets insignificance, she would say. We cannot go silent. With a child on the way Maria's commitment to protecting the park and the monkeys took on a manic sort of energy. She had drawn a connection between the health of the forest and the well-being of her unborn child, and as her pregnancy progressed her output of thought leadership and written correspondence did, too.

At night, though, in the first few weeks after Collymore disappeared, Maria's disquiet since the night of the fires would transform into an all-consuming dread. She would go quiet and sullen, often mid-sentence, her mind cycling through images of the old man stumbling through the bush, collapsing to his knees, settling face down into the forest floor and his insides being torn apart by cats or overrun with maggots. Just as Stanley had feared, Maria began to think of Collymore's vanishing as a terrible omen, and hardly a night passed when Stanley didn't huddle with her on their bunk and tell her that everything was going to be fine, that they had experienced a period of tragic upheaval but that it was over now, and there would be no repercussions—something that would have been much more difficult if Maria had known the truth about Collymore's demise. One day Stanley returned from clearing trails with a gorgeous specimen of heliconia. Maria strung it up on Collymore's bedroom door, and after that the visions of disaster slowly receded.

In the same way that the river dropped a little more every day as the dry season progressed, as time passed the trauma of the professor's disappearance slipped from significance. Maria brought it up less and less often, Stanley offered no more details, and Camp Collymore came under the spell of a dreamlike domesticity, a sense of peace that had been missing ever since the researchers had been living in tents and helping Petrus bless Ant Hill with bottles of beer. Maria turned in early most nights but Stanley stayed up, usually in his hammock or pottering in the nursery and always with a bottle nearby. He remembered everything, but he was also slowly forgetting it all. Even in a place as demonstrably uninterested in human campaigns as the jungle, where vipers lie coiled in wait and the rains collapse the forest and the waters wash away your route home, a child was coming, and the world was full of possibility because of it.

Wout flew in a nurse once a month for checkups with Maria. On her second visit the nurse delivered a letter addressed to the pair and written in stilted prose by the Chair of Anthropology at the university. Collymore was officially presumed dead. He had no children or siblings and his two ex-wives were deceased. The only real inheritance to deal with was the monkey project. The Chair requested that Stanley and Maria continue their late professor's work, if they felt at all capable of doing so, as this would be the best way to honour his memory and cement his legacy. Upon waking the next morning Maria came up with an additional way to honour Collymore. We should name our child after him, she said, to which Stanley could only agree.

21

~

STANLEY HAD NEVER WOKEN TO SUCH SILENCE. Faint light traced the crevice to his cave but he heard none of the usual sounds of the pre-dawn jungle. His fire had gone out and no embers remained. The animals on his walls still slept. Stanley stood and stretched, tested his sore leg, his ears ringing with the quiet. Then he heard a far-off call, the voice of an animal he knew but couldn't quite place, and when he heard it again, a little closer this time, he fumbled in the dark for his machete. The folk tales spoke of a man-eating jaguar who lived in these caves, and although Stanley knew these were just stories, as he waited for the next call he remembered two things: that jaguars are nocturnal creatures, and that he hadn't found this cave until after nightfall. He had no way of knowing who, if anyone, still called this chamber home. He limped to the entrance as fast as his gimpy leg would take him.

When he emerged from his cave the roar of the rainforest reached him. Above the piping of the toucans, the sizzle of insects and the rush of Pikin River, Stanley could make out this strange call a little more clearly now.

Glok, glok.

Stanley gripped his machete tighter, backed up until he pressed against the stone.

Glok, glok.

Footsteps.

Glok, glok.

A man wearing a ball cap, a bow slung over one shoulder.

Stan-ley.

Stanley looked at the man but said nothing.

Fawaka, Stan-ley?

Stanley looked away, into the sky. His eyes watered but he didn't know why.

Mi luku Camp Collymore. *Mi luku* everywhere.

Petrus came closer, held out a Tupperware filled with fish. Stanley ignored it so Petrus placed the container on the ground and came to stand beside him. He pressed the palm of his hand to the rock and then pulled it away, inspecting his skin, rubbing his fingers together as if looking for something. Then Petrus giggled.

What's so funny?

These stones were black. Rain make clean.

How would you know?

Mi tell *yu* this place, Stan-ley. *Mi* make fire come down right here. Petrus looked up into the sky and smiled. Now *yu* live here?

No.

Where?

Stanley didn't answer. He had forgotten that Petrus's story had ended here, among the boulders in the southwest quadrant of the study site. This is where Petrus had prayed for the spirits to descend. This is where the eagle nest had been, where it had been burned to the ground.

Bas-Pey, tell me a story from the Hundred Years War.

San?

Wasn't there a prophecy at the end? Something about people living beneath the nest of an eagle?

Petrus took Stanley gently by the wrist and inspected the underside of his arm.

Yu need medicine.

I don't care. This place, it's part of that story.

Mi make medicine for *yu.*

Bas-Pey, you need to see what's in there. The walls are covered in carvings of animals. There's an old firepit, old wood. The place is clean, like someone used to live there.

Yu find nest?

I'm never going to find the nest, Bas-Pey. I'm just wasting my time. I found a piece of clothing. It was camouflage. People were killed here. I can feel them.

Stan-ley, said Petrus, letting go of Stanley's wrist. One plane come.

They were killed by a jaguar. I thought you were a jaguar.

Yu need to get on the plane.

Bas-Pey, I'm telling you something right now. Something happened in this cave. There were people here and now they're gone. Come in. Come see.

Stanley motioned for Petrus to follow him but the old man took a few steps back.

These stories for children.

Just come in.

No.

Bas-Pey—

One plane come for *yu.* It's leaving soon. Wout tell me—

I don't care about Wout! Stanley slammed his blade into the rock face, causing a shower of sparks. Wout's never been to the fucking jungle!

Petrus pulled a folded piece of paper from his shirt pocket and handed it to Stanley.

My dearest Stanley,

Apologies for the hasty note but you are urgently needed in the city. There is someone here who needs to speak with you, someone very important. It is imperative that you come. The monkey project—everything, in fact—hangs in the balance.

All will come clear when you get here.

With admiration,
Wout deWitt

PS I've secured you a suite at the Hotel Torarica. I trust this will please you. We will visit the casinos afterwards, my treat.

Stanley looked up from the letter.

Is it her?

Suma?

Who needs to speak with me in the city?

Mi no sabi.

Bas-Pey, is it Maria?

Maria? Petrus paused. Maria?

Stanley turned, squeezed himself back into his cave. She's coming back. The morning sun now shone through the crevice, illuminating the back wall of the chamber, and as Stanley collected his things and cinched his pack shut he perceived another shape on the rock's surface, something more recent, a graffiti atop the ancient carvings, right above the spot where he'd built his fire. Stanley stumbled back from the wall, took in the expanse of the image, yelled for Petrus. The graffiti had been made with red paint, which had faded with time, but it still held the ghostly image: a massive eagle, its wings spread wide, its beak open to the side in a silent shriek.

22

~

THE PILOT WAS OF DUTCH EXTRACTION, A BRAWNY young man named Damian with a crewcut and massive hands he had yet to grow into. He wore the starched khakis of Frog Air, a thin gold bracelet around his left wrist and a crucifix around his neck, and he'd refused to get out of the cockpit once he'd taxied back to the radio building. You have thirty seconds, he yelled to the crowd gathered around the cargo door of his Cessna. Benny and Raymond were busy unpacking the hold, doling out boxes of fresh bread and bottles of cooking oil and cases of Morellos. As Stanley climbed in the passenger side of the little plane he heard the pilot mutter *fucking monkeys* under his breath.

Among the many reasons Stanley hated visiting the city—the mosquitoes, the stench of diesel, the church choirs, the diseased politics of post-independence—he held the bush pilots in special contempt. To land a Cessna on nothing but a slim gash in the forest requires vast quantities of bravado, the sort of blind arrogance that is usually beaten out of men in this country by the time they reach their late twenties, when they discover that everything they've built for themselves, no matter their ethnicity, has been sucked dry like a marrow bone by hyperinflation. So Frog Air recruits its pilots exclusively from that cohort of young men who have just completed their mandatory two years in the military and are therefore

still under the impression that they can force the world to cooper-
ate and cohere through brute strength and machismo alone. The
pilots are overgrown children at the helm of rickety single-props
that have been in the air for forty or forty-five years, and they crash
and die more regularly than a *wagi* driver on Saramaccastraat.
They also deliver tourists to bush camps throughout the interior,
yet another reason to despise them.

The roar of the engine blotted Stanley's thoughts. Folded
into the front seat he watched the forest unfold beneath and felt
the nausea quiver in his throat. To a tourist the jungle from above
looks harmless, a carpet of broccoli, but Stanley had long since lost
this impression. For years now he had seen the bush as an undulating carpet of mould, seemingly still and quiet yet expanding ever
outward with a secret agenda. Petrus, who had hitched a ride for a
quick visit with one of his wives and to collect a few months of back
pay from Wout, sat behind Stanley and vomited prodigiously into
a plastic bag, the sour stench of half-fermented cassava flour filling
the cramped cabin. With each anguished splash from the rear seats
Damian's frown grew deeper, and when the pilot banked north to
skirt a thunderstorm and they hit the turbulence Stanley fumbled
for something to puke into and settled on Damian's coffee mug.

In forty-five minutes the timber concessions began. Dirt roads
snaked south into the mould, flanked by occasional patches of
benign emptiness. Then the savannahs, zinc roofs and trash fires
and no trees, the Santimaka River and then the outskirts of the
capital, chicken and pig farms and coconut plantations, plantain
and peanut and palm. Stanley's ears popped as Damian pulled back
on the throttle. Petrus, who had been silent for a time, resumed his
purging, and as the engine dropped Stanley's mind returned. He
remembered that brief moment in the jungle south of the mountain when the trees had begun to walk, the calm he had felt then.
He had believed, for just a second, that he had found proof of his
own psychological deterioration, evidence that the happenings of

the past month had not, in reality, happened. It had been a fleeting sensation. But now, with Wout's note in his pocket and their plane gliding into the core of the city, that hopeful feeling again stretched wide upon his consciousness. *The story is stronger than I am.* She's coming back—to save him, to offer him mercy—and as soon as they came to a stop at the hangar Stanley unlocked his door and threw it open. Ears ringing, knees wobbling, the prop still spinning a disc in the air, he stumbled around the plane and approached the pilot's door. Damian was checking his watch and scribbling something on a clipboard, while Petrus still sat in the rear with his head tilted back, muttering incoherencies to the roof. Damian! The pilot jumped, locked eyes with Stanley through the little window. Damian! She's coming back! The pilot smirked, popped his door. Buy the old man some ginger beer. And if you walk around the nose again you're gonna get sliced.

23

THE TAXI FROM ZORG EN HOOP TO THE WATERKANT took fifteen minutes. Their driver, a bald Hindustani who looked decades older than the man pictured on his licence, prattled on about the coming election. The status quo has a public relations problem, he said. If you are old enough to remember the war, you are old enough to know this boat is not the one to rock.

They raced past the police headquarters and the technical school to Zwartenhovenbrugstraat, where they veered north along the course of the river until hanging a right onto Saramaccastraat. This was the route Stanley had always taken upon landing at Zorg En Hoop, past the RBTT bank, the electric plant, the bustling Central Market that backed onto the river, dust and trash swirling at every intersxection, decrepit vehicles careening in every direction, white *wagis* lining every major road and awaiting their cargo of Maroons bound for the interior. It was all familiar and at the same time utterly foreign, a dreamscape on the other side of his mud-caked window. Every available surface was cluttered with election signs. The cabbie spoke in a continuous stream of propaganda while Petrus held his aching head in his hands.

As Saramaccastraat merged with the Waterkant the chaos of the markets gave way to the Old Town, cobblestoned blocks of Dutch Colonial mansions facing the river, all red roofs and slatted windows and prim dormers and whitewashed facades and pillared entryways, foundations of red brick that were imported in the seventeenth century as ballast in the slave ships. These mansions were originally built by the Dutch plantation owners, who from their second-story verandas could have watched their ships drop anchor and disgorge their sickly human cargo into the New World. Four hundred years later and these mansions were still home to the entrepreneurial.

This is where the driver left Stanley and Petrus. As the two climbed the staircase to Wout's offices they did not speak, save for a shared groan when they opened the front door and were struck full-force by the air conditioning. In the lobby they sat shivering together beneath a frieze consisting of two angels facing each other and puffing away on their trumpets. The cherubic scene, which repeated all the way around the circular room, was the same one embossed at the top of the front page of the national newspaper, *De Vrije Tijd*, which had first offered Wout deWitt entrée into the circles of power. There was a desk next to a large door of purple-heart wood but the desk was vacant, and above it the half-dome of a surveillance camera sat like a bug on the wall. He could smell her. The sharp sourness of her sweat, the beans on her breath, the sweetness of her feet rubbed into the cotton of his hammock. The whole flight and the whole taxi ride, amid the fumes of aviation fuel and the vomit of two people, Stanley had sensed Maria's growing presence, her arrival, her return. Petrus had said nothing since boarding the plane.

They sat for fifteen minutes. Then a disembodied voice echoed through the room.

Our very own monkey man!

Stanley stood, spun around, searched for the source of the voice.

Whoops! I'm sorry. We've had to make a few changes around here since you last visited. Stanley! Welcome!

Stanley continued to turn in slow circles, scanning the wall for the speaker.

Where's Thomas?

Good lord, Stanley, has it really been that long? Thomas was restructured three years ago. Look, bear with us. We're coming to get you now. *Fawaka*, Petrus? *Alasani bun?*

Ai, said Petrus without raising his head. *Alasani bun.*

An ear-splitting mechanical sound, like the grinding of a rusty set of gears, emanated from behind the door. Then the handle turned and the door swung open.

Welcome, said the voice again. But no one was there. Stanley walked to the doorway, peered inside. A small room with steel walls, lit by four sconces, one on each wall.

Go on, Stanley. It's fine. We'll be catching up in no time.

Stanley took two steps into the room. As he crossed the threshold the wooden door slammed shut behind him and another door, this one of pressed steel, slid across the doorway from a pocket in the wall with that same grinding sound, sealing the room with a thunk. Then an identical steel contraption opened in front of him, revealing a thickset Creole man nearly bursting out of an impeccable black suit. The man was so broad that Stanley couldn't see past him, and when the man joined Stanley in the tiny space this second door slid shut again.

Stanley took a step back. The taxi ride had been a shock after more than a year in the bush, but to be suddenly locked in a tiny steel room with an enormous stranger whose intentions were unclear caused a debilitating dizziness to descend on Stanley. He had to put his hands on his knees to stay upright.

Stanley, meet Jason, said the voice, again from some invisible speaker. Think of him as the new Thomas, only with two black belts in place of the teakettle. If you wouldn't mind assuming the pose this will all go a lot more smoothly.

Jason made a twirling gesture in the air with his finger. Stanley managed to turn around and the man patted him down with his gigantic hands. He smelled like pine trees, a scent that only Gillette would try selling to the tropical world. When he was finished Jason tapped Stanley on the shoulder and the second door reopened, revealing a familiar scene.

Stanley. Welcome. How wonderful to see you.

24

THE VOICE NOW CAME FROM THE MOUTH OF A TALL Dutchman, also well dressed in a dark blue suit and a crimson tie, who stood in the next room cradling a large snifter.

It's all very embarrassing, I know. But I view the whole proceeding as obviating the need for a panic room. Instill a little bit of panic in the visitor, my boy, and you've got the upper hand. Wout smiled. Don't just stand there, Stanley. Come in! We've got much to talk about, yah?

Stanley stepped into the office. Wout put down his glass and pulled Stanley in for a hug.

Stanley. You are skin and bones! How have you been all these years?

Fine.

Well, you smell like a latrine. Your next shipment will consist purely of soap and razor blades.

Wout had aged markedly since Stanley had last seen him. His skin had turned translucent, a throng of liver spots bruised his face and his hands trembled. But he still stood six foot six and straight as an arrow.

I'm sorry for the drama. Due to circumstances beyond our control we've had to modify the reception area and add our little antechamber there. And apologies for the intrigue, as well. I just couldn't risk my message getting into the wrong hands. Now, I've called our guest to say you're here. Should be along any moment. Would you like a drink?

Wout handed him a snifter. When Stanley brought it to his nose he choked at the peat.

What was I thinking? You've gone native. Here, let me get you some of that magnificent rum of theirs.

While Wout searched his cabinet for a bottle of *palum* Stanley peered around the room. It hadn't changed since his last visit. The chandelier of golden leaves, the Persian rug atop the parquet floor, the tight-back chaise longue, the velvet drapes pulled to the side of floor-to-ceiling windows, the teak liquor cabinet, always over-stocked, behind a sleek, Danish Modern desk. The decorations on the walls alternated between oil paintings from the Rococo per-iod, picnic scenes and portraits of pale women, and everyday items from the lives of the Trio Indians of the far south, blowguns of black bamboo, a ceremonial headdress of parrot and macaw feath-ers. Stanley and Maria had always laughed together about this room, its admixture of the late Baroque, 1950s Copenhagen and a quasi-colonial adulation of Amerindian culture.

A buzzer sounded.

Aha! Our guest has arrived.

As the slow grinding of the steel doors echoed through the office Stanley took a long swig of *palum*. He inspected his soiled clothing, swept some of the caked mud from his pants, tied one of his shoelaces, tried to smooth his hair which hadn't been trimmed in more than a year. She's not going to care what I look like. She's only going to care that it's me. Stanley drank again from his glass, cleared his throat, brought himself up into as strong and con-fident and apologetic and forgiving and tender a posture as he could.

The office door opened. Stanley willed himself to take a step towards it but his legs wouldn't move. Then a short, skinny

Javanese man entered the room. Mid-fifties, a trim grey suit, a purple pocket square, silver-framed glasses. He could have been the dean of an Ivy League school. He was alone.

Stanley, I want you to meet a good friend of mine. This is General Stuart van Bronckhorst.

The pleasure is mine, said the general, thrusting his hand towards Stanley.

Stanley just stared at the door, watched Jason swing it closed.

General Bronckhorst is one of this country's greatest patriots. Wout handed the general a snifter. But he's here to listen to you, Stanley. Why don't you tell him what you've seen in the bush?

Stanley saw the note Maria had left him, the words he would never get over.

Who have you been hunting these past few weeks?

Stanley saw Maria atop a river boulder, aiming her bow into the waters.

Stanley? Are you there?

A bird.

Wout raised his snifter to his lips. Yes, and what kind of bird, Stanley?

Gonini.

The general narrowed his eyes and put down his glass.

I told you, Stuart, said Wout, shaking his head. The horse's mouth. Our Stanley is an observant man.

Son, said the general. There are plenty of birds in the forest.

Where's Maria?

Who?

Okay, said Wout. Take it easy, Stanley. The general just wants confirmation. How do you know this bird you've seen is a harpy?

Stanley took a gulp of *palum*, put down his glass and slowly raised his hands behind his head. Staring directly at the general, he extended his index and third fingers on both hands, imitating the crown feathers of the harpy. Then he lunged at the general, his eyes wide. The man started, reached for his snifter in an attempt to disguise his alarm.

Stanley picked up his own glass again, raised it to Wout for a refill.

She's attacking my monkeys. She's taken six of them so far. She's probably taking another right now.

You seem concerned, said the general. About these monkeys.

Stanley looked at the man but said nothing.

Son, during the war I survived on monkey meat for weeks at a time.

Gentlemen, said Wout. At ease, both of you. We have all sacrificed over the years, each in our own way. Isn't that right, Stanley? Wout put his hand on Stanley's shoulder, squeezed it. You may not understand this, but that bird you are hunting holds great meaning for us.

She is a metaphor, said the general.

Stanley choked on his rum.

What the general means, said Wout, is that she is a symbol. Her emergence is symbolic. Have you ever heard the stories of the Hundred Years War?

Stanley felt Maria's hand on his forehead, wiping his sweat.

Do you know how it finally came to an end?

Maria's voice, fading in and out.

Amnesty, said Wout. That lovely word. A peace agreement between the rebel slaves and the Dutch.

Stanley felt the heat in his body spike, the blood draining from his head, Maria's cool hand on his chest.

The key to being a successful businessman, Stanley, is to study and understand the setting from which you intend to turn a profit. Everyone remembers the amnesty, but people always forget the prophecy that followed. The story of the bird and her return.

Rumours have reached the city, said the general. Stories of a rebel force amassing somewhere to the southwest.

The Jungle Commando, said Wout, crossing himself as he spoke. They are rising again, just in time to play havoc with the election.

Walking trees, thought Stanley. Bigaman and his soldiers. Jungle Commando.

This has happened before, continued the general. In the late '80s reports reached us of a harpy eagle who proved unnaturally difficult to kill. We all knew the stories, we'd been raised on them as children, but we didn't take them seriously. A few weeks later, satellite imagery revealed a small army of revolutionaries amassing in that very forest. Now we take those stories very seriously indeed.

Stanley closed his eyes, tried to picture Maria sitting over him while he suffered through his fever. As hard as he tried, he couldn't conjure her face. These men, these professional men—even they have been swayed by the story.

The election is just days away, said Wout. There has never been a more important vote in this country's little history. We can no longer survive on the handouts of a few thousand vacationers, my dear Stanley. Ecotourism has failed this country. Its promise has been a pittance. The election must go a certain direction and the result must be safeguarded, for all of our sakes.

Stanley started to cry. At first it was just a few tears but soon he was sobbing so hard he had to bend over, heaving for breath.

What is wrong with him? said the general.

Stanley?

I've been talking with a saki, said Stanley. His name is Two-Moons. He gives me advice. Sometimes he gets things wrong.

This is a waste of my time, said the general. This man of yours is an imbecile, a jungle mouse. Send him back by boat.

I am a scientist, said Stanley. Do you know what the best thing about science is?

Stuart, please.

The best thing about science is that it's true whether you believe it or not.

Wout, said the general, tipping back his scotch and shaking the Dutchman's hand. Reach me when you're ready to take this seriously. We have contingencies in place, ready at my go. We don't have long to waste.

I already killed her, said Stanley, pulling himself up straight and bringing the back of his hand across his cheek.

What?

I buried her at the foot of a *kankan* tree.

The general stopped, shared a look with Wout, who put down his glass. Stanley felt a chill enter the room, almost as overwhelming as the cold he had felt in his cave.

Well done, Stanley, said Wout finally. Well done.

And have you seen her since? said the general.

I said I buried her.

The general took a step towards Stanley.

Be honest, now, son. Has she come back?

Wout rushed to catch Stanley, to ease him to the floor. A snifter smashed on the parquet.

25

THE ROOM SPUN.
If this is true we have very little time, said the general. Up you get, Stanley.

Wout helped him to the chaise.

Where's my drink?

Here.

You brought me here under false pretenses.

I did nothing of the kind.

Where's Maria?

Who's Maria? said the general.

She was his wife. Maria is gone, Stanley. Good Lord.

She's coming back.

Stanley—

She's coming back! I can smell her. She sends me letters.

You? said Wout. You think those letters are for you?

Stanley peered at the old man like he was a stranger.

Stanley, I inspect your shipments myself. Forgive the force of habit, but if this country's history has anything to teach us, it is that many a conspiracy has been nipped in the bud with the application of a little steam. I have read all of Maria's letters, and I can assure you, they weren't for you.

She addressed them to me.

Who else would she have addressed them to? Those letters

were for your boy, Stanley. Your boy. You were to place them on his grave for her.

Stanley closed his eyes, saw the envelopes with Maria's handwriting on them.

Well, except for that first one, said Wout. That one was definitely for you.

Stanley hadn't noticed the seals had been tampered with. When the first envelope had arrived six years ago Stanley had torn into it, delirious with anticipation, desperate for word of Maria's return. But upon reading the letter and then rereading it to make sure, he had stuffed it back in its envelope and thrust it into the most recent data binder, vowing never to read it again. He had done the same with each subsequent letter, filing them into the appropriate binders but without even opening them first.

Listen to me now, Stanley. Hey, monkey man. Listen to me. Let's come back to reality for just a moment. Tell us. Have you seen anything else unusual at Roosvallen?

Stanley opened his eyes.

A herd of two hundred pingo.

This is absurd, said the general.

Stanley, please! The Jungle Commando is building strength somewhere in your vicinity. If nobody stops them there will be another civil war. Do you know what this means for your science, your monkeys? Do you know what that means for this country? We need your help.

Why should I help you?

Stanley—

All you do is send me mouldy bread and rotten fruit once a month. I don't owe you anything, old man.

Wout took a step back, considered Stanley for a moment.

You little shit, he said finally. Where do you think the money comes from for your precious monkey project?

Roosvallen is fully funded.

Yes, but by whom? Stanley, you haven't applied for new funds in more than six years, you haven't published anything in over five, and your university is, well, not your university anymore.

Bullshit.

When was the last time you heard of a scientist who produced no science?

They would have notified me.

Yes, they would have. If they hadn't notified me first.

Stanley looked at his glass of *palum*, saw the rainbow in the slick of grease on the surface. The drink was a beautiful one, a kaleidoscope, a measure of grace.

You will be our man in the bush, Stanley. You will keep your eyes peeled and your ears open. And your little project will continue.

Stanley said nothing, just stared at his glass.

Yah? Stanley?

Ai, he said finally. *Mi sabi.*

Wout walked to his desk, opened the top drawer. The general joined him and the two spoke in low whispers.

Take a moment, said the general.

There is too much to lose.

Just think this through!

The Dutchman returned to the chaise, held out his hand. In his palm sat two devices, one black and the other white, each about the size of a thumb drive.

Take one, Stanley. Keep it with you. Help us.

Now the general laughed.

My dearest Wout, our country is officially lost. I've been witness to many instances of misappropriation of public funds over my years—you and I have been responsible for many of them—but this is entirely different. This man of yours is going to call us in on a herd of jungle pigs. We will fry bacon. I will get court-martialled and you will go to jail.

Stuart—

It will accomplish nothing.

He's had a shock. He's had too much to drink.

Wout, your man just admitted to taking advice from a god-damn monkey.

What other choice do we have?

Wout sidled closer on the chaise.

This is a satellite beacon, Stanley. To use it, slide this cover open and press the red button here three times. This will signal us with your location. Listen to me now. If you find out where their camp is, use this. And then you must run.

Stanley looked at Wout, stared at him as if he might be able to see through the old man's face. He could, in fact, see through him now. Wout had never been interested in the monkeys or the science. He had agreed to help Collymore all those years ago with this very moment in mind, to ensure he'd have eyes and ears on the ground, bought and paid for, when all hell broke loose in this country again. A good businessman to the end.

What happens when I press the button? said Stanley.

It will signal the helicopters. They will deliver their payload to the exact location within the hour.

Payload?

Hellfire, son, said the general. You will bring the fires of hell down on those jungle-loving bastards.

26

STANLEY SLEPT OFF THE *PALUM* IN HIS HOTEL ROOM. Wout had promised him a suite but instead had booked one of the rooms on the ground floor, across the hall from the casino, and the bells and whistles and blasts of laughter eventually woke him, his head splitting, his body stiffened by the absurdly conditioned air, his thigh aching badly. Before he'd left Wout's offices the old man had insisted that Stanley see the nurse about his leg and the rash on his arms. Wout had summoned her from somewhere in the building, and when she'd arrived, pushing her way in through a hidden door in the wall, Stanley had immediately recognized her as the same woman Wout had flown to Roosvallen once a month to examine Maria during her pregnancy seven years ago. Jamaica was her name, and when Jamaica had realized that Maria intended to have her baby in the bush, she'd sucked her teeth and shaken her head. When Maria had explained that the women from Wintigron and Konkoniston had promised to travel upriver to assist when the time came, Jamaica just laughed. You people are crazier than the Dutch.

Stanley was sure that Jamaica remembered him after all these years. She had said nothing to him other than hello, and had kept her eyes lowered as she inspected his belly and rubbed the analgesic into his bruise. But when he winced at the pain she trembled, closed her eyes to gather herself, and he knew she had placed him. She could do nothing for his rash.

Now that he was fully awake he detected a new noise above the racket of the casino. Drums, and the voices of many people. He pulled himself out of bed and when he peered out his window the pool-deck was abandoned and so was the poolside bar. Then a crackle of explosions, like fifty guns being fired in rapid succession. Instead of taking his first hot shower in more than five years—an experience he had quite frankly been dreading—Stanley pulled on his soiled clothes, limped through the lobby and out the front door.

The commotion came from the north, on Wilhelminastraat, and it was growing louder. The concierge and the valets were nowhere to be seen and the street was empty. *Bangbangbangbangbang!* Without thinking Stanley felt in his pocket for the device Wout had given him, turned it over between his fingers. A civilian war. There was nothing Wout or the general or their crony friends could do about it now. But then Stanley saw the people, hundreds of them turning the last corner on Wilhelminastraat and marching towards him, a sea of purple T-shirts and black caps fronted by three enormous men, their skin painted purple, bass drums slung over their impressive bellies, mallets like toothpicks in their huge hands. The mouths of every man, woman and child were wide open in song, and after each ear-splitting explosion a thick red smoke rose up behind them.

The demonstration thundered past the Torarica, sweeping more and more people into its wake. Stanley allowed himself to be dragged along and when the rally reached Independence Square the people swarmed onto the lawn like fire ants. The sun was beginning to set. The Presidential Palace was bathed in a soft light, its arched beams turning pink, the nation's coat of arms affixed to the centre gable a little less dull than usual. Fencing had been erected around the palace, behind which stood an imposing line of government soldiers in black-and-white camouflage and red berets, machine guns at the ready. The people now pressed themselves up against the chain-link, continuing their chants, the drummers increasing their pace, the whole extravaganza building towards some kind of crescendo Stanley could not understand. He hung back near the street next to the statues of former presidents, felt the familiar anxiety rise in him, the acquired agoraphobia that all field scientists are forced to negotiate. As hundreds of people filled in behind him and he scanned for an escape route, a great roar went up from the crowd. A spotlight had appeared on the second-story balcony of the palace. The French doors swung open and a coterie of well-dressed women and men emerged. Then from two banks of speakers on either side of the square came a crashing drumroll, so loud that many in the audience cringed and had to cover their ears. Thirty seconds later, a small Creole man stepped through the doorway and onto the palace balcony, toward the microphone and into the light, and the crowd lost their collective mind.

The incumbent president waved, his stature seeming to grow by the second, and as he began his speech, in a surprisingly deep and commanding voice, a hush fell over the crowd. Stanley spotted someone just a few feet behind this man, someone who towered over the other delegates on the balcony, an old white man dressed in a blue suit and a crimson tie. Again Stanley fingered the device in his pocket, imagined an entirely different scene to the destruction Wout and the general anticipated and hoped for, this crowd and that palace and that little man waxing lyrical, all of it going up in flames.

Partway through the speech a woman screamed from somewhere in the back of the crowd. Stanley turned and saw a melee on the ground not twenty feet from where he stood. The fight was a one-sided affair, three young Creoles on their knees getting punched and kicked by twelve or fourteen people, Hindustani and Chinese and Dutch and Creole themselves, men and women, all of them unified in purple and black. The three tried to get away but the crowd tightened around the skirmish, and as they floundered like fish in the bow of a boat Stanley noticed that all three wore yellow T-shirts with the same design on the back: a red graphic, the shape of an eagle, its wings outstretched.

27

To the dismay of all involved, Damian was assigned to fly Stanley and Petrus back to Roosvallen the next morning. The skies were clear and there was no wind but that didn't stop the two from vomiting nearly the entire hour. Damian had come prepared this time with buckets.

Collecting his pack at Petrus's hut Stanley avoided going inside. He did not want to see the picture of Maria on the wall, her smile and his happiness, the luck and happenstance of their lives back then in full bloom. As he climbed into Petrus's boat and pushed it off the rocks Stanley spotted the latest tour group walking along the shore, approaching the swimming hole from which one of them was more than likely to be dragged later, their body racked with spasms and gasping for breath. Heading upriver in the bow, leaving the city and the citizenry behind him, Stanley sensed the world fitting back together like a jigsaw puzzle. He still didn't know how to complete the picture, but the pieces had begun to slot in of their own accord—except for one piece, of course, which Stanley was pretty sure he'd never find. Perhaps *I* am this missing piece. Perhaps my job is to figure out where *I* should go. But no. He patted his pocket, felt the device there. Now is not the time to change course.

Petrus veered towards the beach at the bottom of Ant Hill and Stanley hollered, waved his arm to the south. Petrus righted the boat, aimed it at a small break in the trees upriver from the beach. When the boat scraped up onto the rocks at Anyumara Falls, Stanley leapt out as best he could and hefted his pack, shivering as the cool air of the rainforest goosebumped his skin.

Stan-ley, said Petrus. Where *yu* go?

To find the monkeys.

The nest?

Yes, Bas-Pey. Of course. The nest.

Remember what I tell *yu*. Pay attention. And if this no work *yu* must pray.

Yes, Bas-Pey.

On his way up Kawati Top he heard Petrus's boat growling back to the island, but down the other side the riot of the rainforest resumed. He began to feel badly for Petrus. The puzzle of this place will never fit together for him. Stanley hiked down to Pikin River to begin his search from there. He walked for two hours, zigzagging east to Main Street. When he was sure there was nothing in the southern quadrants he took Pancho Villa north to Jag Junction and headed west across the top of the bamboo patch.

Then he heard a splash, looked up, and there was Johan.

The troop was all around him, feeding in the crowns of three *Pourouma*. Charlie? Stanley didn't bother with a headcount. He just ran beneath the Longfellows and trained his glasses on every juvenile he could find. Mignon, Suri Rama, Athena. Charlie, where are you, little man?

And that's when the memory returned.

When Maria's water had broken two months early, she and Stanley had been clearing trails together in the north near the Lolopasi. She had tried to yell to him but in her panic couldn't muster her voice, and when she radioed him Stanley didn't understand what she was saying. They met in the middle of the trail, just as they always did when clearing new pathways, but now Maria was walking on her tip-toes and tears were pouring down her cheeks. Stanley piggybacked her out. All the way back to the Voltz, up and down Kawati Top, past Anyumara Falls to the beach, which was now fully above water. By the time he'd pulled *Pasensi* from the reeds and placed Maria in the hull she was passing in and out of consciousness and blood was slipping down her thighs. He raced up to the house, radioed the island, then returned and pushed the boat into the water. But *Pasensi* would not start. Stanley pulled and pulled but the engine refused to turn over. He screamed at the motor and Maria screamed, too, fully conscious now, revived by the pain of a contraction. Finally the boat garbled to life and Stanley steered it into the main course of the Cariban. The waters were low and the current weak, but even so Stanley lost control of the vessel a number of times, careening off hidden boulders, Maria curled up and howling in the hull.

Somehow Stanley managed to crash *Pasensi* into the rocks at the top of the rapids. He screamed for help and Benny, Raymond and Petrus came running. A few tourists came running, too, but when they realized the seriousness of the situation every one of them stopped to watch. Benny reached the boat first but when Petrus saw Maria lying there, ribbons of blood sloshing over her, he shoved Benny out of the way, plucked Maria from the boat and carried her to the pavilion like a sleeping child.

Benny radioed the villages, called for the women of Wintigron and Konkoniston, but it was two months too soon. The women were still at their inland gardens. It would take a day just to reach them.

Nobody is coming, said Benny. They are sorry but nobody can come.

Stanley found Charlie a few feet off the ground, sitting in the low curve of a liana, nibbling on a slug. Stanley knew then that the bird had killed Marilyn and that Charlie had lost his mother. He dropped his pack and sat with the monkey, who twittered when Stanley opened his squeaky camp chair. Hours passed, Stanley didn't care how many. He just wandered wherever Charlie wandered and fended off the memory. Then, between rumbles of thunder, he heard voices to the south, from the direction of the Voltzberg. Male voices. Surely the Boyz.

He heard chirping, too.

Stanley looked up. Two-Moons, in the fork of a *Pourouma*, not ten feet above Charlie.

No way, said Stanley. I don't care what they're doing, Two-Moons. I'm where I'm supposed to be.

Two-Moons chirped again.

The Boyz can arm all of Brazil, I don't give a shit. I'm staying right here.

Petrus placed Maria on a table under the yellow lights of the pavilion. Raymond fetched a bucket of water and some towels and Benny tried to reach the city on the radio. As gently as he could Petrus lifted Maria's knees and spread her legs. She groaned, then came alive with another contraction.

She must push, said Petrus.

What about the tourists?

Accountants.

Benny? said Stanley.

Stanley?

Sweetheart, it's going to be okay. You need to push.

I can't.

Benny? said Petrus.

Benny stuck his head into the room.

The doctor is at the airport. They say if the contractions are more than five minutes apart, she should not push.

They are definitely less than five.

What if they're less?

The hum of insects.

Benny! What if they're less than five?

The whirr of bat wings beneath the thatch.

They say she should try.

I can't.

You can, Maria. The doctor is on her way.

The doctor isn't here!

Petrus is here. Sweetheart. Petrus is here.

Maria pushed. The sound that came from her travelled the course of Stanley's limbs and buried itself in his belly.

Harder, said Petrus.

I am!

You're doing great.

Harder!

Maria stopped.

No stop, said Petrus.

No stop! said Raymond.

I can't.

Stan-ley, said Petrus.

Maria, you need to keep going. You can do it. Then it'll be over.

It's too soon. It's too soon.

Stan-ley!

Maria! Push! Now!

Maria screamed.

A minute passed.

Raymond stood and left the room.

Petrus raised his head from between Maria's legs, tears streaking his cheeks.

Stan-ley.

His boy was stillborn. Purple papery skin, a tiny road map of veins and arteries, curved spine, a miniature jutting nose. Stanley's first thought was that he looked like a baby bird. Then Petrus turned him over and Stanley saw something that sent him crashing to the floor. Partway along the baby's back was a black and gaping wound, as if the flesh had been melted by a flame.

Shut up, Two-Moons! Please!

Stanley covered his ears with his hands, closed his eyes, rocked back and forth in his camp chair. He would banish the memory, the impossibility of it all, just as he'd been doing for the past seven years.

Why are you still punishing me, Two-Moons? I'm doing the right thing.

Stanley sensed a commotion in the forest around him but he ignored it, continued his rocking.

It's not possible. It's not possible! It had nothing to do with me.

Then he felt something press into his shoulder. Stanley dropped his hands from his ears, opened his eyes and a quake went through him.

The muzzle of a Kalashnikov.

The trees were walking again.

FROG-LICKER

1

WHAT'S YOUR NAME?
Do you have a name?
She's going to kill them all.
Names aren't important. Mine's Stanley. You're beautiful. How did they catch you?

She's hunting them to death.

Did they climb up and swing after you in the trees? I tried that once. Did they follow you from below and just wait for you to fall asleep? Catching me was easy. They didn't need to go hunting. I'm sorry. I just figured it out. You were young. That's how they caught you. They shot your family and wrapped that chain around your neck. I get it now. We don't have to talk about it.

They had made him carry his own pack. This had seemed strange at first—Stanley had always imagined hostages being stripped bare of their possessions—but as the hours wore on he realized where they were taking him and he understood their reasoning. His pack was heavy, and Bigaman would probably demand whatever was inside. The rains came and quickly turned torrential. At the West Platte they marched through the storm, steam rising from the wet stone, and he saw the Voltzberg shrouded in mist and stippled into the pools of rainwater. Down the other side and into the bush they bypassed the trail to Camp Schumacher and continued into the jungle south of the mountain. The lekking site was quiet—no birds, no Romanesque flashes of orange—and when they passed through the spot where Stanley had witnessed the gun drop and emerged into a small clearing filled with bare-chested soldiers and roughshod huts and hammock stands and piles of weapons and ammunition half-covered with tarps, he felt a door closing behind him and began to panic. He turned, tried to run, and received the butt-end of a rifle to his forehead.

When he came to, Stanley found himself in a cage made of green bamboo at the edge of the clearing. In the enclosure with him was a female brown capuchin monkey, a rusty chain padlocked around her neck.

2

THE ITCHING KEPT HIM AWAKE THAT FIRST NIGHT. His rash was beginning to weep in places, but the worse discomfort came from the bites he'd received while he'd been unconscious. His body had been swarmed by tiny flies, and he knew their bites, knew they were always a problem near human settlements. On the island they had been maddening, slicing microscopic holes into his skin and depositing their saliva like liquid fire while he smoked and drank with the Boyz.

Did you get bitten yesterday? Why aren't you scratching like I am?

By sun-up the men were busying themselves throughout camp, hauling water or rolling propane tanks or stuffing duffel bags, huddled in groups around the trunks of trees, taking turns doing pull-ups to the low branches, their biceps quaking at the end of each set. At the weapons caches two or three soldiers sat on stump stools, playing cards or wiping down their AKs. Occasionally a superior would pass by and the men would snap to attention. Everyone ignored Stanley in his cage.

Everyone, that is, but the boy.

Stanley spotted him on the far side of the clearing. He was younger than the rest by at least three years, and when they locked eyes the boy disappeared into a hut and reemerged moments later carrying Stanley's orange tarpaulin. The boy smiled, shook it open, and ran all the way across the clearing towards Stanley, the tarp fluttering behind him like a cape. When he reached the cage the boy wrapped the tarp around himself and screamed obscenities at Stanley. Fuck you! Fuck you! At the first utterance the monkey squeaked a terrestrial predator alarm and leapt to the far corner of the cage.

Eventually, as if called by a dog whistle, the soldiers congregated in the middle of the clearing. They formed eight lines of eight and stood with their hands at their backs. Stanley pushed himself up to watch the gathering, spilling the plate of fried cassava that had been left for him overnight. The door to the hut next to his enclosure swung open and Commander Bigaman walked into the sun.

Two days from now, we will be heroes.

A great cheer went up from the ranks.

Three days from now, we will be legends!

Bigaman walked down each aisle inspecting his troops, clapping many of them on the back. In his hand was the same hardcover book.

Liberation is at hand. And in these final days of our oppression it is more important than ever to remember those who went before us, those brave souls who slipped their shackles four centuries ago and made a home for themselves in these glorious forests.

At this the soldiers bowed their heads. Stanley picked up a piece of cassava and threw it over to the monkey. Bigaman resumed.

Last night I smelled smoke. At first I thought I was dreaming, that I was smelling the wood of their palace as we burned it to the ground.

Another cheer went up.

But then I woke and realized, no, this was not a dream. Someone had lit a fire. Someone had broken my cardinal rule and signalled the army's birds.

Bigaman continued walking but said no more. Stanley pushed

himself up to his knees, leaned on the bamboo, clawed at his ankles. A few of the soldiers shifted their feet, clasping and unclasping their hands.

If the spirit of Kwafunu were to appear before us, who would he point to?

Silence.

Tell me!

A soldier slowly raised his hand.

I killed a snake, he said. I just wanted to cook it.

Christopher?

No, said the soldier. No.

Where is Christopher?

The tarp boy stepped out from his line.

Christopher, show this soldier his freedom.

Christopher unslung his rifle and shoved the muzzle into the soldier's stomach. No! Please! The boy escorted the man out of the clearing and into the jungle. A minute later, boom.

You will notice that our numbers no longer concern me, said Bigaman, returning to the front of his men. It is the strength of our bodies and the quality of our minds that will deliver us now. Tonight we welcome the final member to our commando. You will witness his devotion at sunset.

3

I DIDN'T EXPECT YOU TO SMELL. I'VE SPENT MANY years with your kind, and aside from the shit I never noticed a smell. What is that? Is it your hair? Is it your breath? It's not bad, it's just there, you know? Like a sound, or a personality.

It's still in my pocket. Can you believe that? They didn't even pat me down. Jason would be horrified at the unprofessionalism. Wout would say this is all the proof he needs of their inferiority. I've still got it right here. I could blow us all to smithereens, anytime I want.

Do you know where the eagle lives?

What? You want to see it? I shouldn't take it out. I really shouldn't. But don't worry. I'm not going to use it here. Well, I don't think I am. I guess you never know. Hellfire, son. Hellfire.

I'm looking for the nest of a harpy eagle. Can you help me?

Late that afternoon when the shadows were long the rebels reconvened. They sat cross-legged on the ground, facing Commander Bigaman's hut, and when the man emerged this time nobody cheered.

There is one simple thing the fascists in the capital do not understand, said Bigaman. They do not understand that we are only interested in peace. Unfortunately, in order to have peace in our hearts we must pay the price of war with our bodies. So we have read the stories. We have armed ourselves and we have taught ourselves to fight. And there is one man who has helped us more than any other towards this peace we seek.

A man emerged from the opposite side of the clearing. He walked slowly, a solemn look on his face. As he approached Stanley stood, gripped the bars, squinted into the setting sun.

It can't be.

Mr. Hank! said Bigaman, and the soldiers hollered a welcome. Hank joined Bigaman at the front of the crowd and the commander received him with a hug.

The capitalist dogs would have us believe that we are six tribes, that we are divided and powerless. After all, the whites wrote our history. They assigned Ayano to the Santimakans. This is the great injustice we seek to amend. Because four hundred years ago we were not divided. We were one.

Hank listened to Bigaman with his head lowered. Stanley didn't know if he should hide in the corner of his cage or call out to him.

We may be from different rivers. Our mothers may not have shared a garden. But do we not cure ourselves with the same medicines? Do we not tell our children the same bedtime stories? And did our ancestors not suffer together? We may be mixed, but now we are united. This man represents our heritage more than anyone.

The men cheered. At their sudden outburst the monkey made another terrestrial alarm and leapt onto the ceiling. She began turning cartwheels, flipping over and over, her five limbs spinning her upside down and then right side up, her chain clanking against the bamboo and becoming hopelessly entangled. Hey! Stop it! Hey! But it was too late. Hank looked over and saw Stanley in his cage. The two stared at each other for a few seconds. Then Hank lowered his head again.

Mr. Hank. Not long ago I asked if you would take a bullet for us. What was your answer?

Hank looked up.

Yes, Commander.

Now a few of the men hollered. Some smiled and leaned forward, others grimaced into their chests.

On your knees, then.

Hank knelt.

Christopher?

The boy stood. He carried a white yoghurt container with the lid on. At the sight of the container the men closest to the boy scrambled away.

Bring it here, boy.

Christopher delivered the container to Commander Bigaman and then returned to his seat.

Mr. Hank, every soldier here has suffered the way you are about to suffer. But you are all of us in one man. You may not believe me now, but you will. Give me your left hand.

Bigaman shook the container and the audience gasped. Then the commander knelt beside Hank, carefully peeled off the lid, took Hank's hand by the wrist and guided it into the container. Hank closed his eyes and a great cry went up from the men.

The monkey resumed her flailing. Stanley fell back from the bars of his cage. As Hank's screams rang out, Stanley figured out what was inside the container.

4
~

CALM DOWN. CALM DOWN. STOP SPINNING. IT'S OVER.
They carried Hank past Stanley's cage and into
a neighbouring hut. As they passed a spasm went
through the man's body, straightening it like a plank of
kapok wood. His left arm was swollen as if someone had inflated
it with air.

Listen to me. I need your help. How long has it been since
you were caught? Do you remember seeing a bird? She would
have been larger than any other bird in the forest. No, she
wasn't beautiful. Why would you ask me that? She would have
had these feathers on top of her head. Look, see? Like this. Do
you remember?

A pair of macaws screeched overhead. More thunder rumbled
from the south.

Talk to me. Think back. Remember your family. I know, it's
hard. Was there ever a place in the forest you would never go?

One of the rebels slipped a plate of cassava flour mixed with
water under the bamboo.

Do you want this? I'll give it to you if you talk to me. You can
have it all if you tell me what I need to know.

In the latter days of Collymore's tenure at Roosvallen, when
the professor was regularly engaging the animals of the forest
in raucous debate, the Maroons began referring to him as the

frog-licker. The old stories told of a poison-arrow frog whose skin was so toxic that just one touch could scramble a man's mind.

Night fell. The rains came and Stanley's fever raged. He and the monkey shook in the wet and the cold.

5

~

S TANLEY WATCHED FROM THE KITCHEN AS PETRUS snapped the cap off a *jugo* of beer and began pouring it, slowly, over the tops of the bottles. This was the third day of offerings, the third day of submission, and Maria was still locked inside the nursery with the tiny body of their child. Stanley listened to Petrus's chanting, his pleas drifting through Camp Collymore and accompanying Maria's wailing in the way a cello accompanies a violin.

Three days earlier in the pavilion, after Petrus had helped Stanley to his feet and Maria had passed into unconsciousness, Stanley had put his lips to his wife's cheek. I'm sorry, he whispered, over and over as he wept. I'm sorry. He knew she couldn't hear him, and this was a good thing, because she might have misinterpreted his words at that moment—might have detected a small measure of guilt buried in his apology—and that would not have been a good thing. To acknowledge a link between Collymore's tragedy and this one would be to succumb, to morph into some kind of believer, and even now, watching Petrus from the kitchen, Stanley refused to set himself that sort of trap. He would not join the old man at the foot of the palm tree. What the hell was he praying for, anyway? His son was already dead.

But as the days progressed and Maria continued her wailing he began to wonder if Petrus was continuing to prostrate himself from morning to night not because he expected some sort of signal from the forest, a sign that balance had been restored, but because he was waiting for something entirely human to occur, for Stanley to walk outside and join him in mourning. On the fifth day Stanley stood, walked outside and came up behind the old man.

Without looking, Petrus handed the bottle behind him. Stanley took it and poured some into his hands, rubbed it into his hair, his beard, his face. Petrus's voice grew louder, and for the first time in five days Stanley couldn't hear Maria's crying over the chant. Stanley closed his eyes and Petrus's voice swept into his mind, curled its way down his throat and into his lungs and his guts. He felt suddenly weak in the knees and had to bend over. A sneak attack; clever man. But there was no stopping the memory— Stanley hadn't yet learned the trick about pain—and now he surrendered to it. He threw Collymore against the sharpening rock, and as he did so he crumpled to the ground. He saw the blood in the creek, Maria's blood in the boat. He saw the wound in Collymore's leg and in the skin of his boy, his baby bird.

We must bury him, said Petrus, offering Stanley a hand. We must bury your child as soon as we can.

Then, from inside the house, the radio crackled to life. Benny's excited voice echoed through Camp Collymore.

Stanley! Maria! We found his things! We found the professor's things!

6
~

ONKEY, MONKEY, YOU SAY YOU'RE TRYING BUT I don't think you are. Are you watching? This morning might be our last, so please, just think. Where should I look? Is it to the north of Pikin River or to the south? Should I be searching above the Lolopasi or is it the swamps of the northeast she calls home? Where is it? Jag Junction? Main Street? Somewhere in the Kawati Hills? Think!

Do you remember an old man? All the animals talked to him. I'm sure your family did. Some of them even spoke in verse. I have them all back at camp. He transcribed them right into our data. Group scan, group scan, group scan, and then a poem composed by a trumpeter bird. I remember a few of my favourites. One was about a snake who had swallowed a pingo but couldn't digest it. My wife, Maria, she loved the one about the tamarins, and how their hands were red from all the finger-painting. We mocked the old man, but some of the poems were really smart, really beautiful. There was one about a baby bird. I think it was the tapir who came up with it. A rhyme about a baby bird who had fallen from its nest.

Stanley stopped. His eyes began to burn.

Monkey.

Monkey.

My baby bird.

7

HELP ME DIG!

Stanley dove to the ground at the back of his cage and started clawing at the earth.

Monkey! Come and help! I have to get out of here!

He scraped through a few inches of soil but then his fingertips grazed the basalt, so he leapt up and pulled on the bamboo bars. He shook them so hard the cage shuddered, but the enclosure was well made and wouldn't give. He reached through and grabbed the padlock on the door, wrenched at it. Nothing. In the clearing some of the men had stopped to watch Stanley's futile escape attempt. Every time he yelled something at the monkey the men burst out laughing. When Commander Bigaman emerged from his hut the soldiers dispersed.

Ignore this fool, said Bigaman. These are the thrashings of a dead man. The forest does not belong to science any more than it belongs to the swine in the capital and their resource companies.

Stanley slumped down with his back to one of the cage walls. He thought of Collymore. He now understood that the old man's ravings had carried meaning with them, that even though it was impossible, the professor had indeed learned something important about the forest, and during his last months at Roosvallen he'd been desperate to communicate this new-found education to his field assistants. She's coming back. The animals, or the rebels, it didn't matter whom—they had given Collymore a warning. They knew the eagle would rise again; they just didn't know when.

Time doesn't matter, thought Stanley. He threw his head back against the bamboo. He did this three times. Time doesn't matter! Why couldn't I see it sooner?

The monkey in Stanley's cage *ke-junked*, as if she had just bitten into a ripe piece of fruit. Stanley turned to face her. She *ke-junked* again, louder this time, and held his gaze.

Ke-junk.

Stanley frowned.

Petrus doesn't know what he's talking about, monkey. Pay attention. That wasn't me paying attention back there. That was me remembering something from the past. Two very different things.

Ke-junk.

I can't explain it to you. I just . . . it's not as easy as it sounds. Not for me. Not for someone like me.

Ke-junk.

Who would I pray to, anyway? Empty bottles? A palm tree? You? Should I pray to you, monkey?

Out in the clearing, four men had raised a makeshift flagpole and were shovelling dirt back in around its base. Fluttering at the top was a yellow flag with the shape of an eagle, its wings outstretched, painted in red.

Ke-junk.

Okay, I'll try. I'll try! Just shut up and let me try.

Stanley knelt and faced the flagpole. He closed his eyes and brought his hands together at his chest. His lips moved but no sound came out. He remained in this position for five minutes before slumping to the ground.

I don't know what I'm doing. This is ridiculous. I feel ridiculous. Monkey, listen to me. Just because nothing else has worked doesn't mean this will.

Ke-junk.

That's not an argument. Process of elimination is not an argument.

Ke-junk.

He tried again. This time he lasted ten minutes.

You know the worst part? You know the real problem with this? It's not the lack of proof. Not having evidence is a problem, but it's not the worst part. The worst part is that I'm wasting my time.

Ke-junk.

Okay, okay. Fine. I'll give it another try.

He knelt again.

Then a rattling sound near his head caused him to spin around.

Christopher stood at the back of the cage, dragging the muzzle of his rifle across the bars.

You should have been praying a long time ago, said the boy. Now I have surprise for you.

From behind his back Christopher produced the white yoghurt container. Stanley leapt to his feet, ran to the far side of the cage. Christopher followed him around.

If you yell, I will fill your cage with bullets and tell them you were trying to escape while they were eating their lunch. If you play along, maybe you live until Bigaman kills you and eats your monkey.

Ke-junk. Ke-junk. Ke-junk.

I know, I know, said Stanley. Monkey, I hear you. Time doesn't matter.

Stanley dropped back down to his knees, brought his hands together.

You really are *fukkup*, aren't you? Christopher opened the lid to the container and dipped a long stick inside. When he pulled the stick out, a black bullet ant was clamped to the end with its massive pincers.

The boy smiled.

Jungle roulette, he said.

Stanley closed his eyes. He said one word, the only word that occurred to him.

Please.

Christopher whipped the stick at Stanley. The ant went flying but hit one of the bars of the cage and dropped to the ground.

Huh, said Christopher, watching the ant scurry away. Lucky frog-licker. He dipped the stick again, and Stanley said the word to himself again. Please. Please. And the third time he said it something shifted inside him.

The next bullet ant sailed through the bars but missed Stanley high and to the left. It came close to hitting the capuchin, who squeaked and leapt away.

Please.

Stanley did not know who he was speaking this word to, but the more he spoke it the more he wanted to speak it. With each utterance he felt more and more alone and yet completely enveloped, just as he had felt that night in the boulder cave when he had sensed a presence but couldn't put it into words.

Please.

He no longer cared who he was pleading with. It might have been this awful man-child, Christopher, or Commander Bigaman. It might have been Professor Collymore, or Maria, or his stillborn son. It might have been his cage-mate, this monkey. He didn't know and he didn't care. All that mattered, he realized now, was the asking.

Please.

Christopher fired another ant towards Stanley. It hit him square in the chest but failed to grab onto his shirt, tumbling down his torso until finding purchase near the zipper of his pants.

Money shot, said the boy.

The monkey twittered. Stanley opened his eyes and looked down. And just as he swept a panicked hand across his pants and the ant went flying, Stanley heard a *whump*, looked up and saw Christopher's eyes roll back in his head. The boy dropped the yoghurt container and followed it to the ground.

Someone stood in the shadows behind Stanley's cage.

Maria?

The figure stepped closer. Stanley scrambled to his feet.

No, it's you! Professor! You're alive!

The man limped into the clearing. He wore camouflage fatigues. The sun gleamed off his shaved head and his face was twisted in pain. His left arm fell limp at his side.

Boy, you *fukkup*. Hank grimaced as he pulled a set of keys from his pocket.

8

~

H E RAN.

He went south into the bush a few hundred feet and found the old hunting trail, just as Hank had said he would. From there he tracked east, and just when he thought the trail would continue all the way to Santimaka it veered north and Stanley picked up his pace. He stopped every five minutes or so to listen, and he said that word again to himself, please, please, as he tried to stop shaking. The trail circled north around the rebel camp and soon he had stumbled into the lekking site of the cock-of-the-rock. He found himself surrounded by beautiful orange birds, some on the ground in flamboyant mid-performance, others perched and waiting their turn.

Listen. Listen. Nothing.

He splashed through a small creek, saw the bandstand of Camp Schumacher through the trees on his right and then burst onto the West Platte. Not wanting to expose himself he skirted the edge of the rock face, crashing through throngs of pine-apple plants and opening up his shins to their spikes. Before he had left he had demanded that Hank release the monkey, too, and when Hank had refused, told him there was no time, Stanley had grabbed Hank by the shoulders and smiled and told him time doesn't matter, there is always time, it just depends on how you think about it. Something about this nonsensical statement struck a chord with Hank—perhaps the toxins were still circulating his brain—so he fumbled through the keys for the smallest one.

Get out of Roosvallen. Tell Benny and Raymond and Desmond and Petrus. Take a boat, do not call a plane. There is no time.

Why help me?

I'm not, Hank said with a sneer. I help the older ones. I was born to make this sacrifice. Benny and Petrus and the others, they make theirs already.

Once he had reached the Voltzberg Trail Stanley could run full-out, and although his thigh was still bruised his muscles had warmed to the point that he no longer felt them. He crossed Earthsea Stream and then Neverland and Wonderland, stopping often to look behind him. It would not take long for them to notice he was gone. Perhaps they would send Christopher after him. Perhaps Bigaman had already ordered the boy's execution. Through spider monkey territory, through the giant heliconia patch and across Bedrock Stream, he began to recognize the forest around him, and when he came to a halt at Asgard, saw the intersection of Main Street a few hundred feet ahead, he nearly broke into sobs. Please please please please please.

He raced through his study side, and as he arrived breathless at the bottom of Ant Hill he saw Petrus's boat moored to a tree. The waters had swallowed the shoreline jungle and were now halfway up the hill. Stanley slogged through the river and then the mud, and once he felt the sun on his back he called out for Petrus. Coming over the top he saw the front door of Camp Collymore swung open, the old man standing in the doorway.

Bas-Pey! I know where it is! I've found the nest!

Stanley blew past the old man and ran straight for the camp library. He ignored the overflowing buckets, the flooded floor, the black mould growing up the wall where his hammock hung.

Fawaka, Stan-ley. Where have *yu* been?

Stanley inspected the spines of the data binders.

Stan-ley?

Bas-Pey, you have to get out of here. You have to get out of Roosvallen.

Tell me, said Petrus.

They caught me.

Suma?

The day you dropped me off. The Jungle Commando. They held me for three days.

San? Stan-ley, where?

Wait, just wait, Bas-Pey. Here!

Stanley pulled a binder from the bookcase, one of the early ones from his first year in the forest. Then he pulled the two on either side of it and threw all three onto the data table.

I know where the nest is. Professor Collymore knew, too, in a way, but it was just too early back then. Stanley flipped through the binders, page after page of monotonous group scans. Where is it? Where is it? It's in here somewhere.

Petrus came to stand next to him.

Stan-ley, everything fine?

Bas-Pey. They took me to their camp. They are planning a revolution and it's about to begin. You need to get out of here.

What camp?

Stanley kept flipping.

Their camp. In the jungle south of the mountain.

Petrus placed his hand on Stanley's shoulder.

Stan-ley. Do not speak of that place.

Bas-Pey, that's where they are. Just past the lekking site. There's about sixty of them. They're preparing to take Roosvallen, and then the capital.

Stanley threw one of the binders to the floor and opened another, continued flipping. Then he slowed, began reading the pages more carefully.

Here, here, it's around here. Look, Bas-Pey, the poems. Collymore's poems. They're right here.

He found the one about the snake who had eaten too much. He found the one about the tamarins and their love of painting. But there were more than he remembered, pages and pages of yellow paper filled with stories of giant armadillos who wished to be free of their armour, black pumas who couldn't climb trees, a pygmy anteater who hated the taste of ants, and a herd of pingoes that smelled not of shit and musk but of rosewater and chrysanthemum. Each of the poems was signed by a different animal, in Collymore's handwriting. In his last few months this was the only data the professor had bothered to record.

Here it is, Bas-Pey. The one written by the tapir.

Stanley read aloud from the binder:

A baby bird who cannot yet fly will crash to the ground in the
    blink of an eye.
A baby bird with two broken wings will certainly make a big
    mess of things.
A baby bird with too much mass will come to a halt in a forest
    of glass.
A baby bird who cannot be saved will come to a rest in a baby
    bird's grave.

A forest of glass!

Stanley leapt from his chair and saw that Petrus was already opening the front door. The two rushed down the hill together.

Get in your boat and drive north, Bas-Pey. All the way to the coast.

Ai. Mi sabi.

Tell everyone on the island to do the same.

Petrus turned to face Stanley.

Stan-ley, what *yu* do?

Bas-Pey, don't worry about me. Just go as quickly as you can.

9

BENNY DELIVERED THE ITEMS HIMSELF. WHEN Maria heard the fat man's voice over the radio she had unlocked the door to the nursery, and when she heard his voice at the top of Ant Hill she emerged into the living room for the first time in five days. She handed Stanley the blanket that swaddled their dead child. The blanket was so light it might have been empty.

Maria opened the front door for Benny.

Show me, said Maria. Show me what you've found.

That morning, Raymond had been leading a Belgian family to the Voltzberg when one of the children, a six-year-old girl, had vanished. Her parents, who had five other kids under the age of ten, only noticed their daughter was missing when the group slowed to wade across one of the many streams that criss-crossed the trail. No one knew which direction the girl had gone, so Raymond and the father decided to split up and follow the stream north and south, while the mother and her other children would retrace their steps along the Voltz. Raymond went south, and after twenty minutes of picking his way along the bank and calling for the girl he made a strange discovery: a day pack, exactly like the one Professor Collymore had used, lying on top of a flat stone.

Raymond lifted the pack, and as he did so he noticed an odd set of indentations on the stone beneath. Something about this observation put a fear into Raymond, a fear he hadn't felt since childhood, and he forgot all about the missing girl. He rushed back to the Voltzberg, and when he returned to the trail he found the Belgians huddled in a tight circle around the missing girl, her mother's face streaked with tears, her father's blank and rigid. Apparently, their daughter had spotted a giant armadillo just off-trail and wanted to see if she could ride it.

Benny presented the day pack to Maria and Stanley, while Petrus looked on. There was no question it was the professor's gear. Maria slumped to the floor, burst into sobs, pulled the pack towards her.

Stanley felt he might vomit.

San? said Petrus.

There's one more thing, said Benny.

Maria looked up.

Benny dug in his pocket and pulled out a bloodstained field sock.

Raymond find this, too.

No, said Stanley.

Maria took the sock in her hand. Stanley reached for it but he was too late.

Oh my God, said Maria. Maria pushed herself to stand, held the sock up as if she were inspecting a new fruit. Stanley reached for the sock again but Maria wouldn't let him.

Petrus motioned for Benny to leave.

Maria looked at Stanley.

What is this?

Stanley's eyes burned. He should beg her to be quiet. He should plead with her to let this pass.

What haven't you told me? said Maria.

Do not succumb, thought Stanley.

You were there. Oh God, Stanley. What happened to Collymore?

Do not tell that story.

Are you going to answer me? What happened to the professor?

Stanley just stared at his wife. He couldn't find the words. Instead he started to weep. The truth, he thought. The truth would only be worse.

Maria nearly collapsed. Petrus caught her.

No, no, no, no, no.

Petrus helped Maria to the bottom of the attic ladder. She gripped the side rails, shut her eyes, began to shake.

Maria—

A sound came from Maria's throat, as if she were choking on air.

I . . . have to . . .

Sweetheart, please.

She started to climb.

Maria?

What have you done?

Nothing, said Stanley.

What have you done!

Nothing!

Maria let loose a terrible moan, pushed open the attic door.

Tell that to our boy.

The attic door slammed shut and Maria began to wail. Her cries echoed through Camp Collymore. Stanley looked down at the swaddle in his arms. The howl of Benny's outboard drifted up from the beach.

Petrus hefted his rucksack, walked to the front door.

We must go, he said.

Maria, it's time, said Stanley.

I have already lost my child, cried Maria. I will not watch this forest swallow his body.

Stanley looked at Petrus, who shook his head.

He says you must come with us.

This place is diseased, Stanley. Collymore was right. It destroyed him and now it's destroying us.

Stanley came to the bottom of the ladder.

Sweetheart, please.

He had the infection. The same as Collymore. We both saw it.

I don't know what I saw.

Stanley, you always know what you saw.

Stanley knew Maria was right. Their son had contracted leishmaniasis in the womb. He also knew this was biologically impossible.

There is no other explanation, said Maria after a time. The forest wants us to leave.

Maria—

Just ask Petrus.

Stanley looked at Petrus, who looked away.

Ask him. He'll tell you what happened. He understands this place better than we ever will.

You're not thinking straight, Maria. You need to come down and help us.

Now the attic door swung open and Maria appeared in the square of light.

Maybe I *am* thinking straight, Stanley. Maybe I'm having a moment of complete fucking clarity. We are being punished. Because of you. You want an explanation. There it is. He had the same infection. It's impossible, but he had it.

Stanley peered up at his wife. From his position at the bottom of the ladder Maria looked like someone he barely knew, not quite a stranger but close to it, like someone at the other end of a very long trail—a trail he'd just cut, a trail he'd never set foot upon until now.

We are being punished, said Maria again. The forest wants us to leave.

The attic door slammed shut again. The walls of Camp Collymore shook. Stanley crouched down, closed his eyes, tasted bile in his throat. This trail, he thought. How long until the forest reclaims this trail?

Petrus unlatched the front door, stepped outside, closed the door quietly behind him. Maria's voice thundered down.

We were going to give him the same name. They were going to share a name!

Stanley saw the blood on the sharpening stone, the professor's limp body.

We are being punished.

Stanley saw Two-Moons in the trees, witnessing all.

This is the only explanation. The only one!

No, said Stanley, opening his eyes. He pushed himself to standing, put a foot on the lowest rung of the ladder. Maria, these ideas, you have to stop them. He started to climb, pulling himself up with one arm. Stop it with this story. We are not being punished. Do you hear me? It wasn't my fault. It wasn't anyone's fault. You weren't there. You have to believe me.

He reached up, pushed on the attic door. It wouldn't budge.

This has nothing to do with Collymore.

He pushed harder but the door wouldn't open.

Please. Sweetheart, come down. I can't do this by myself.

Go with Petrus, said Maria, her voice quiet and shaking. Return our son to the soil. That's where he belongs now, in the belly of this place. In the ground with the rest of the spirits.

IO

~

AFTER LEAVING PETRUS AT ANYUMARA FALLS, and after insisting one last time that he and the Boyz get themselves as far away from Roosvallen as possible, Stanley hiked up Kawati Top, down the other side and then veered south on Domineestraat. The sun was dropping and the caracara birds had begun their lament. He spooked a family of trumpeters and passed through a troop of squirrel monkeys but did not see any capuchins. He stopped to listen five times, and each time he heard no caps.

Good, thought Stanley. Charlie and the Longfellows will be safe.

When the *kankan* grove opened up before him he raced through it, felt the warmth of the sun reflected back to him by the sacred trees, and when he reached the *kankan* with the bottles at its base he dropped to his knees and righted the forest of glass. Seven years ago, Petrus had chosen this tree. Stanley had never asked how; he had just followed the old man into the grove without a word, cradling his swaddled boy and trying to shade his tiny body from the relentless sun. When Petrus stopped it seemed that he had stopped at random, and perhaps he had. He pulled a *jugo* of Parbo from his rucksack and the two men started digging with their hands, and as Stanley clawed at the earth Maria's accusation lay heavy on him like a termite nest in the crook of a tree. When the hole was ready Petrus motioned for Stanley to lay the body of the boy in the bottom. Both men wept as Stanley did so. Then the two pushed the soil back into the hole and patted the surface smooth. Petrus snapped the cap off the bottle and began his prayers, but Stanley took a few steps back from the tree. When Petrus reached behind him with the bottle, Stanley refused to take it, and when the prayers were over, only Petrus's face was wet with beer. The old man stood, pulled Stanley in for a hug, muttered a few words of reassurance and told him to bring a new bottle to this tree every year as a blessing.

Now, seven years and eight bottles on, Stanley stepped back from the tree and peered into the canopy. Sure enough, way up in the crown he spotted a great mass of sticks and branches. It looked like no nest he'd ever seen before, impenetrable and arresting, a fortification without equivalent in the natural world. Tears burst onto Stanley's cheeks as he took in the sight. He hadn't thought to look here. Why hadn't he thought to look here? Collymore, the tapir . . . someone had written a poem about a place that didn't yet exist, or a place that had existed in the past and that would exist again in the future. Time doesn't matter. The only thing Stanley could be sure of was that this poem was the most important piece of data ever recorded at Roosvallen.

Kneeling at the foot of the tree, Stanley pulled a flask of *palum* from his pack and twisted off the cap. Then he began sprinkling the sour rum over the tops of the other bottles, and as he did so he rubbed some into his hair, his beard, his cheeks. He understood his burden now, the thing he'd been carrying all this time—that he was responsible for Collymore's death, and that here, in this forest of stories, this meant he was also responsible for the death of his child. Maria had been right; this had been his punishment. Now, finally, he would grieve his son.

When the flask was dry, Stanley slipped his hand into his pocket and retrieved the small device Wout had given him. He pushed back the cover, revealing the red button, and looked up into the canopy again, took in the vastness of the eagle's nest one final time. The stories are wrong, thought Stanley with satisfaction. The rebels are nowhere near here. Wout will not get what he wants, but I will. His thumb hovered over the button as he waited for his eyes to clear, as he waited for the right words to arrive in his mind, the words for his son and his wife, for the professor and the spirits of the forest, a plea not for mercy but for forgiveness. The words arrived and Stanley spoke them. Then he pressed the button three times, placed the device among the bottles, and ran.

BEYOND THE GROVE THE JUNGLE HAD GROWN dark. Stanley stumbled back up Domineestraat to the Voltz and picked his way home. When he arrived back at camp he went straight to the door of the second bedroom, removed the sodden towels from its foot, and pushed it open. Inside, he lay down on the lower bunk. Even though it was improbable after all these years, Stanley could smell Maria in the sheets that still dressed the bed, in the pillow and in the walls of the room.

When he and Petrus had returned from burying his child, they'd found Camp Collymore abandoned. *Pasensi* was gone and so was Maria. She had left a note on the kitchen table but the note hadn't said much, just a simple command and a few cryptic words for Stanley to ponder the rest of his days at Roosvallen.

Please stay with the monkeys. The story is stronger than I am.

That night, after Maria had left, Stanley had woken frequently to the sound of an outboard motor. Every time he heard it he rushed from his bed and threw open the front door, convinced it was the sound of Maria's return. Now, lying here seven years later, revelling in the sweet scent of his long-lost wife, he heard a similar sound, a distant growl and a rolling thunder, becoming louder and louder and then taking on qualities he'd never heard before, *thock thock thock thock thock*, until the sound nearly collapsed on top of the bedroom, rushing over Ant Hill with an ear-splitting sweep like that of a toppling tree. The sound faded—the birds were headed south and to the east—and just when all was quiet again the walls of Camp Collymore shuddered, Stanley's bunk shook, and the air filled with muffled booms.

NATIVE SON

I

~

STANLEY WOKE TO THE PIPING OF THE TOUCANS. HE
had dreamt of nothing, having slept more deeply than he
had in nearly a year, and just by the trilling of the insects and
the warmth in his bunk he could tell the sun had been up for
at least an hour. He dragged himself through to the kitchen, poured
himself a glass of water from the tap, and as he lifted the cup to his
mouth he noticed the rash on his arms had faded. Pouring himself
another drink he also perceived a lightness in his body, especially in
his forehead, almost like vertigo but without the alarm, and walking
outside to take a piss he realized his fever had broken.

Back inside he emptied the buckets of rainwater out the side
door. Then he dumped the contents of his expedition pack onto
the floor. Leaving behind the cassava flour, the cooking implements, the butane canisters, the extra batteries and the orange tarpaulin, Stanley fetched his day pack from a cubby and repacked it
with only the essentials. He refilled his water bottle from the tap
and pulled the freshest set of field clothes from the clotheslines.
Pulling on his boots and slipping his machete into its sheath, and
leaving the lanyard with the fire-starter and the whistle around
his neck as a sort of memento, he pushed open the front door and
made his way down Ant Hill.

As he approached Anyumara Falls, Stanley slowed, expecting
the capybara and her young to be somewhere nearby. He was

about to step off-trail, to go around the rodents' favourite drinking spot, when he saw Petrus's boat pulled up in its usual spot, on the rocks in the pool below the falls. In the hull was the old man's blue cooler, which was always filled with bottles of cold water and Popsicles, refreshments for tourists returning from the Voltzberg Mountain. Passing the boat and hiking up to Kawati Top, Stanley grew angry at his friend, who had obviously ignored his warnings and was now in even more danger. Down the other side he saw Petrus walking towards him along the Voltz, his bow slung over his shoulder and his machete in his hand.

Bas-Pey, what are you doing? I told you to leave.

Ai, mi sabi. But there is a tour group coming. I did not want to leave them.

Petrus, forget about the tourists. They have to fend for themselves. You need to go back to the island and tell everyone to get out of Roosvallen.

Petrus turned, looked back down the trail and frowned.

Okay, he said, letting out a long sigh and nodding. *Mi gwe.*

Good. Bas-Pey. Thank you.

Domineestraat, Hollywood Boulevard, the Danforth, Fifth Avenue, Downing Street. Stanley said the names of his trails aloud as he passed them, and with each one he felt more at home. Stanley had accomplished what he had set out to do, he had completed the hunt and protected the troop, and whatever happened next was of no consequence. He arrived at Treefall Creek, where the swamp had reached its seasonal peak, and as he crossed the rotten log Stanley spotted the Brazilian tapir. She was standing alone in the underbrush and watching him, as she had done so many mornings in the past.

Stanley slowed, stepped off the log and began to speak.

Your child and mine, he said to the tapir, they are still here. They are still a part of the forest. They are buried in this soil. The spirits are not separate from us, tapir. They *are* us, all of us, the animals and the people and the children and the trees and the river and the fruit. We are the ones rustling in the bush, fighting and losing and dying and being born. We are the ones who carry everything into this place, and we are the ones who leave it all behind when we go. We don't get to choose whether we believe in the forest, tapir. Even when we don't believe in it, we do. Yours is the earth and everything in it. That's Kipling, tapir. It's us. You and me. It's us!

The tapir didn't move for the entirety of Stanley's speech. She just looked at him and occasionally stomped one of her hooves. But once he was finished he took another step towards her and she bolted, thundering into the bush.

Stanley searched the southern section of his site for the next two hours. Coming up Saramaccastraat he paused on the Voltzberg to drink some water before heading into the northern quadrants. Then he heard a commotion further down the trail. Human voices, many footsteps, the sound of something being dragged across the ground. Moments later a group emerged from around a bend in the trail. He recognized them, but only barely.

Shike led the way, limping severely as if he'd just twisted his knee. He held his machete in his good hand and carried a heavy pack on his back. His uniform was torn open at the shoulder, the edges of the fabric blackened as if it had been burned. When Shike spotted Stanley in the middle of the trail he yelled and raised his machete, not recognizing him at first, and at the panic in his voice the tourists behind him yelled, too, a few of them crossing them-selves and murmuring prayers in Swedish, one of them dropping to his knees. All of their faces were smeared with black soot, some of them wore blood-soaked bandages on their arms and legs, and their clothing was similarly tattered and torn, much more than usual after a simple climb to the summit of the mountain. Bringing up the rear were Frank Lampard and Alberto. Frank Lampard dragged a sleeping bag behind him, which Stanley thought strange. Alberto's shirt was off, revealing a blistering burn the shape of a termite's nest on his torso. The same black grime coated both of the boys.

When Shike realized it was Stanley up ahead he relaxed, resumed his limping, and as the group approached Stanley moved to the side. He wanted to ask them what had happened, but as they passed and he registered the fear on the black faces of the Swedes and he saw that the sleeping bag being dragged by Frank Lampard was not empty, in fact it was filled with something very heavy and long—when Stanley saw all of this a shudder went through him and he tried to speak but couldn't. One of the tourists, a middle-aged man, broke into sobs as he passed, and another one reached out and grabbed Stanley by the shoulders. The stories, said the man, a wild look in his eyes. The stories they tell us are true. As Frank Lampard passed, Stanley saw something poking out of the top of the sleeping bag he was dragging: a shred of camouflage clothing perfectly matched to the Roosvallen bush.

Stanley returned to the trail, watched the sad procession inch its way west and felt the urge to vomit once again. As he ran to the sacred *kankan* grove for the second time in less than a day, he realized the jungle south of the mountain must have been laid to waste by a conflagration so indiscriminate that not only had it destroyed the rebel camp and Bigaman's revolutionaries but also Camp Schumacher, where generations of tourists had hung their hammocks and listened to tales of the forest. And that inside Frank Lampard's sleeping bag was the desecrated body of a man who had led the Boyz deep into the wilds of their ancestors, a man who had probably saved Stanley's life.

2
~

WHEN THE UNDERSTORY OPENED UP AND THE sun warmed his face Stanley stopped running.

How can this be?

He had expected a scorched landscape, soot and cinders and smoking stumps. Instead the trees stood just where he'd left them last night, their buttress roots butting up against one another in that rare and unnatural way.

He went directly to the foot of the *kankan* with the bottles at its base, the tree beneath which he and Petrus had buried his stillborn son. He peered into the canopy, searching for the massive eagle's nest he'd seen the night before, but saw nothing untoward in the high branches, nothing to suggest a nest had ever been there. Looking down he saw that the bottles were all still upright. The black device Wout had given him sat among them, the cover pushed open, the red button beneath.

Stanley stumbled through the copse of trees, searching for the other *kankan*, the tallest in the stand. When he arrived at its base he dropped to his knees and began clawing at the earth between the two largest buttress roots. In thirty seconds the dirt gave way to a bed of limp feathers and the flank of an avian torso blanketed with maggots. One stiffened foot poked out of the ground, the tarsus gone slack, the talons dangling like pieces of jewellery. He did not dig down to the head.

Stanley lay back, stared into the canopy, listened to his blood rush.

I killed the bird. I buried her here. She rose from the dead. I found her nest and destroyed it.

That was the story.

Stanley closed his eyes. Yesterday he had spotted an eagle's nest above his son's grave. Now the nest was gone. Yesterday he had condemned these trees to ruin. Now a different part of the forest had been destroyed. Over the last few months he had witnessed many impossible things. He had invented a philosophy, time doesn't matter, to deal with the resulting uncertainty. He thought he had figured things out. But no amount of circular logic would help Stanley now.

Had he imagined everything the day before? Was he imagining things now? Was someone else—some*thing* else—imagining everything for him? Hopelessness descended, and at the same time another feeling—a sense of complete and utter freedom—also made itself known. Which one would win out? Stanley wasn't sure. All he knew was that among all the questions circulating his mind, one in particular demanded more attention than the others:

Which part of the story was the story, and which part of the story was true?

Stanley struggled with this impossible question for a long while. He did not grow hysterical, though, as he had in the past when the jungle had thrown him. He just sat with the uncertainty, allowed it to settle deeply into him. And then slowly, after one hour, maybe two, a small measure of understanding began to course through Stanley like sap through the sapwood of a cotton-wood tree. He remembered sitting in Wout's lobby with Petrus, who had accompanied him there to collect on his back pay, even though Petrus was not on salary with Wout but with the domestic conservation agency. Stanley remembered the story Petrus had told him about his own search for the harpy in the 1980s, about the Dutch businessman who had plucked him from the brothels and offered him more money than he could spend, about the days and nights he'd lived in the jungle, about the boulders and the prayers and the fires of the spirits that caused a great conflagration and that chased him into Pikin River with their heat. He remembered Maria's voice as he suffered with malaria more than seven years ago, those hallucinatory stories of the Hundred Years War, of rebel slaves and jungle hideouts and an eagle vowing to return. And he remembered the faded red paint in the black boulder cave, the shape of the *gonini* atop the ancient carvings, the wood and the firepit and the remnant camouflage clothing—all of it indicative, he now understood, of a destroyed rebel camp.

Stanley remembered Jason's molestations and the arrogance of the general and the stink of the scotch in his glass. And Wout reaching out his hand, opening his fist, and revealing two devices, not just one.

3

S TANLEY FOUND THE OLD MAN WAITING FOR HIM IN the kitchen of Camp Collymore.

Stan-ley, *mi* bring *yu* gift.

I'm tired of fish.

No *fisi*. Memories.

Petrus held out the photograph of the four of them, the one that had been tacked to the wall in his hut. The researchers and their jungle grandfather. The smiles, the happiness, the bright future before them.

Stanley knelt at the kitchen counter, rifled through the bottles and cans beneath.

You can keep that, Bas-Pey. Those are your memories, not mine.

Stanley stood, a fresh bottle of *palum* in his hand. Then he half-filled two cups with water from the tap and reached for the bottle of *stroop*. Sitting down opposite Petrus, Stanley glugged rum into his glass while Petrus squeezed *stroop* into his. But then the old man looked up and motioned for the bottle of booze. Stanley shrugged, handed it over, and Petrus poured a healthy dose of rum into his own cup.

Then he told Stanley a story.

The day before, at Anyumara Falls, Petrus had listened to Stanley's warnings to get out of Roosvallen, and he had watched

Stanley climb Kawati Top. But once Stanley had disappeared down the other side of the hill, Petrus had set off after him. He tracked Stanley all the way to Domineestraat. He saw him take the trail south. And then Petrus headed east along the Voltz. He went as fast as he could, splashing across the creeks and spooking a troop of spider monkeys and arriving at the West Platte in record time. Down the other side towards the foot of the mountain, now Petrus slipped into the understory and took greater care with his footsteps, tracing the old hunting trail as it veered south. He passed Camp Schumacher, where he spotted the Swedes' hammocks. He slipped past the lekking site, which was empty of birds. And then, just as the sun dropped and a gloom descended on the jungle south of the mountain, Petrus saw a tree, two trees, that appeared to be walking.

He killed the rebel scouts with little fanfare, making sure his arrows severed their windpipes so they wouldn't be able to warn their comrades. Then he crept forward, keeping low and hidden, until he reached the edge of a small clearing.

In the middle of the rebel camp stood an enormous Maroon, larger than any man Petrus had ever seen, even during his days running with gangsters in the city. This man read aloud from a hardcover book as forty or fifty soldiers bustled around him. Petrus was surprised to see Hank among the men, dressed in camouflage fatigues and hefting two duffel bags brimming with weaponry.

For fifteen minutes the giant Maroon hollered something about a prophecy, the return of a great power. Then he retreated to a hut on the opposite side of the clearing and slammed the door behind him. Next to this hut was a makeshift cage made of bamboo. Inside the cage sat a boy no older than twelve.

He's just a child, thought Petrus. What kind of heathen would imprison a child?

From his chest pocket Petrus pulled the device Wout had given him. As he pushed back the cover and his thumb hovered over the red button, Petrus thought back to that brothel where he had taken refuge after the botched jewellery theft in 1988, where he had first met Wout deWitt. The Dutch businessman had made a remarkably persuasive sales pitch, one that Petrus was unable to ignore.

There is a *gonini* at Roosvallen, Wout had said. The tourists have confirmed it. You look like a good Maroon, yah? You must know what this means.

Wout had been right. Petrus knew the stories of the Hundred Years War as if they were his own biography; aside from the prayers, they were the only thing he remembered from his childhood in Konkoniston. He recalled the tales of shamans who could summon noise and light from the air, of turncoat slaves and double agents slinking through the bush, of gruesome torture at the hands of the Dutch, of Ayano and his *obiaman* Kwafunu cutting the reeds and claiming the rivers for his people. Most of all he remembered the heroism of the escaped slaves, those brave souls who returned to the plantations from which they'd fled to murder their overseers and to help more of their people to freedom. Those slaves, who would come to be known collectively as the Maroons, founded makeshift villages on the remote shores of the rivers, just as their ancestors had done in the jungles of West Africa, and for decades they waged their slow war of recompense from the bush.

Without fail, the Maroons chose their village sites very carefully. The rebel slaves would only light their fires beneath the nest of a harpy eagle, the land beneath which they considered sacred.

Every year during the dry season, the Dutch sent war parties into the jungle to put down the insurrection, but one by one these parties were decimated. The Maroons fought bravely, protected by their *kunus*, the spirits of the ancestors, and the Dutch became hopelessly bogged down by endless ambushes, bouts of malaria and dengue, and an unwelcoming forest that, with its thickets of vines and mile-wide swamps and swarming insects, seemed to yearn for them to leave. The war continued, on and off, for a century. When the Dutch finally capitulated, agreeing to abolish the slave trade and make peace with the Maroons, the two sides signed an amnesty agreement, a contract that still held sway today, four hundred years later.

The collected stories of the Hundred Years War ended with a prophecy: that if this amnesty with the Dutch were ever broken, if the Maroons ever became disenfranchised again, the harpy eagle would return and seek vengeance with a vicious rebel army of her own.

This *gonini* will bring civil war upon us, said Wout, pressing his case to the young Petrus while the two swigged cheap martinis and watched the girls dance. Do you want your country to go down in history or in flames?

Petrus took the job. The money was irresistible for a young father, as was the opportunity to escape the city where he was a wanted man. But his task was not just to kill the eagle or to find its nest. Not exactly. His task was to find the headquarters of a new rebel force known as the Jungle Commando. As the legend suggested, the eagle would lead him straight to it.

It took him two weeks to find the nest and destroy it. Much of what Petrus had already told Stanley about this period had been true—his gradual awakening to the power of the forest, his awareness becoming honed like a beam of light, his burgeoning belief in the spirits of the ancestors, his new-found faith that through prayer one might achieve anything at all. He had followed the monkeys for days, he had seen the harpy attack them, he had put an arrow through her chest and he had witnessed her resurrection. But what he had left out of the story the first time around was that when he had finally found the eagle's nest, in the crown of a tree high above the boulder caves, he'd also found a bustling camp of rebel soldiers beneath it. Petrus had spotted thirty-five or forty Maroons dressed in camouflage fatigues and carrying rifles.

They were taking shelter in the caves. They had made their home beneath the nest of a *gonini*, just as their rebel ancestors had hundreds of years before. Between the two largest boulders they had raised a yellow flag bearing the insignia of a bird with its wings spread wide, a symbol of revolution in red paint.

Petrus did not, as he had originally claimed, sit beneath the nest and pray for three days, imploring the spirits for help. Instead he had found a hiding spot on the outskirts of the rebel camp, and once he was sure he was well hidden he pulled the device Wout had given him from his backpack. The beacon was the pinnacle of 1980s communications technology, an ungainly piece of equipment that weighed fifteen pounds and resembled a military field radio. Petrus raised the antennae and flipped a series of switches on the front panel, just as he'd been taught. Then, stealing one last glance at the eagle's nest and making sure the rebels hadn't spotted him, he flicked open a silver latch, revealing a small red button, and prepared to run for his life.

4

STANLEY POURED HIMSELF ANOTHER GLASS OF *palum*, fingered the photograph on the table, while Petrus completed his tale.

The black fires, said Stanley.

Ai.

It wasn't the spirits.

Petrus sipped his rum.

It was the spirits and it was not.

Stanley thought for a moment.

These are your people.

Petrus smiled.

Stan-ley, you never talk like Europe man. Don't start now.

But how could you betray them?

Petrus held Stanley's gaze. Stanley thought he saw the old man's eyes water.

These are not my people, said Petrus finally, clearing his throat. I'm sorry, Stan-ley, but if *yu* had children *yu* would understand.

Bullshit, Bas-Pey. The Boyz have children. Lots of Kwebo out here have children.

Ai, out here. Children *na busi*. They live in the bush.

So?

My children, my grandchildren, they all live in the city. They don't know the old stories. They don't care who is buried under which tree. They don't care who cut the reeds. Stories do not buy gasoline.

Stanley sensed this was a depressing thought but he wasn't sure why.

Those are my people, said Petrus.

But you are their ancestor, said Stanley.

No, said Petrus, taking a long swig of *palum*. My children have no ancestors.

Stanley sat quietly with that thought while Petrus continued to drink. The same was true of his own son, wasn't it? Only for different reasons? His boy had no ancestors because he had never lived. Did that make sense?

No, of course it didn't. Because Stanley was still here. Stanley was his son's ancestor. Maria, too.

Eight years, said Stanley after a time.

Ai.

You helped bury my child.

Ai.

You couldn't trust me.

Stan-ley, *mi* trust no one in the jungle. Petrus took another long drink. But *mi* trust no one more than *yu*.

Why didn't you tell me the whole story?

Mi want *yu* to find the nest. That is all.

I wouldn't have told anyone.

If *mi* tell whole story, *yu* no believe. *Yu* must believe first, then search.

A bird that comes back from the dead? How is that more believable than the truth, rebel soldiers, a revolution?

She does come back to life, Stan-ley. That is not the hard part. The hard part is believing *yu* can kill something that does not die.

Stanley winced at the twisted logic.

If you'd told me the nest would be above a camp of revolutionaries I would have taken you to it a week ago.

Petrus shook his head.

I would have.

No, Stan-ley. The nest will no be there if *yu* look.

Bas-Pey . . .

Did *yu* see the nest when *yu* were there?

No.

Yu were there for three days.

So?

Some hunter.

I wasn't looking for it then.

Ai, yu were.

I wasn't looking for it there! I found the nest, Bas-Pey. It was in the *kankan* grove. In the tree above my boy.

Petrus placed his empty glass on the table.

Yu see?

What?

Yu were looking for the wrong thing. Always, from the start, the wrong thing.

I don't understand.

Stan-ley. *Yu* were trying to kill something from the past. Not even forest spirit can do that.

Stanley pushed himself up from the table, walked to the sink, peered out at the forest that had encircled him for so long. Without conscious effort his mind returned, as it always did, to Maria, to her belief in the story of the earth as a living organism so complex it deserved to be revered. Maybe this was all just earthly complexity, thought Stanley—the bird, his monkeys, Commander Bigaman, Hank and the Boyz. All varieties of the impossible, his rational mind and his imagination, the grief he and Maria would always share. Perhaps it was all just complexity, worthy of reverence.

Stanley smiled. He began to consider something he had never considered before, and as he did so a peculiar lightness surged through him. Petrus was right—and he was also terribly wrong.

Stanley had imagined the eagle's nest above his son's grave, that much was clear. But—and here's the curious part, the part that made Stanley burst into laughter as the significance sank in, the part that ultimately convinced him of his sanity and relieved him of his burdens both—the fact that he had imagined the eagle's nest made the truth of it no less real.

He had finally laid his son to rest. He could feel that now.

So, Bas-Pey, said Stanley after a time, his breath calming, his eyes still fixed on the jungle beyond the walls of Camp Collymore. Was it there when you looked for it?

San?

Yesterday. In the jungle south of the mountain. Did you see the nest before you signalled the helicopters?

Petrus threw back the last of his *stroop*.

Ai.

It wasn't in your story.

Ai.

Then why should I believe you?

Petrus giggled, held out his cup.

Why not?

5
~

THE MAROONS HELD THE FUNERAL AT MOEDER-
vallen, Mother Falls, the most sacred space in Kwebo
cosmology. Villagers from Wintigron and Konkoniston
made the journey south to pay their respects, and for many
of the women it was their first visit to Roosvallen since they had
heard about Maria and Stanley's tragedy seven years before. Back
then they had left their gardens half-planted and arrived three days
later by the boatload, all of them dressed in spectacular *pangis* and
painted head-to-toe in white chalk. Now all the villagers and the
men from the island wore the same white chalk, a sign of reverence
and innocence in the face of the spirits, and they danced next to the
rapids while the Roos Boyz played their *kawina*. Raymond was in
magnificent form, his voice traversing the registers as effortlessly
as a musician wren, lingering on the notes of mourning like a great
tinamou. The Boyz would return his words, echoing their leader
like a forest full of trogons, and then they would all laugh together,
a flock of obnoxious jacana birds. The words they sang were the
same ones they sang for the tourists, evoking their ancestors and
thanking them for their resistance, their unimaginable struggles,
but now the rhythm was slower, more a lament than dance hall or
reggae.

Stanley watched Petrus as the Boyz drummed and sang. He
watched the old man's lips move to the hymns.

A Kwebo funeral ceremony would normally last for days, but given the recent upheaval the villagers had decided to conduct a truncated ritual. They would mourn all fifty of their brave brothers and sons by blessing the body of just one—the bravest one of all—in the traditional way. Two hours into the singing and dancing four men emerged from the shoreline bush carrying a body wrapped in muslin. The women had worked a miracle on the corpse. For the next three hours the Maroons held Hank aloft, passing his body back and forth and wailing like woodcreepers when they were each forced to let him go. The connection between Hank and their freedom-fighting forebears was lost on no one, and it was dusk before the last person, an elderly woman from Wintigron so tiny and parched that the slightest of winds might have blown her to dust, allowed his body to be removed from her grasp. The same four men then carried Hank back into the bush, to be buried in a grave they had dug the previous night.

Later that evening, blitzed on *palum* and stumbling up to his front door, Stanley collapsed on top of a fresh delivery of provisions. Among the boxes of rotten produce and bags of mouldy bread he found a handwritten note from Wout.

My dearest Stanley,

Greetings from a city that can breathe again.
 You didn't know it, but you started it all. When we heard the eagle had risen we knew that something terrible had been resurrected in that jungle of yours. This may sound like superstition and fantasy, but only if you have never lived through something like the late-1980s in this country. Those days were worse than anything you could have conjured with your imagination. Those years made us believe anything was possible.
 The last time she rose up, we almost lost our country.
 I am sorry for not trusting you completely, dear Stanley,

for switching off your beacon. But after that performance in my office I became concerned. You reminded me of your old professor, I have to say. I do hope you've managed to pull yourself out of that particular spiral. Please understand, Petrus has been our man in the bush for almost thirty years now. I couldn't possibly leave him out of the loop. Whatever he told you, whatever story he employed to convince you to help, please do not allow it to sink your friendship. Together you have performed a sacred task. Operation Gonini is complete! Let us pray we don't hear from her a third time.

    We are all, everyone in this country, forever in your debt.

Happy monkeying,
Wout deWitt

PS Why is it so difficult for a country to get over its past? We must move on! This is not the opinion of a rich man. This is the opinion of a local man, a native son. You are a native son now, dear Stanley. Maybe that's why you spend so much time with the monkeys. Animals do not dwell on the past like we do. Perhaps you are wise to stay so long in the bush.

6

~

SOMEHOW STANLEY WOKE AT FIVE O'CLOCK WITHOUT a hangover. On Kawati Top the sun peeked through the trees and Stanley wondered how much longer it would take for the bamboo season to arrive, how many more weeks until the forest would sleep again. As he did every year around this time he yearned for the boredom of those days circling the bamboo, staring at the wall of green and wondering what the monkeys were doing inside. He had brought the bow and the quiver of arrows with him. Over the past few weeks he had rediscovered many long-lost skills, and he had vowed not to lose them all this time around.

He'd also brought the letters. Before leaving camp he'd pulled six data binders from the library shelves and shaken each one out over the floor. From the binders fell six envelopes, all the letters unread but one.

At the bottom of Domineestraat Stanley passed the lone heliconia plant but didn't linger. Instead he walked straight into the *kankan* grove, straight to the tree where his boy was buried, and once there he pulled Maria's letters from the top of his pack and gently placed them among the bottles. Standing back from the base of the tree Stanley felt he should do something or say something. But the truth was he had already done and spoken many things, and enough was enough, so without a word he turned and walked north from the grove.

He found the Longfellows heading up Broadway, just west of the patch. He rushed over to the amphitheatre just in case some of the animals were sweeping through there. Sure enough, Johan and Beatrix were down near the ground when Stanley arrived. They *ke-junked* when they saw him. Jerry came through, followed by the fuzzy-butts Suri Rama and Athena, and then the old lady, Lucy, slinking among the branches.

And then Charlie appeared.

The morning after burying his child, and twelve hours after Maria had left Camp Collymore, Stanley had stumbled back into the jungle, still drunk from many days and nights of *palum*, his mind and body equally shattered by the happenings of the previous week. He had decided to obey Maria's command and not follow her out of the park, even though he was desperate to speak with her, to convince her to shift the blame for their loss away from their jungle home and whatever spirits held court there and onto a more rational locale—in other words, to shift the blame away from him. This would have solved nothing, of course, but that morning Stanley existed in that in-between place, with reason to his left and superstition to his right, and it would take him another day or two to extricate himself from that crushing binary. *The story is stronger than I am.* Soon he would rediscover the absurdity of that statement and his faith in rationalism would be renewed.

At least, that's what he had hoped at the time.

That morning he had found the Longfellows up near the Lolopasi, moving east towards the lowland swamps, and as he performed a headcount and then began his IDs he saw something strange, something remarkable. He spotted an ungainly lump beneath Marilyn's chest, and as he trained his glasses onto the female and slowly turned the focusing wheel he saw that this lump was no lump at all but a newborn monkey. The infant's eyes were still closed, its face was wrinkled and pink and its tiny hands gripped Marilyn's hair. There was a blotch of white on the end of its skinny tail.

Little monkey, said Stanley as he wept. Welcome to the world.

Stanley opened his notebook and recorded the birth, the first in the troop since the researchers had arrived. It was his job to name the infant, and in doing so he would hew to Maria's wishes while simultaneously rejecting her accusations, her superstitions. The new monkey with the flash of white on its tail would be named Charlie—in memory of their son, of course, but also to honour their old boss, Professor Charles Collymore.

Seven years on, Stanley stood in the amphitheatre and finished taking his IDs, watched Charlie amble back over to Broadway and disappear into the density. He did not see Moses or Agnes or Dustin or Costanza or Banana or Marilyn, and when he conducted a headcount he always came up with thirteen. He didn't know what this meant. He didn't understand why the monkeys who had been killed hadn't come back to life now that the bird was gone. But this ignorance sat quietly with him now, not as an agitation or a source of anxiety, as ignorance had his entire life, but as a comfort or a balm, the sense that Stanley wasn't alone anymore in some mad pursuit of perfect knowledge. He searched the canopy a few times for Two-Moons, thinking he might ask him, but he would never see the white-faced saki again.

An hour later he heard voices coming from the south. He left the monkeys and hiked down to the Voltzberg, and as he approached the thoroughfare a deep male voice boomed from somewhere up-trail. Stanley heard the clatter of equipment and many footsteps so he turned, scanned for a good hiding place, and ducked down between the buttress roots of a *kankan* tree.

Sneaking a peek over the top he saw Petrus appear around the corner, his machete in one hand, his pack slung over his opposite shoulder. But it was the next person to emerge who made Stanley smile. General Bronckhorst, dressed immaculately in formal military garb, with a black cap, white gloves and carrying a silver walking stick. Behind the dapper general marched a phalanx of heavily armed soldiers two-by-two, forty at least, in red berets and black-and-white fatigues.

It's time to go home.

Slipping the bow from his shoulder, Stanley pulled an arrow from his quiver and quietly nocked it. I will become a part of this forest, he thought, raising the bow and bringing General Bronckhorst into his sights. I will be welcomed into the soil by our son. But then Stanley lowered the bow and carefully leaned it against the trunk. Leaving the arrow nocked and ready he unsheathed his machete, and as the soldiers neared his hiding spot he knocked the hilt against one of the buttress roots. A low boom rose up the trunk. Petrus slowed—he'd heard the signal—so Stanley waited two minutes and tapped again, a little harder this time, and the boom went straight through him.